THE *Rule* BOOK

RULE BREAKERS SERIES

JENNIFER BLACKWOOD

Entangled Publishing, LLC
2614 South Timberline Road
Suite 109
Fort Collins, CO 80525
Visit our website at www.entangledpublishing.com.

Embrace is an imprint of Entangled Publishing, LLC.

Edited by Candace Havens
Cover design by LJ Anderson
Cover art from iStock

Manufactured in the United States of America

First Edition May 2016

embrace

To Mom, I love you.

Chapter One

Starr Media Handbook Rule #37
The following words are strictly prohibited when posting on social media:
Damp
Smear
Pustule
Secrete
Fester
Vomit
Slurp
Genitals
Moist

I stopped reading halfway down the list as my "I made it to my second day in my first big girl job" latte turned uneasily in my stomach. Why anyone would create a post using those words in the first place, well, it was beyond me. Definitely got the gist, though, and my client, Craig Willington, the supposed next George Straight (in about five years, give or take), would not be using *moist* to refer to his grandmother's cornbread, or anything else for that matter. A shudder rippled under my skin just from seeing the words *moist* and *genitals* next to each other on the page.

I slumped back in my ergonomic swivel chair that had most likely cost more than one-month's rent in the city, and rocked back and forth, fanning the two-inch-thick Starr Media Employee Manual with my thumb. I'd only held a few jobs in college, mostly at minimum wage retail establishments to pay for my one-click and shoe addiction, but never had I encountered such a detailed list of rules. Brogan Starr ran this company on a tighter leash than the Pentagon during a national security threat.

"Newbie. What's your status on the manual?" Jackson, the first assistant to Mr. Starr and overall grinch of a person, rounded the corner of my desk and leaned a manicured hand on the stack of paperwork towering over my sad-looking outbox bin.

"Almost done, only" —I glanced down at the manual— "forty more pages." It had taken me all of yesterday afternoon and this morning to get this far. At this rate, I'd be done by the end of the work day. I was itching to get past all the logistical first-week training so that I could start what I was hired to do—work with social media accounts.

Okay, so that would be more of a side job while I fetched coffee orders, made copies, and did everything else that came along with the job of Second Assistant, but there was an upside to my newly attained post-grad-school title. With an MBA and a focus on social media relations, I'd been given the opportunity to prove myself with a one-client caseload and eventually work my way up to marketing director. In a few years. If the stars aligned, and Venus was in retrograde.

"Let's take a quick tour. Before I go to lunch." His voice held all the enthusiasm of someone waiting in line at the DMV.

"Great. I can't wait to meet everyone. I thought maybe we could do lunch at Luigi's…" I trailed off as I took in Jackson's expression.

His eyebrows morphed into two cartoon-like squiggles that clearly said, *oh honey, not happening.* "First off, we will not 'do lunch' together. Ever. Second"—he tapped my Starr Media Employee Manual—"you must not have gotten to rule 738."

Someone check the thermostat, because it just got chilly in here. I decided the safe thing to do was to ignore his jab and instead asked, "You know all the rules by heart?"

"Just that one in particular. The Antichrist really outdid himself with that one." Jackson sneered. In the past day and a half, he'd referred to our boss as "the Antichrist" more often than his actual surname. Said something about how it was the office nickname.

Things I'd learned about Brogan Starr based off of my two-minute Wiki research (aka stalking) a few days before I started:

> 1. He was the youngest CEO to start a Fortune 500 company
> 2. He grew up in Bellevue, Washington
> 3. He finished top of his class at MIT at the age of 20
> 4. He had a *very* nice chin—pretty much the only feature visible in his profile picture with him wearing a Seahawks hat and Ray Bans.

I had yet to meet *the* Mr. Starr, who had been holed up in his office all of yesterday and today, so I'd form my own opinions on the aptness of the Antichrist moniker whenever he decided to make an appearance in broad daylight.

Confused at Jackson's mention of the rule, I flipped

through the employee manual until I reached the number he'd rattled off.

Rule #738

Employees must not, under any circumstances, store fish or any food items with garlic in the company refrigerator. Employees will refrain from consuming garlic items during work hours.

I set the manual down and stared blankly at Jackson. Then back at the manual. Then back at Jackson, words unable to form in my state of duress.

Dear God. This man was a monster. Shudder-worthy words were one thing, but garlic? Images of delicious breadsticks and savory pasta danced in my mind, taunting me. Guess that meant no afternoon jaunts to Luigi's. Their garlic pizza was the best in the city, but definitely not worth losing my job over.

Meeting Mr. Starr was no longer necessary to determine my fully formed opinion. The office nickname was well deserved.

Jackson tapped his foot in a hurried staccato rhythm and let out an exaggerated sigh. "I don't have all day. Do you want the tour or not?"

I shot up from my desk and grabbed a pen and paper to take notes. With the avalanche of information cascading in my direction these past two days, I needed to write down the important "don't do these or you get canned" CliffsNotes in the spiral I borrowed (okay, I totally stole it) from Zoey's room yesterday morning. "Yes."

A field trip around the office was much better than being stuck in this two-person isle of seclusion.

We walked past the main entrance and into the other portion of the office where the rest of the employees at

Starr Media were stationed. Pristine white tile gleamed in the lighting, and the walls were painted a trendy steel gray, occasionally dotted with pictures of our most esteemed clients. Jackson picked up his pace to a power walk and rattled off explanations the same way a guide would on a Hollywood sightseeing tour—bored, informative, and over-rehearsed. Somehow, that was less than comforting, and "please don't let this be a revolving door position," and "crap, I need this job more than air" rolled around in my head.

He pointed to a small room on the left and didn't bother to stop. "Here is the copy room. We each have our own codes. If you lose yours, you're subjected to the wrath of Glinda. Don't piss her off."

I nodded and scribbled a quick "don't cross Glinda" into my notebook, adding a double underline to the note.

After passing a few more doors where Jackson mumbled descriptions under his breath, we reached the back half of the office, which contained fifteen or so cubicles with posh chairs, exposed brick walls, and cement flooring that gave it an industrial chic feel. A hum of fingers hitting keyboards, ringing phones, and low murmuring voices filled the space, a completely different vibe than my post in the stuffy entranceway. Action happened here—the dynamic of people creating and orchestrating ideas practically zapped like static electricity in the air. This was where I wanted to end up. This was the place to be.

The energy shifted as a few people glanced up from their paperwork, studied me for a few seconds, and then went back to what they were doing.

Jackson pointed to each desk, starting from the back and working his way to the window. "This is Amy, Fred, Patricia…" the list went on, much faster than I could scrawl on my paper. The verdict was out on whether or not Jackson was doing this on purpose or if he normally talked like he was on triple fast forward.

As far as introductions went, this was what I would classify as a drive-by—fast, chaotic, and one that guaranteed zero chance of remembering anyone.

"Hi." I waved. A few grunts sounded from a couple of the cubicles toward the window, but everyone else kept their head down and continued working.

All right. A lively bunch. I clutched my notepad to my chest and pushed back the burning desire to sprint from the room and hide under my desk, popping Skittles and hoping they put me into a sugar coma.

College had made for an easy environment to meet like-minded people. I'd assumed that since we were all working for the same company, I'd hit it off right away because, hey, couldn't we all just band together and say "stick it" to the garlic-hating man? But it was becoming increasingly apparent I had to earn my way up the social ladder as well.

"Hurry up, newbie." Jackson was already in the hallway that led to our desks, and I hustled out of the bullpen to catch up to him. The power walk had turned into a half sprint just to keep up with him as we weaved our way to the front entrance.

As soon as we got back to our desks, he plopped down in his chair and began typing something on his computer. "When you're done with the manual, I need you to make a coffee run. Two pump vanilla latte with soy milk. Extra hot."

My head shot up. This could be it; I could finally have a chance to meet the mysterious Brogan Starr. "Is that Mr. Starr's drink?" Sounded like a drink for someone with a stick up their ass. Scratch that, ass was one of the pre-determined no-no words. *Behind*, then. Mr. Starr had a stick up his *behind*.

"No, mine."

I swallowed back a smart-*behind* response. Grunt work was part of the whole working my way up the totem pole in the social media business, that was expected. Play the game, move up one peg at a time, and one day, I'd be able to share my own ideas for improving networking. Until then, I was Jackson's...*female dog*.

See? Fast learner.

"No problem." I even managed to plaster a smile on my face, just to show how delighted I was to be here. Which wasn't too far from the mark, because nothing made me happier than a steady income fresh out of grad school, especially when I could put more toward Mom's medical bills and, okay, the occasional use of my one-click finger for online shopping.

Twenty pages later, I decided to take a break and get Jackson's coffee. I glanced his way as I walked toward the elevator, and caught myself before I could shake my head at his slouched figure. His feet were propped on his desk as he fiddled with something on his phone. Cell phone use during work hours was prohibited—as stated in rule forty-seven. But I guess that rule didn't apply to first assistants.

The elevator opened and Jackson shouted, "Soy milk. Extra hot or you're fired!" before the doors closed.

My job now rested in the hands of a barista and their ability to heat blast the shit out of Jackson's latte. Excellent.

I slumped against the metal bar at the rear of the elevator and rested my head against the wall. An upbeat eighties song droned over the intercom, and it reminded me of something Mom would lip sync to in the car. A sad smile wobbled at the corners of my mouth. It was pathetic how much I missed her—I mean, a twenty-four-year-old should be okay living a couple hundred miles from her mom. As it was, a whole month apart proved I was a total mama's girl, especially given her current condition. Before I could pull out my phone to give her a quick call, the elevator doors sprang open, and I hustled out the door to get Jackson's latte before I gave him any reason to fire me on my second day.

By nine thirty, I'd made it back to the building and learned that downtown really did have a Starbucks on every block. Being technologically savvy (or as my mom liked to say, "addicted"), my fingers itched to take a snapshot of downtown Seattle and post about my first week at Starr Media. I frowned, remembering the strict policy prohibiting posts about the company on personal social media. Pretty much, working at Starr Media was the equivalent of being part of Fight Club. Heavy emphasis on the first rule.

As I entered the elevator, I chanced a glance at the mirrored wall and cringed. The misty Seattle air upped the frizz factor of my curls, and my thick mass of hair was quickly transitioning from a "before" to an "after" shot in a Chia Pet commercial.

I blew a stray piece out of my face as I balanced the to-go container with Jackson's and my coffee and tapped my foot impatiently, waiting for my floor. For such a large building in the heart of downtown, the elevator moved at a banana slug pace, the digits of each floor flashing overhead as it ascended. When it finally got to the fortieth, I took a second to adjust my grip on the coffee container and my purse and made my way out. Both feet had just made it past the opening when the door zipped shut behind me, almost taking my purse in the process. I let out a yelp and stumbled forward, spilling a bit of coffee in the process. Holy mother of Moses, it was like I was in a giant arcade crane game. I straightened my jacket and adjusted the coffee cups, shaking off the incident. For an archaic elevator, it definitely made sure the door hit you on the way out.

Jackson looked up from his computer and smiled when he saw the coffee in my hands. "Looks like you just learned a lesson from old Betsey."

"Who's Betsey?" I handed him his drink.

"Our beloved elevator." There was a silent *duh* added on to the end of that. "And here's a hint: she only bites people who deserve it." He pursed his lips then took a pull from his soy-hope-he-choked-on-it latte.

I looked at the elevator again, my heart still beating frantically against my chest. "Good to know."

Why wasn't that in the manual? *Rule #768: Do not stand in elevator more than two seconds after the doors open. You will get chomped.*

Someone with so many rules should include something on the carnivorous elevator.

I cupped my own coffee in my hands and took a deep pull of my triple shot espresso.

"When do I get to meet Mr. Starr?" I stared at my desk, which only had a manila folder with Craig Willington's information, my large stack of liability papers to be signed, and the employee handbook. I'd imagined my first few days on the job to be chaotic, buried in paperwork (the exciting kind, not the signing-my-life-away kind), like I'd seen in all my favorite TV shows, but it was much more anticlimactic in real life. If my life were a hashtag right now, it'd be #whompwhomp.

If I were able to post about my job, that is.

"He's already in his office and doesn't want to be disturbed."

"Oh." I frowned. Meeting Mr. Starr was at the top of my to-do list. The faster we met, the sooner he'd see I was capable and give me a larger workload. Judging by the constant annoyed expression affixed to Jackson's face, he didn't seem too keen on the idea of me making it past this week, so I needed to get someone else on my side.

"Don't worry, Lacey, you'll meet him soon enough."

"Lainey."

He waved his hand dismissively, and the fluorescent lights glinted off his manicured nails. "Whatever." And then he muttered something that sounded a lot like "not that I'll need to get to know your name, anyway."

Um, that was not comforting. Whatsoever. Even though asking about previous employees was decidedly a bad idea, I just couldn't sign another confidentiality waiver until I knew what exactly I was up against. "How long was the last person in my position employed here?"

"Two weeks."

I swallowed hard. Okay, no big deal. Maybe they were a total dud and lacked the skills to be a second assistant. "And the person before that?"

"A week."

Well, crap. "Oh." I kept a smile plastered on my face all the way back to my desk, not wanting him to see me sweat. Seriously, was this how other companies in Seattle worked? Revolving door positions, everyone as disposable as a to-go cup?

This position was not dispensable to me. I had to make this work, so I had to show Mr. Starr just how invaluable I could be.

I plopped down in my swivel chair, and after signing my life away with the paperwork, I pulled up Craig Willington's media account. Jackson had shown me how to gain access to the Cloud drive with all pre-approved photos from each celebrity. As part of my job description, I was in charge of posting on their social media sites and building their fan base.

Craig had sent over three pictures this morning—selfies on his boat, taken with his girlfriend, country music star Miranda Rivers. He had a blocky chin with a smattering of stubble, and the gap between his two front teeth was ten shades of charming. Miranda was in her typical peach-colored eye shadow and ruby red lips that glistened in the sunlight. I let out a sigh and stared wistfully at the photo. If I were reposting to my own page, I'd tag it #lifegoals. But this wasn't my personal account—made apparent by my lack of arm candy and dismal bank account. Ah, the glamorous life of a postgrad student. Once I paid off Mom's expenses, I'd be in the clear to make poor life choices with my newly acquired cash flow. In the meantime, "getting crazy" was code for

Netflix and frozen pizza.

My legs bounced as I hunched over the desk and stared at the images, deciding what to say. This was my first account, my first post, and I really wanted to get it right. Craig had fifty thousand followers—a smaller following than other clients in the firm, but I planned to change that. They deserved to be as entertained by him as much offstage as at a country music concert. After Jackson gave me his account yesterday, I went home and looked up all his music and live performances. This guy was heading straight for platinum records. It was only a matter of time.

Mulling it over for a few minutes, I decided on:

Craig_Willington: *Sailing into the sunset with my lemon drop, @MirandaRivers.*

I smiled, satisfied with my idea. Fans would totally eat that up since "Lemon Drop" was his latest chart-topper. Within minutes of hitting send the post already had two thousand likes and shares.

Jackson strode over to my desk a few moments later and plopped his perfectly pressed khakis on top of my notes I'd taken from the manual and our whirlwind office tour. When I didn't acknowledge him in the amount of time he deemed appropriate, he cleared his throat loudly and shifted on the desk, crinkling my notes. Asshat.

I looked up at him, pressing my lips into a smile. "Yes?" My mother always told me to kill 'em with kindness, and I wasn't about to get sassy on my second day with someone who smelled of arrogance and a few too many spritzes of Dolce and Gabbana cologne.

"As much as I love babysitting, I take my lunch at eleven thirty, which means you take yours at twelve. During that time, if there is an emergency, text me. Do not go to Starr—he doesn't like to be bothered by anyone when he's working on a new project, especially by a newbie like you." He scribbled down his number on a sticky note, tore it off the pad, and plastered it to the bottom of my computer screen.

"Don't screw anything up, *capisce*?"

"Okay." I mean, really, was there anything else to say? Jackson wasn't rolling out the welcome mat. Not that I expected him to—I had to earn it here and was determined to show him I was more than capable. I wouldn't have minded a little polite chit chat, though.

"Good. Wouldn't want to get canned your first week," he singsonged as he pressed the button to the elevator.

No pressure or anything.

Just as the elevator doors opened, another employee rushed through the hallway, almost sprinting to my desk. Phil? Or maybe it was Darrel? All the names from the earlier tour blended together. "I need these signed by Mr. Starr within the next forty minutes or this client is going to terminate services." He shot a nervous glance toward the closed door and sucked in his blotchy cheeks as he held the manila folder out to me.

Jackson had given me strict orders to not contact Starr, no matter what. "Did you email him?" I asked.

A bead of sweat trickled down the guy's forehead. "Yes. No answer."

Okay, this was so not in my wheelhouse, but I knew someone who could help…

Jackson stepped into the elevator, either failing to hear the conversation happening ten feet from him or just plain ignoring his coworker's plea. Either way, poor Phil/Darrel/Whoever was in for a huge disappointment when he learned that second assistant privileges didn't extend to things like talking to the person who I'm actually assisting.

"Jackson, wait!"

But the doors slammed shut, and I was on my own.

Crap.

Chapter Two

Starr Media Handbook Rule #332
Staff at Starr Media must dress professionally at all times.

I'd lucked out and not had a single call during Jackson's lunch. Phil had managed to get Mr. Starr's signature, no thanks to me, just as Jackson made it back from break. He breezed through the elevator, sipped the contents of his Diet Coke can through a straw, and leveled me with a glare.

"Thirty minutes. Don't be late," he said, flicking his hand toward the exit.

I pushed back from my desk and beelined it to the elevator. Once I left the building, I took a big gulp of Seattle air. I was still getting used to the weather here. Although it rained in Portland, Seattle air was stuck on a seemingly constant mist setting.

Instead of picking up Luigi's, I opted for the safer option of the sandwich shop next door. As a precaution, I decided to get my turkey Panini sans onions, even though those weren't on the list of prohibited food items. Just to make sure I wouldn't be late getting back to my desk, I brought the sandwich back up to the break room, which was empty—surprising since twelve seemed like it'd be prime lunch-eating time. In fact, everything about this side of the office was eerily quiet. Maybe I'd watched too many office sitcoms in college, but wasn't there supposed to be laughing and joking around? People taking coffee breaks around the water cooler? Reality was a huge buzzkill.

This morning's tour of the company flashed like a montage in my head as I remembered everyone's bored expressions and total lack of acknowledgment. I hadn't thought about popularity since high school, but this felt an awful lot like being demoted to the bathroom stall during lunch time.

I sat down at the table and unwrapped the Panini and frowned. Breadsticks would have hit the spot. Although, no amount of breadsticks was worth giving up a steady income, not even Luigi's. Still, I gave a spiteful glare to my sandwich.

Just in time to take me out of my garlic grieving, someone walked into the break room. The first thing I noticed was his hair. You could tell a lot about someone based off the length and style. And the clean-cut, lightly-styled golden brown hair that the guy in the plain black tee sported spoke volumes. It said "I look like I'm not trying too hard, but I carefully crafted this look of perfection for at least fifteen minutes this morning."

The second thing I noticed was this guy should be reamed for violating the dress code policy. Not that I was complaining—because, really, those tatted biceps deserved to be on full display at all times.

I mentally catalogued everyone I'd spotted during Jackson's drive-by office tour. He most definitely wasn't part of that whirlwind of name-drops, because I'd remember those high cheekbones. And those tattoos. His arms were covered from each wrist with intricate markings, disappearing under the sleeve of his T-shirt. Some were words, some were pictures I couldn't quite piece together without creepily staring at him. Decidedly, all were hot as hell.

He smiled at me and walked over to the water cooler. He procured a teabag from his pocket, plopped it into his black coffee mug, and filled it with water. The *glug glug glug* of the cooler cut through the silence, and I quickly swallowed my bite of turkey sandwich, preparing myself for if this guy wanted to talk — unlike the last five people who took one look into the break room, saw evidence of human life, and booked it to the elevator before I could even manage a *hello*. For people working at a social media agency, they were oddly... antisocial.

"You're new here." It was a statement. One that held the suggestion that this happened more often than my purchases from ShoeBinge.com. I'd deleted the app from my phone the minute I learned Mom's diagnosis a month ago and was still thinking about those rhinestone heels.

"Second day." I smiled. Finally. Someone to talk to. Besides Jackson and his awesome ability to give the evil eye over his computer screen.

"How are you liking it so far?" The muscles in his bicep bunched together as he took a sip of his tea. *Ovaries, meet arm porn, your new best friend.*

I folded the wax paper of my sandwich wrapper in half and creased the seam with my thumb. "It's been nice. I made it through the employee manual...finally."

"Learn anything good?"

I looked up from the wrapper and eyed him. "You're breaking the dress code in at least two ways."

He looked down at his clothes and then back at me, smiling. Two dimples indented his cheeks, and I realized how incredibly unfair it was that someone could be that gorgeous and not airbrushed by professionals in a magazine.

"Guess I am."

"You've met the boss. What's he like? Uptight like that rule book?"

His lips tipped up in one corner as he regarded me with his piercing brown eyes. "I don't know if uptight would be my first choice."

I chuckled. "Really? I hear he's called the Antichrist."

His brows rose. "Oh, really. That one's new to me."

"Huh." I fiddled with the wrapper. "Jackson said it was a pretty well-known nickname around the office." Maybe the guy worked in a different department than everyone else. Heck, he was a lot nicer than all the other employees I'd (not) talked to yesterday and today.

He let out a loud laugh that echoed throughout the break room. "Very interesting. Thanks for the heads up." He grabbed the string to the tea bag and absentmindedly dunked it in the water. Veins corded deliciously up his arms and my brain went into zombie mode. Except instead of my inner monologue chanting *must eat brains,* it was *must touch veeeeeeins.* "What's your name?" he asked, bringing me out of my stupor.

I cleared my throat, heat tingeing my cheeks. "Lainey Taylor. Newly appointed second assistant to the Antichrist."

Mr. Dimples mashed his lips together, and I couldn't tell if the glint in his eyes was because he was amused or slightly annoyed. Maybe a bit of both. Great, I guess I was back to square one with making friends here. He backed toward the door and leaned against the frame. Really odd. Where I came from, people tended to give their name after someone else introduced themselves. This guy? Nada. I doubted 200 exits up the I-5 corridor were enough to see a shift in social customs.

He bit down on his full bottom lip and looked like he was really enjoying this awkward silence that had me squirming in my seat. I balled up the sandwich wrapper just to give my hands something to do. Really, these people needed to work on their social skills. Where was the welcoming committee? Mental note: start welcome committee if one doesn't exist.

"It's really nice meeting you, Lainey," he said.

He put his hand on the doorframe, and just before he left the room, I called, "Do I get your name?"

"You can call me the Antichrist." And with that, he breezed out into the hallway and disappeared into his office.

My heart screeched to a halt, and that turkey Panini turned to a solid brick in the bottom of my stomach.

Shit.

I tried to come up with anything to say to smooth over the situation, like a "ha ha just kidding, I totally knew it was you the whole time, old buddy, old pal" (cue maniacal laughter), but all I could do was stare at his retreating form. For the love of all that's holy, I just called Brogan Starr—*THE Brogan Starr!*— the Antichrist to his face. I lowered my head to the table and kept it there. If it was possible to die of mortification, now would be as good of time as any. Well, I'd better pack up my desk now. Bet I set a new record.

Chapter Three

A girl is only as strong as her closest girlfriend.

My best friend Zoey was curled up on the loveseat, watching a rerun of *Gilmore Girls* when I entered our downtown apartment at nine that evening. The crazy thing about leaving at eight thirty was that there were still people flitting about the office that late, meaning I needed to step up my game if I wanted to make a good impression.

She glanced up from the TV and frowned as she took in the drastically more disheveled version of this morning's look. "Should I even ask how your day went?"

"If you mean the day in which I called my boss the devil to his face? Nope, don't want to talk about it." But she already knew this after I'd sent an *SOS Kill me now* text promptly after the incident had occurred.

She just nodded. That was one thing I loved about Zoey. She never pushed for more information before I was ready to dish. "Leftovers are in the fridge," she said.

I froze and took a deep whiff, checking for any evidence of smoke or burned food. Nope, just our raspberry vanilla wall plug in. Not a hint Zoey had touched a spatula or a pan. "You cooked?"

She snorted in response, and I relaxed. Zoey had been demoted to preparing cold meals only. Anything else was a fire hazard. "I felt bad about you moping around, missing your mom, so I went and got Luigi's. Just make sure to brush extra good tomorrow morning so you don't get in trouble with the Antichrist."

Zoey and I had been best friends since she moved in down the street from me in seventh grade. She'd had the same bike as I did, and held a fierce love for New Kids on the Block, and we decided from that day forward, we were brain twins. After we both graduated college, she was offered an interior design job in downtown Seattle the same week Starr Media had offered me my job. So it was only fitting we moved in together.

"You're the best." I dropped my purse on the counter and excavated the takeout box from the fridge. Sweet, delicious breadsticks and angel hair pasta with shrimp in a cream sauce. My stomach let out a loud growl in response to the beautiful aroma hitting my nose.

I sat next to her on the couch and propped my legs on the coffee table, shoveling food into my mouth. One of the early seasons' episodes was playing, where Rory was still with Lap Dog Dean. Zoey always hated when I used that reference, but I found it very fitting.

She pointed at the screen and said, "Now there's a man who won at life when he went through puberty."

"I think all the guys won at life on this show."

"Amen."

Dean was busy throwing a hissy fit about Rory needing to study. "I seriously don't understand what she sees in him,"

I said. Anyone who got in the way of a girl and her books deserved to be dumped, right there, on the spot.

She stole a breadstick out of the takeout box and waved it around as she talked. "Hot guy, has that whole caveman thing going on." She lowered her voice to a gristly croak. "Me like Rory. Me stake my claim. It's all very primal."

"Yeah, that doesn't do a thing for me."

"That's okay, I'll keep him all for myself, thank you very much." She took a bite of breadstick and smiled.

I polished off the last of the pasta and the final breadstick and dumped the box into the trash. It'd been a couple days since I'd talked to my mom and decided I'd call her before she went to bed.

Slipping into my room with my secret stash of Doritos, I dialed her number and lay down on my bed. I imagined she was in the same position, most likely watching TV.

She picked up on the second ring. "Hello?"

"Hey, Mom." I shoveled a Dorito into my mouth, trying my best not to chew directly into the phone. Mom always complained that I chewed too loud, said I got that endearing quality from my dad (one of the nicer put-downs when it came to him). Five years ago, before he left us, I'd laugh and take pride that I was anything like my dad, but nowadays the thought that half my genes came from him soured my stomach.

"Hey, love bug." She paused. "Jesus Christ, are you in a hail storm or something?"

"Eating." I said with my mouth full.

"Are people around? You're upholding our family name by at least covering your mouth, right?"

I rolled my eyes and swallowed. Even this sick, she was able to crack jokes. High spirits were definitely encouraging. Maybe treatments were going better than before I left for Seattle.

"Just Zoey in the other room, and she doesn't care how loud I chew my food," I teased.

She let out a long sigh, but I could hear the grin in her voice when she said, "Gives me the warm fuzzies knowing I taught you great manners."

My smile faded. She was able to joke about it, but just how much longer would I have with her? Stage two ovarian cancer wasn't a walk in the park. Chances weren't super high at the moment that she'd be giving me manners lessons in the future. I threw the chip in the bag, my earlier hunger extinguished.

"How are you feeling?" I managed to ask over the lump in my throat.

I knew the answer. Chemo had taken my once vibrant mom and turned her into a zombified version of herself. Soft curves were replaced with harsh points. Easy smiles were fewer and farther between.

It'd taken every ounce of willpower I'd had to leave Portland after her diagnosis. But an entry level position at Starr Media paid twice as much as anything I could find in my hometown. Renting Zoey's uncle's apartment for dirt cheap was a no-brainer.

Dad had been out of the picture for years, picking up his life with the secretary he'd been seeing long enough to have kids with who were almost my age. He obviously wouldn't be any help or support to my mom during her battle.

Mom's insurance only paid for part of her treatments, not to mention the insanely high hospital bills racking up, and her savings from her fourth grade teaching career didn't even begin to cover the costs. Now that she was out of work, it was either let her drown in debt or chip away at it little by little with my help.

"Just feeling a little under the weather today. I go in for another treatment on Monday."

I nodded, and then remembered she couldn't see me through the phone. "I'll transfer money into the account next week, okay?"

My mom began to protest. "You don't have to—"

"Mom." We'd been through this at least fifty times since I'd decided to take the job at Starr media. The only way I'd live so far away from her was if I could contribute part of my salary for her treatments. Otherwise, no dice. There was no way I'd let my mom worry about money when she was already fighting to stay alive.

"Thank you, sweetie." She cleared her throat, and I wondered if she was as close to tears as I was. "I'm going to go lie down for a bit. Love you."

These phone calls always put me on edge. I was just waiting for the other shoe to drop, for her to say treatments hadn't worked and that I should come home immediately. There was so much I wanted to say to her—*how am I supposed to move on if I lose you? I'm not finished learning from you yet. I need you, Mom.* I kept those to myself because right now she needed someone to be strong for her, not a blubbering mess. Time to enforce my favorite mantra: fake it till you make it. "Love you, too." I gritted my teeth and pressed the end button.

I brushed away a few rogue tears that managed to spill over my lids. Was it really worth it to take this job and be hours away from Mom? A gnawing doubt clawed deep inside me, the worry that I'd made the wrong choice not to spend this time with her. But it was either that or add years to the payment process.

I shook my head. No use thinking that way. Mom was going to make it, and I'd taken this job to ensure we wouldn't be in debt until I hit AARP age.

Zoey knocked softly on my door and cracked it open a bit. "Everything going okay?"

I tossed my phone onto my nightstand with a heavy sigh. "She's just having a hard time with chemo." My voice wobbled as I said, "Wish I could be there."

She opened the door wider and came to sit on my bed. The bed dipped under her weight, and I laid my head on her lap.

Zoey pulled my hair out of its makeshift bun and began to braid sections of my curls. Her fingers smoothed the kinks from the rain and the hair tie and made deft work on the left side of my scalp. We'd been doing this since we were twelve, although when I braided her hair it looked like something out of a Michael Jackson music video.

"Guilt is a useless emotion, Lain. You can drive yourself crazy wondering about the what-ifs."

I bit my lip to smother a smile. "What are you, a fortune cookie?"

Zoey was one of those people that doled out great advice, but it was more of the "do as I say, not as I do" variety. While I had a worn copy of Whitman I'd taken with me while backpacking across Europe with Zoey and my mom for a semester in college, Zoey had spreadsheets and checklists, planning out every single day down to fifteen minute intervals (I wish I were kidding)—something my fly-by-the-seat-of-my-pants self still needed to master. She had an answer to every what-if, maybe even a backup plan to the backup plan. Worked great for her career.

She ignored my joke and continued. "You're doing what's best for you and your family at the moment. Just remember that."

I nodded. "I know. If anyone will pull out of this, it's her." I had a feeling I was saying this more for my own benefit. Zoey probably had my mom's recovery date penciled in somewhere in that planner of hers.

"Focus on something that you can control. Help your

clients, stop calling your boss the devil, things like that." A smile twitched at her lips.

A laugh escaped through my nose. Yeah, I really needed to work on that last part. "Man, it's like you should be a psychologist or something."

She squeezed me tight. "I'm here to psychoanalyze any time you need."

Chapter Four

Starr Media Handbook Rule #224
Phones must be answered in a professional manner.

There came a time in every postgrad's life where thoughts like "what the hell am I doing with my life?" and, "grad school in no way prepared me for this; I want a refund," pummeled you harder than a torrential downpour during monsoon season. For me, that moment happened when Jackson disappeared through the elevator doors during lunch on my fourth day in the office.

I sat there in the quiet, the gravity of the situation hitting me full force. I was alone, the same as every other day this week. And for those terrifying thirty minutes, I had no clue what I was doing. The phone had yet to ring while Jackson took his break, and I was hoping that my lucky streak would continue for the duration of my employment at Starr Media. This was a Fortune 500 company, and at this moment, I was trusted with the phone. Me, the person who was terrified to call the pizza place down the street to order delivery. But my phobia would have to take a hike, because answering the phone was an unfortunate requirement of the boss's assistant.

My lucky streak ended when the phone rang within one minute of Jackson escaping to lunch. I stared at the receiver and then gave a hopeful glance toward the elevator. Chances were at a firm zero percent that Jackson would come back and help me with the call.

You have your MBA. You can answer a damn phone.

Right. This was just like ordering a meat lovers special with double-stuffed crust—terrifying, but doable in the case of dire hunger, or in this instance, needing to keep a job. I squared my shoulders and picked up the receiver and answered the phone as Jackson had earlier this morning. "Starr Media, this is Lainey. How may I help you?" Okay, not horrible. I tapped my pen along the edge of my desk, needing somewhere to place this nervous energy.

"I don't care if you're the damn pope. I want Brogan Starr. Right now. Preferably his head on a stick."

My hand froze, and I dropped the pen. *Well, hello, ray of sunshine.* "I—uh—sorry, I didn't get your name."

"Jonathan Gizzara." There was a silent *who the hell doesn't know who I am?* added onto the end of this statement. "My client Guy Wells is not happy with his recent ratings, and Starr will answer for this. Do you know what it's like to be bent over and—" He continued with a slew of expletives and a few sexual positions a novice wouldn't dare try in the bedroom.

Due to my lack of recent history in this department, this conversation was especially excruciating. At least *someone* was getting some, although I really didn't need to hear about it in explicit detail. "Sir, as fascinating as the play-by-play of your sexual experimentation is, I don't see how this pertains to Mr. Starr…"

"Not the sharpest cheddar in the cheese factory, are you, sweetheart?"

My molars ground together as I fought to keep my composure. On my off time, I'd tell this jerk just where to stick his cheddar cheese. But, since I did need a paycheck at the end of the month, I swallowed down my irritation. "Mr. Starr isn't available right now."

His voice climbed a few octaves. "What do you mean he's not available?" I cringed and held the phone a few inches from my ear to save myself from early hearing loss. "Where's that pissant, Jackson? He at least knows how your damn company works."

"He's at lunch right now. I'd be more than happy to leave a message for Mr. Starr." I forced myself to smile as I said this, which helped keep my tone cheery and upbeat. Otherwise, I'd inevitably slip into sarcasm that I doubted Gizzara would appreciate. I'd learned that trick from watching Jackson during his hundreds of calls. He was all smiles until he ended the call, then it was back to his broody, insufferable self.

"You tell him that if he wants to keep his top-grossing clients and prevent a colossal shit storm of lawsuits he'll be buried in until he's fifty, he should pick up the damn phone."

My pulse pounded in my ears, and the back of my neck flamed. Jackson had specifically told me not to disturb Brogan, but this sounded important. Against my better judgment, I added, "I'll make sure to do that." It *may* have come off a little snottier than intended.

The line went dead before I could tell him to have a nice day. I hung up and groaned, resting my head in my hands.

I'd aced Microeconomic Foundations, Marketing Management, and Management Communication Speaking, but did that prepare me for agents asking questions about their client's ARPUs and threatening colossal shit storms? Uh, no, it did not.

In fact, after the fourth fumbled phone call, sweat rolled down the small of my back, and I prayed that a power outage would strike our building. Or a strategically targeted EMF. No need to be picky at this point. By eleven fifty-eight, I'd convinced myself that my shiny diploma could now function as toilet paper in case of an emergency. Calling my boss the devil *and* screwing up phone calls? Thin ice didn't even begin to describe my current predicament. Maybe shaved ice? No, not even that. One single ice cube—that was melting on a hot stove.

200 miles from home in a strange city with a coworker who was annoyed with me at best, and a boss with more rules than my drill sergeant dad, it was looking like this job maybe wasn't the adventure I had envisioned the real world would be. Just me, Dolce and Gabbana Overload Jackson, and the Antichrist. My own island of happiness. I'd get right on buying kazoos and party hats, but I was sure noise-makers were banned under some rule in the manual.

After I'd fumbled through a few more calls with agents, thankfully ones less angry than Gizzara, Jackson breezed through the elevator door at exactly twelve.

"Keep the company intact?" He took a sip from his Diet Coke and set it on his desk.

I folded my hands together and tried to remain as calm as possible when delivering the news. "There was an issue."

His brows lowered. "An issue," he repeated. "What kind of issue?"

"Jonathan Gizarra called," I said slowly, bracing for how Jackson would take this.

His jaw tensed, and his Adam's apple worked against the top button of his dress shirt. "And you put him through to Starr, right?"

I hesitated, thumbing the sticky note with his name between my fingers. "No. You told me not to bother him."

"Oh my God." Panic flared across his face, and he sat down at his desk and began typing madly on his computer.

"Oh my God," he repeated, this time more frantic than before. Blotches of red dotted the pale complexion of his cheeks and neck. "I will make this right, but you screw this up one more time and you're out." He pounded a few keys on the phone and pulled the receiver to his ear. "Go to lunch before I change my mind about firing you."

I bit the inside of my cheek, pushing back the hot sting of tears, and grabbed my purse. It had been a long time since I'd disappointed someone. In fact, I was fairly certain the last time had been when I forgot to send a thank-you card to my Aunt Ruth in seventh grade, and my mom laid major guilt trippage on me. My livelihood at my first job that actually counted for something was currently being sucked down an industrial grade toilet.

Logic told me to spend my lunch outside of Starr Media, and I paced around downtown with my homemade peanut butter and jelly sandwich until the jitters from the past thirty minutes subsided. I'd never really considered myself an anxious person, but between this job and my mom's illness, it was enough to fray the nerves of Bob Marley.

By the time I returned to the building, my lungs could fully expand, and the constant urge to bash my head against something had subsided. Mostly.

Jackson's lips curled into a sneer when I sat back down at my desk. "I fixed the problem. Next time try not to be"—he motioned toward me—"you." He pointed to himself and cocked his head in an overly dramatic fashion, one that just begged for a slap in the face. "Think to yourself 'what would Jackson do?' That should be your new mantra."

"Got it."

"I made a list of people who you always put through to Starr. If you make it past next week, you'll need it."

"Thanks." But that was a big *if.*

. . .

I managed to float under the radar for the next two days, keeping busy with file work and making myself scarce at the exact time I knew Brogan would be leaving his office for a meeting. Having access to his schedule came in very handy for keeping mortification levels to a minimum.

Fifty folders were spread out before me, waiting to be filed in the floor to ceiling shelving system. This was the closest I'd come to venturing into the office with my coworkers who performed various other jobs for the company. With the odd looks they gave me as they passed me in the lunch room last week, the chances of finding a friend here to grab drinks with after work were slim to none. Which was fine because I had Zoey, but having more than one friend in the city wouldn't hurt either.

I was busy alphabetizing the clients' folders in the depths of the cavernous file room when a voice cut through the silence.

"Jackson put you on file duty?"

I had actually finished my work, but when Jackson saw that I had a few extra seconds to do things like breathe and squeeze in a thought like *I might make it through today without ODing on caffeine*, he didn't waste any time wheeling over a cart of files and telling me they needed to be categorized according to last name and the year they signed.

I glanced up from my work to find a woman who was maybe in her late twenties, wearing a Pepto-Bismol pink sweater and zebra print rimmed glasses. She smiled down at me and said, "Zelda."

It took me a few seconds to process. Was that her name or was she professing her love for the fictional character?

The woman must have noticed my bafflement because she added, "My mom was *really* into playing the video game when she was pregnant with me."

I blew my bangs out of my face and extended my hand to hers. "Lainey. No cool anecdotes about my mom's pregnancy, although she did eat a lot of bean burritos."

Zelda grinned, and her lip piercing glinted in the fluorescent lighting. "How are you liking it here so far?"

"Besides making an ass out of myself in front of Brogan Starr and pissing off an agent?" I cringed. It had been all I could think about for the past two days. I'd tossed and turned last night, trying to come up with the perfect thing to say to make this blow over. Unfortunately, the only thing that came to mind was changing my name and moving far away from this city—because that surely wouldn't be a pain in the ass or get me any closer to paying Mom's bills. So, mortification it'd be. "Everything is going okay, I guess."

"Happens to everyone—the pissing off agents part. They're impossible to please, so don't beat yourself up over it."

I nodded. I suspected that she was telling me this to make me feel better, but I'd take it. "Just getting used to everything."

She leaned against the copy machine and gave me a warm smile. "I haven't seen you in the staff room. You should come join me. I take my lunches at noon."

"I take mine then, too, but I think I'm the social pariah."

Her brows furrowed. "Weird. I didn't see you in there this week."

"I was there. And so was Brogan. When I made an ass out of myself."

"In that staff room?" She pointed to the room across the hall from the file room.

This was news to me. Nowhere on the Jackson Office Tour From Hell was there mention of staff rooms. Emphasis on the plural. "No. The one across from my desk in the front of the office."

Her face screwed into an awful grimace, but she quickly covered it with a chuckle. "That's Brogan's area. No one uses it but him, unless we're out of creamer."

I covered my face in my hands and groaned. Why hadn't anyone told me this? "I was wondering why people were looking at me so weird!"

Of course Jackson wouldn't, because in his mind I wasn't sticking around long enough to fraternize with other coworkers. This whole hazing thing was going to come to an end the second I started learning more about the company.

"Come hang out with me today, and I'll introduce you to everyone."

The first genuine smile I'd had in days edged at the corners of my lips.

"Can I ask you something?" I flipped my thumb across the folder in my hand, one question gnawing at me ever since my horrible first meeting with Brogan.

She nodded. "Sure."

"Does the staff have a nickname for Brogan?"

Her brows scrunched together, and her tongue ran across her lip ring. She stood in silence for a moment, most likely wracking her brain for an answer. "Like what?"

"The Antichrist?"

Her lips quivered as a smile broke out on her face. "The what?"

"Antichrist," I said, a little more hesitant this time.

She bent over at the waist, clutching her knees, laughing. It took her a few seconds to compose herself. She straightened and wiped the stray tears running down her cheeks with her sweater sleeve. "No. Brogan's an amazing boss. A little eccentric with all the rules, and scary as hell when bothered during one his deadlines, but everyone here loves him."

Yeah, everyone but Jackson, apparently. And, of course, he was the one that had trained me. Not the other fifty employees that thought Brogan was a decent boss. I smothered the urge to crawl underneath all the paperwork and not come out until everyone left for the day. "Good to know."

"Well, I have to get these to the copier before a meeting." She waved her stack of papers in front of her. "Come hang out at lunch, okay?"

I nodded, and before I could say anything else, she was gone in a pink blur heading in the direction of the copier.

Two hours later, I grabbed my salad from the fridge and headed to the correct staff room, cringing when I walked past Brogan's personal eating area. How stupid did he think I was, eating in there the whole week after I'd had the nerve to insult him? And why the heck was I still employed? Because unless he'd had a brain aneurysm, a guy who wrote a 300 page manual of painfully detailed rules (none of which, curiously, mentioned his personal lunch room) should have fired me ten times over by now.

I still couldn't get the flex of his muscular arms as he gripped his coffee or his adorable dimples out of my mind. If he were just some random guy at a bar, I'd definitely let him buy me a beer or three before taking full advantage of him in my queen size bed back at my apartment. That said, he wasn't a random guy at a bar. He was my boss, and according to rule twenty-seven, completely off-limits.

Um, reality check, girl. Who's to say he'd be interested in you or your mouth that decidedly should never open around him?

Right. Duh. The rule was no big deal, because obviously my imagination was fifteen steps ahead of reality.

In the *actual* staff room, employees lounged in the chairs, smiling, talking, and looking happier than I'd seen them the first day. I was starting to think that people were only miserable whenever Jackson was in a ten-yard vicinity. I could get on that bandwagon, for sure.

Zelda was on the end with an empty chair beside her. She beamed when she saw me, and patted the chair. "You came!"

I gestured around me and gave a wry smile. "I made it to the right place this time."

"Everyone, this is Lainey, Jackson's second in command." She pointed to a guy in a mustache shirt with a goatee. "This is Eddy." She motioned next to him to the guy in a beanie and thick black-rimmed glasses and said, "Clarence." And the two people sitting next to them she introduced as, "Tina and Ashley."

A few of them looked fairly familiar, and I was certain the girl in the polka dot dress had given me mad side-eye when I was in Brogan's coffee station yesterday. "Nice to meet you." I clutched my salad harder and forced a smile, praying that I'd have a warmer welcome than the one I'd had when Jackson gave me the office tour.

They all chimed in at once with, "Welcome," and "Great to have you on the team."

Relieved at their greetings, I pulled the chair out and sat down, digging into my salad.

"Thanks."

"Did Jackson not tell you about the staff room again?" The guy with the goatee shook his head and gave a knowing look to the other people in the room. "Typical."

I nodded, and they all groaned. That made me feel infinitely better than I had a few seconds ago. At least I wasn't the only person to be duped by him.

"Number one tip—besides don't listen to Jackson's negative garbage, obviously—is to get on Glinda's good side. She is the copy guru and can fix any problem."

The guy nodded toward Zelda and said, "She's the tech queen. Any glitch in your system, she can have it fixed within an hour."

Zelda blushed and repositioned her glasses on the bridge of her nose.

"Just don't surf porn on the work computers. Someone did that last month and caused a system-wide virus. Starr wasn't too happy when he turned on his computer and found a bunch of vaginas on his screen."

They all laughed at this.

"Good to know."

I sat back, finally feeling comfortable, for the first time in a week.

Chapter Five

Lainey Taylor Rule of Life #2
Never trust Betsey.

The bustling chaos of tourists, businessmen and women, and locals getting in a midday workout flooded downtown. As I'd only commuted to the office before and after standard working hours, I avoided most of this traffic. There was something satisfying about being lost in the shuffle, just another person with somewhere to be, something to do. Here, I could be anonymous, discard the label of Professional Worrier over my mom's health and financial spiral, and just let go for a few minutes.

I'd successfully made it through the two-week mark at Starr Media, a miracle that I think took Jackson by surprise. Heck, *I* was surprised.

The conversation with my mom last week still lay heavy on my chest, and I'd wished there was something I could do besides work my unpolished fingers to the nubs. Even with Zelda's protests, I'd decided to do lunch on my own today.

Thirty sacred minutes to sort through my thoughts about Mom.

She was scheduled to be in a doctor's appointment during my lunch, so I sent off a quick *I love you and am thinking about you* text as I navigated through the heavy foot traffic. The early October sun warmed my face even with the biting chill in the air. I cinched my favorite Chanel belted cardigan tighter around my waist and snuggled into the warm fabric. The fog had burned off and left a cloudless, blue topaz sky in its place. This was the first time in the past few days I'd been able to really breathe, deep breaths that didn't feel like tiny holes punctured my lungs.

After finding a bench in Wyatt Park, I pulled out my salad leftovers and scanned the expanse of lush greenery. A guy wearing tweed sat on the bench across from me, yelling into his Bluetooth about stock portfolios. Two moms with newborns made loops around the park area before disappearing into a coffee shop. And a pair of street vendors shot each other evil glances when they thought no one was looking.

This area of Seattle was feeling a lot like Portland, minus the eccentric flair—nobody could beat the "Keep Portland Weird" mentality. Plus, they didn't have Voodoo Doughnuts, which was a shame, because everyone should experience a Cock-N-Balls at least once in their life.

A calm blanketed my frayed nerves, and I gave myself this brief moment to believe that everything would be okay. I slouched down in my seat and took a second to close my eyes and rest my head on the back of the bench.

Everything was going to turn out fine. Mom would get through chemo like the champ she was. The only thing that worried me was her being alone during this process. In a desperate attempt, I'd tried calling my father and telling him about Mom's diagnosis, but he'd brushed me off, too busy with his new family. His *other* life. It was still hard to stomach the idea of having a half-sibling almost the same age, and to think that every time he'd been on a "business trip" he was actually spending time with their family. His family. Someone who'd claimed he was an open book had hidden chapters riddled throughout. Seriously, it sounded like something from a soap opera, not a downtown Portland neighborhood.

My phone rang, hammering through the trip down memory lane. I pulled it out of my purse, frowning when I saw Jackson's name on the screen. The dude was pushing it with encroaching on my only thirty minutes of solitude in a ten-hour workday.

"Hello?" I balanced the phone between my ear and shoulder as I readjusted my purse on my shoulder.

"Two lattes, extra foam. Be in the conference room in ten." His haughty tone sent a jolt of annoyance down my spine.

Before I could say anything, the line went silent. I glared at my phone and shoved it into my purse, muttering under my breath. What a jerkoff.

Ten minutes. It took at least five minutes to get to the fortieth floor with a crowded elevator. Which meant I had to find the nearest coffee shop and get two lattes made in half that time. Okay, no big deal. There were a dozen Starbucks in a one-mile radius.

I got my order and sped back to the building. Five minutes until whatever was going on in the conference room. I was totally golden. To top it off, the elevator was empty, which meant I'd have a straight shot up forty floors.

Just as the elevator doors were in mid trash-compactor mode, a hand stuck between the two slabs of metal, and the doors retracted. Just yesterday, I saw a secretary from another company get hammered by the doors. They had no mercy except, apparently, for my boss.

My heart sunk faster than a penny in a wishing well as

I eyed Brogan. He gave a tentative smile, one that seemed polite, but I could really tell he would rather be anywhere else but here. (*Because you called him the devil, you idiot!*)

The doors closed and "Tainted Love" softly played in the elevator. I stared at the coffee cups in my hand, my purse on the ground, the smudges on the elevator door, trying to keep my mind busy, but the silence was too much to handle. I couldn't just ride up forty floors saying *nothing* to the man who'd hired me.

"We meet again," I said, and cringed at how stupid I kept sounding in front of him. Seriously, a Master's degree, and that was the best I could come up with. Cheesy chitchat usually only made an appearance with red wine and too many shots of tequila. The guy had hired me to help with the basics, and this wasn't exactly showcasing my competence.

"Yep. Just out for a quick walk." He nodded and picked at an invisible piece of lint on his sleeve.

Did he pass by me in the park on his walk? Oh God, had he seen me chewing? My mom's chiding about my eating habits suddenly didn't seem so stupid.

I chanced a quick glance his direction. Since that awful encounter in the break room the other week, his hair had been neatly trimmed into a stylish cut that accentuated his face. Brogan was all strong angles and broad shoulders. Normally my reaction to forced proximity with a hot guy in an elevator was that of a) glee b) praying I didn't have horrible coffee breath, and c) the obvious hope of said hot guy jamming the big red stop button and proceeding to give a mind-blowing elevator romp.

A completely irrational, unfair thought process since he was really the *only* person I was not allowed to go for. Besides the thirty other men that worked for Starr Media. As the old adage went, the person you embarrass yourself in front of the worst is the person you want the most. And Mr. (anti)

Antichrist was looking particularly appealing today.

He shifted and took his hands out of his pockets as I stared straight ahead, trying not to make eye contact in the mirrored doors. Oh, this was going to be a very long ride in silence.

I stared at the little red numbers climbing, each one taking its time. Should I say something else? It'd be rude not to, but then again, I was the one that made an ass out of myself and insulted him. Maybe I should just keep my mouth shut like Jackson instructed.

"Nice day, huh?" Okay, so I failed at taking my own advice. Awkward silence gave me hives, and I always felt the need to fill it.

He clasped his hands in front of him and looked down at me. "Yep. Enjoy it while it lasts—supposed to be a rough winter."

"I don't mind rough," popped out of my mouth even as *Noooooo don't you dare say that!* tried to lasso my tongue. If I wasn't carrying coffee, I'd be pulling the hood of my cardigan over my head and pretending I'd melted into the elevator.

The dimples made an appearance, and I could tell he was using every bit of restraint not to laugh. "Is that so?"

"That was way too far down the 'that's what she said' rabbit hole to even begin to redeem myself. Can we let that slide?"

"My duty as CEO entails letting comments like that go."

I didn't get it. He seemed friendly enough, social, so why did this guy have so many rules to abide by? I'd expect it from someone who hated people, enjoyed making them sweat—not a guy who was still kind to a person who insulted their character. Then again, my dad had thousands of rules in our household and was well-liked by the community, and look how he turned out.

"About the other day…" I started and trailed off.

Somehow "I'm sorry for calling you the Antichrist to your face" didn't feel appropriate here.

"Yes?"

Ugh. It'd be so much easier if he'd say, "Don't worry about it. Let's start over." But this was real life. Of course he wouldn't let me off the hook that easily. The edges of the to-go container dug into my palms as I gripped it for dear life. "I'm sorry for calling you"—I swallowed hard and managed to look him straight in the eye—"the devil."

His lips mashed together, and it looked like he was holding back a laugh. "Technically, you called me the Antichrist."

"Technicalities."

"The devil's in the detail." A smug smirk etched across his lips. Damn him and those glorious dimples.

I groaned, and my feet ached to run anywhere far, far away, out of this damn elevator. "Okay, if I apologize another five times can we never mention anything involving Satan again?"

He chuckled and raised a hand, seeming to brush our previous interaction off, like it hadn't been a big deal. "It's refreshing to be insulted every once in a while. Everyone is a little too nice to me when they know I'm around."

"I'm still really sorry. You're not at all what I pictured."

"No? And what did you picture?" His voice deepened, the question a challenge. If he weren't my boss, I'd almost believe this brushed on the side of flirting.

A stick figure with an even larger stick deeply rooted up their ass. Someone with premature male pattern baldness. Someone that didn't have delicious dimples or full sleeve tattoos.

This time I kept my thoughts to myself. "Just not you."

Instead of the casual attire he'd worn the first time we met, a tailored black suit with a light blue button-up fit snug on his body, like a rich, Italian glove. There was a lot to be said for a man in a well-fitted suit. Such as *yum,* and *I'd tap that like a friggin' maple tree.* Nothing quite got my salivary glands going like a hot guy dressed up. My gaze inconspicuously traveled to his arms, working down to where his hands were tucked into his pockets. Which then got me thinking about the man bulge threads on Pinterest, and how Brogan should really wear his pants a little tighter.

He cleared his throat.

Warning bells blared between my ears. *Abort mission. Move your eyes up before he thinks you're staring at his package.* Which, let's face it, I totally was.

This thought process should not be happening because, yeah, he happened to be my boss. A boss that I'd already made a crap first impression with, and an equally shitty second one by the way this was going. That was enough reason to stay the hell away from inserting him into my solo shower time entertainment.

Our gazes met in the mirror, and he lifted a suggestive brow, and that sly half smile ticked at the corner of his mouth. Yep, my boss just caught me checking him out. Yes, I was going to freak out in the bathroom as soon as I booked it off this elevator ride from hell.

The elevator picked this moment to have mercy on me and stopped at the fortieth floor. Brogan motioned for me to exit the car first.

I walked out, Brogan tailing close behind, when I realized I'd set my purse on the ground. I rushed back in, cradling the to-go container that held the two coffees, and reached down for my purse. The doors were still wide open, a minor miracle, and I bolted out.

Brogan stood there, waiting, while I booked it out of the elevator. I hadn't gone one step before the door zoomed shut behind me. Phew. Made it.

We both started toward the conference room, but I was

immediately tugged backward. What the…? The hairs rose on the back of my neck.

No, it couldn't be.

I pulled harder, and a chill ran through me as I heard the distinct sound of fabric ripping.

Oh no.

Betsey, how could you do this to me? Didn't she know that this was my favorite cardigan she had locked in her stupid Jaws of Life? I'd spent two hours in line on Black Friday and elbowed past old ladies to get this. I wanted to shake my fist at her. I wanted to do the Dawson ugly cry. I wanted my damn cardigan back.

I pulled a little harder and heard another rip. *I'm sorry, Betsey, did I say Jaws of Life? I meant beautiful doors of metallic glory.*

Brogan kept walking toward the conference room and called behind him, "You coming?" He looked over his shoulder and did a double take, his brows furrowing. "Everything all right?"

Totally okay. I often stood with my favorite Chanel cardigan in the elevator door just for kicks. "I'm great."

"Then let's get to the meeting. Can't be late." He jutted his thumb at the conference room and continued walking toward the sweet refuge that was just out of sweater-snag reach.

"Yes." I moved forward, trying again to pull my cardigan out of the iron talons of the door, but I was rewarded with another soft rip in the material. It took everything in me not to whimper and break into a frenzied game of tug of war with the elevator over my beloved sweater.

He was almost at the conference room door. If he disappeared into it even for a few seconds, I could get my top free. *Keep walking, just a little more.*

As if he heard my thoughts, he stopped again and turned around.

I froze mid tug, trying my best to keep my face void of any indication of my inner freak-out. This was the most messed up game of red light green light ever.

"Are you sure you're okay?" he called back to me, almost at the conference room door.

My heart raced as I tried to come up with a reason, any reason to get him out of sight so I could properly lose it over the situation. "I realized I left something downstairs. I'll meet you in there."

"All right," he said slowly, still unsure. "Timeliness is important, so try to be quick."

Play it cool. He has no clue you're stuck in Betsey's death grip. "I won't be late," I reassured him. "Punctuality is my middle name. Well, it's actually Jane, but it might as well be punctuality." A laugh bubbled up, notes of hysteria mingling with the loud guffaw.

Oh God, just shut up so he walks away and you can get away with some dignity left. I smiled and said, "I'll meet you in there before it starts."

He nodded slowly and turned toward the conference room. "Sounds good."

Things I'd most likely find on my desk by the end of the week: a random drug test form and a formal letter terminating my employment.

As soon as he was out of sight, I turned toward the elevator, set the coffees on the floor, shimmied out of my sweater, and tried pulling again. And, again, another soft rip started at the bottom hem.

"Please, Betsey, what did I ever do to you?" I begged.

I tried prying the doors open, but they wouldn't budge. "I will give you anything if you just give me my sweater back." That included offering Jackson as a human sacrifice. Anything to get this back.

I pressed the down button and figured if the doors opened,

it would plop into my welcoming, broke as a joke arms. The hum of the elevator car moving was a comforting sound. Yes, the doors would open, the sweater would drop, and I'd make it to the meeting in time.

"I promise to take the stairs every day from now on if you just spare the sweater. It's Chanel, for Christ sake," I pleaded.

I was reduced to bargaining with a hunk of metal. Stupid Betsey.

The fabric of my sweater must have gotten caught in the internal mechanisms, because as the elevator arrived, the cardigan shot to the top of doorway in a mangled heap and a horrible ripping sound confirmed this accessory was toast. A mix of a wail and a groan edged up my throat as I stared at the article of clothing. I stood there, stunned. It was like one of those terrible videos on YouTube of men dancing in thongs—horrifying, and yet I couldn't look away.

The doors flew open, and my cardigan dropped right in front of Jackson's feet.

He pursed his lips and stepped around it like it was road kill. "Typical," he said, his stupid pert nose pointed to the sky. "I told you, Betsey only gives what she thinks you deserve." Then he was off to the conference room while I stood there, staring at the mound of black cashmere on the floor.

I gathered up the tattered fabric, squeezed it to my chest, and promised myself that I'd give it a proper burial in the bottom of my closet once I returned home tonight. Shoving the garment into my desk drawer, I followed Jackson into the conference room and took the only available seat at the oversize round conference table.

The other employees, who'd either ignored my existence or gone out of their way to avoid me the first week, were now smiling, and all said hello to me when I sat down. They didn't bother saying hi to Jackson, which the grinch didn't seem to notice, or he just didn't care.

Brogan glanced over at me, and his eyes widened a fraction as his gaze dipped below my shoulders to the very low-cut top I'd had on under my cardigan. They quickly flickered back up to my eyes, and he cleared his throat and shifted restlessly in his seat. I couldn't be 100 percent certain, but if I wagered a guess, that quick flit of movement to my chest erred more on the side of *bang me* than *you're breaking office dress code*. Or that might have been a heaping serving of wishful thinking with a side dish of "I need to get some."

Down girl. He's your boss, not an office pervert.

He focused on the rest of the employees, who were talking amicably amongst themselves. As soon as he started talking they quieted down, and all seemed to be raptly listening. "Let's get this meeting started, shall we?" His tone held an authoritative air while still remaining friendly. That is exactly how I would describe Brogan—commanding but also approachable.

"Melissa, what do we have on projections for the new year?"

She shuffled papers in front of her and said, "We're slated to have at least forty new clients by next June."

"Triple it." Brogan said and nodded toward the guy sitting next to Melissa. "What do you have on our return on investment projections, Gabe?"

"I'm still working on it, but it looks like we'll double our profits by the end of the fiscal year."

Brogan nodded, pleased. "That's what I like to hear. Have the numbers on my desk by Friday."

Gabe smiled and gave a quick chin bob, which I assumed meant "sure thing" in dude talk.

He worked his way around the table, each person sharing their reports from their specific departments.

"What other news do we have?"

Someone chimed in on an idea to save Starr Media money

by cutting services that were weighing the company down and not providing much in terms of profit.

"That's a really great idea. Get on that as soon as you're done with analytics."

I glanced around the room in awe. Odd, everyone seemed happy to be there. Nothing like the classes I'd taken in college, where students stared at the clock the second their butts hit their seats. No one was on their phone, perusing social media. No one was flicking pieces of paper or focusing on their computers. Every set of blue, green, hazel, and brown eyes was cast toward our CEO, hanging on every word he said. The only exception was Jackson (surprise, surprise). Then again, if it didn't involve making people regret the day they were born, I doubted it would elicit more than an eye roll from him.

After each member gave input on their division of the company, Brogan stood and smiled at everyone, the dimples making an appearance.

"Keep up the great work, team." He clasped his hands together, and everyone pushed away from their seats and strolled out of the conference room.

As I gathered up my computer, I realized Brogan and I were the only ones left in the conference room.

He cleared his throat and asked, "Did you get what you needed?"

My head shot up to look at him. He was standing by the floor to ceiling window, light pooling around his features. "Needed?" If he'd read my thoughts at that exact second, he'd know that what I needed involved less articles of clothing and more chocolate (because chocolate is always the answer, no matter the question).

"You said you left something downstairs earlier."

"Oh, yes."

"I know you've read the manual, so I'm assuming you understand you're violating dress code right now?" There was a teasing quality to his voice, and I was fairly certain this was payback for my smartass remark the first time we'd met. His gaze dropped below eye-level for a fraction of a second again…and was that a groan? It was so quiet that if I'd been breathing at that moment I might not have heard it. But there was definitely a noise coming from his direction.

No, I had to be imagining things. Brogan Starr did not just look at my chest and groan. Right?

"Yes, sir. I'll get right on covering it up." I crossed my arms and his eyes widened the slightest.

He swallowed hard, his Adam's apple sliding along his throat. "Yes, I think that's a good idea." Something about the heated stare sent goose bumps skittering across my skin. A guy hadn't looked at me like that in a long time—or at least, for most of my college career I'd been too busy with my nose in a textbook to notice. No, this had to be a hallucination caused by my epic dry spell. I was making more out of this than it was. Poor guy was just giving me a hard time, and I was turning it into one of those steamy romances I'd just read on my tablet.

Just as I reached the door he called out, "I couldn't help but notice you didn't add anything in the meeting." He grabbed a stack of papers from the table and tapped them against the surface. His thumb ran across the edge of his papers in a smooth, steady pattern. "Participation is highly encouraged."

"I didn't know if it was my place to say anything." Seriously, my days employed were in the single digits. What did I have to contribute to this meeting? I was Brogan's assistant. Everything he needed to know, I'd already relayed to Jackson, who then gave that information to him.

"Did you list Latte Fetcher on your resume?"

I cocked my head and studied him for a moment, not quite sure what to make of this question. Was I *supposed* to have listed this? Last time I checked, my degree was worth more than basic beverage delivery services. "Of course not."

"Right. I've read your credentials. Many times. You have fresh ideas, and meetings are a chance to share them. It's how I grow my company." He leveled a look at me, with enough ferocity to sucker-punch the breath right out of my chest. A few years ago, during my backpacking trip across Europe, I'd thought I'd met some of the most stunningly handsome men on the planet. I mean, come on, *accents*. That alone was enough to send my swoon meter into the red. But Brogan had such an intensely gorgeous face—even with his lips currently set in a frown— paired with an equally impressive body, and an air about him that could command a room. Every expectation I'd formed about what was truly attractive in the opposite sex was shattered. Brogan Starr broke hearts…and with those delicious forearms, quite possibly beds—not that I'd be finding that out.

He tapped his papers against the table again, and my attention snapped back to him. All congeniality left his face when he said, "Show me I didn't make a mistake hiring you."

"Right." I frowned. I'd get right on that. Looked like I had a lot of work to do if I wanted to keep my job.

• • •

"We gather together to honor the short life of Chanel Cardigan Black Friday Find. Your time on our poor Lainey's shoulders was cut short, but you were with her through rain and overcast days." Zoey grabbed a cupcake from the package and took a ceremonial bite. "Do you have any words, Lain?"

Another tradition we'd started in high school was clothing funerals. Whether a fashion trend died before we were ready to let go (I will never get over the baggy jeans fad) or something was beyond repair, we'd honor our favorite outfits by giving them a proper good-bye. We started out with sparkling cider freshman year, and by the time we reached college, it was boxed wine and Hostess cupcakes.

"You were a great sweater. You kept me warm on cold days."

"Dependable as a good boyfriend," Zoey chimed in.

I swilled my wine. The sad part was that I wouldn't be able to afford anything that nice for a long time. I tried to take good care of my clothes, especially now, with my budget tighter than a pair of Spanx. "More. I didn't need to put out for her."

"I'll drink to that." She raised her wine, and we clinked glasses.

"To the best sweater a girl could ask for." I took a sip of wine and tossed the coat into a cardboard box in my closet. I'd save it for a later date, when maybe in all the spare time I had (ha!) I'd take up sewing.

Zoey handed me the last cupcake in the container and asked, "Want to watch an episode of *Gilmore Girls*?"

"Only if it's a Jess episode."

Anything to get over the fact that work wasn't all that it was cut out to be, and that little problem of not being able to get my boss's brown eyes off my mind. "Deal."

Chapter Six

Starr Media Handbook Rule #263
Animals are not permitted on Starr Media premises.

"Come in to my office," Brogan says, his harsh voice piercing through the intercom.

"Yes, sir. Is something wrong?" I slide past the door and lean against it.

He frowns and furrows his brows as he pages through papers on his desk. "Your work performance is not up to Starr Media quality lately. I'm not happy with your progress."

Sweat trickles down the curve of my spine, and I'm gasping for air. The room is closing in on me. I need this job more than anything—he must know that. "But I've done everything you've asked of me."

"I want more," he demands, hunger in his eyes.

"What do you want?" I don't have more to give.

He rolls up his sleeves, revealing one delicious tattoo at a time, and gives me a dimpled smirk. "You."

My alarm buzzed on my phone, and I shot straight up in

bed. My bangs were matted against my forehead in a soggy clump, and my heart continued to pound against the wall of my chest. What the ever-loving hell was that? I mean, I guess I was still shaken from the meeting yesterday, but naughty office dreams about my boss were the last thing I needed.

I groaned and looked at the time. I still had four more snooze button presses before I had to roll out of bed. I collapsed back on my pillow and tried to lull myself back to sleep, rolling to my left side. Then the right. I tried fluffing my pillow and pulling my hair into a bun. No use—my body was jacked up from the weird Brogan dream. I groaned and rolled out of bed, resigned to the fact that I would not be getting any extra Zs this morning. Fine. Time for plan B. Liquid sustenance.

Morning didn't start until I'd ingested at least four cups of coffee and they'd had time to kick in. Mom claimed she'd never drunk coffee while pregnant with me, but I was convinced that my addiction stemmed from main-lining the stuff in the womb.

With disheveled hair and sleep shorts and a tank, I lumbered my way out of bed and shuffled out to the kitchen. Coffee was already brewed and my favorite cup—*I would cuddle you so hard*—sat next to the pot, clean. Zoey was one of those annoying people that loved mornings, evidenced by her habit of doing sun salutation crap on a yoga mat in the middle of the living room while I pressed the snooze button seven times. At this moment, though, she was a goddess. Anyone who brewed morning coffee could do no wrong in my book.

Cup number three had just been consumed when Zoey bustled into the kitchen, humming something under her breath.

"She's alive," she said, moving toward the fridge and taking out a container of yogurt.

"Merrr," I mumbled and stuck my hands out in front of me, stiffly, doing my best Frankenstein impression. One more cup and I would be eighty percent functional. After I'd tossed and turned last night, replaying the great sweater demise and wrestling with the fact that Brogan wasn't completely convinced he'd made the right choice hiring me, it was well past three by the time I fell asleep.

"Did you eat anything? That rocket fuel's going to burn a hole through your stomach on our run." She pushed a Tastytart (or as I deemed it "cardboardtart" in terms of flavor) across the counter, and I just stared at the foil-wrapped pastry. Off-brand food sucked when I'd been spoiled the first twenty-three years of my life. Which automatically made me feel guilty for that thought crossing my mind, because the least I could do was give up Poptarts to save money for my mom.

"Run?" I feigned ignorance. Maybe if I played dumb, she'd take mercy on me, and I could get away with not working up a sweat before heading to the office. My strategy had succeeded a total of two times, both while Zoey was recovering from a wine bender. Chances weren't looking too good at the moment.

Her lips twitched, but she held her ground, her hand planted on her unfairly perfect hourglass waist. "I distinctly remember you promising to be my running partner this morning."

I pointed my Tastytart at her and took a bite out of the corner. "You took unfair advantage of my wine-induced state last night." It was cruel and unusual to ask promises from a person taking pulls directly from a box of Franzia. We kept it classy.

Even though I was currently feeling the not so pretty after effects of all that wine, I had a hard time saying no to Zoey. We'd always ran together in college, since our campus wasn't always the safest at night and early morning, and the routine had stuck when we moved to Seattle.

"I didn't realize my best friend would leave me to fend for myself to get abducted on the streets of Seattle and end up on an episode of Dateline. They'll find my body parts chopped up and stored in the freezer of some guy who neighbors describe as 'nice, but just a little off.' Do you really want that for me?"

Good lord she was in fine form today, laying on the guilt thicker than extra-chunky peanut butter. Really, it was impressive. Sixteen more ounces of coffee and I'd be able to come up with a worthy retort. Until then, it was zombie nation up in my noggin. "Fine. One more cup of coffee and I'll be ready."

"Sorry, cutting you off. Can't have you yacking all over when we run the waterfront." She grabbed my mug and poured the rest of my coffee down the sink.

"The service in this place sucks," I jeered. I scooted off the stool and headed toward my room to get dressed while Zoey chuckled to herself in the kitchen.

Waterfront Seattle was devoid of the usual hustle and bustle at six in the morning. Much like Portland, a lot of the active business professionals ran along the water. The November chill cut straight through my bones until we were well into our second mile along the bay.

Zoey hated running—something I never understood because she was always so excited up until the point our feet hit the pavement—and she was puffing along with short, shallow breaths.

I'd run cross-country in high school and college, and when I ran, everything fell into perspective. I hadn't been able to get out all week because of my crazy schedule, and the twitchy desire to let off steam had become so bad that I was willing to sacrifice an extra hour of sleep for some much needed exercise.

I was contemplating my goal of finding another deal on

Black Friday in a few weeks when Zoey elbowed me in the ribs. I tore out one earphone and shot her a look. "What?"

"Look at that tall, dark, and give me some of this." She nodded toward a man running toward us, and I fumbled a few steps.

No.

Why?

Of all the spots in the city at the crack of dawn, not just any tall, hot guy was running my way. No, that would be totally awesome and fair of the universe. This man with the sweat soaked gray T-shirt, the material plastered to a set of nicely toned abs, was none other than the friendly neighborhood anti-antichrist.

A dog loped beside him, pulling at the leash to go faster. At my estimation, we'd intersect in the span of fifty steps.

Crap. I knew it was pure coincidence, running (oh, the irony) into him on a morning jog, but my personal vanity would not allow him to see me in such a disheveled pre-makeup, pre-hair-taming state.

This chance meeting could not happen—no, *would* not happen—if I could help it. I pushed Zoey off the paved path and into grassy area with a few large oak trees and waist-high shrubs.

We were well-hidden from view when she asked, "What the hell?"

"That's my boss." I whispered.

"The Antichrist?" She moved to peer around the tree, and I grabbed her shoulders and pulled her back.

She let out an exasperated sigh and threw her arms out to the side. "Come on. He doesn't know what I look like. Why can't I take a little looksee?"

"Because someone staring at you from behind a tree is creepy."

She raised a brow. "So is hiding from your boss behind a

tree," she deadpanned.

"Touché, but I'm willing to let that one slide if you are."

"Yeah, that's not going to happen any time this decade."

She peered around the tree again and let out a low whistle. "I'd totally hit that if I were you."

"Rule book," I reminded her. Which he expected everyone to stick to. Everyone but himself, apparently.

"Screw the rule book. Maybe he could even smack your ass with it."

I chuckled. "You're sick."

She wagged a finger at me. "Resourceful."

As Brogan ran past the tree, the dog went nuts, pulling at his leash and barking in the direction of where Zoey and I stood hiding. I ducked deeper into the bushes, trying to conceal myself properly. Brogan pulled him back and lightly reprimanded him and then went back to long, purposeful strides.

He seemed to be off in his own world, his eyes unfocused and jaw clenched as he ran. If he'd seen us, he didn't give any indication.

"I think I like this view even better." She nodded toward Brogan's retreating figure. His calf muscles strained against his skin, and the fabric of his shorts molded against his ass on every step.

For a few seconds I let myself consider what the routine of Mr. Starr looked like. If he was up this early and stayed at the office until nearly midnight during the week, I doubted the man got more than a few hours of sleep a night.

This was my first real clue to what he liked to do outside of work. He ran. And he was a Seahawks fan. I was two steps closer to writing his biography. Something about him made me want to know more—okay, maybe it was the fact that I was a snoop, but still, his ability to be so nice and yet so powerful intrigued me. My guess, he was a freak in the bedroom and unleashed some of that pent-up boardroom aggression on whoever was lucky enough to be tangled up in his sheets. That sounded deliciously amazing right about now.

Hello, your boss is literally the worst person to fantasize about.

I shook it off and chocked it up to being severely dehydrated. Yes, I was incredibly thirsty, and Brogan was definitely not my brand of Gatorade.

Boss: check

Already made a bad impression. Twice: check

Needed money more than sex: hesitant check

Plus, there was no ignoring the whole 300-page manual filled with insane rules that were better left for a *SNL* skit. Past experience had taught me that a person with that many rules came with a lot of baggage. And his did not need to take a layover in my thoughts (okay, brain, this is the part where you take a hint).

By the time we'd made our two-mile trek back to the apartment, I only had time for a quick rinse off. No time to wash my hair, so I'd pulled it back and hoped for the best.

I was almost functioning at full capacity when I took the light rail to work. I wiped the last of the sleep out of my eyes and entered the building.

Just as I pushed the button for the elevator, Brogan walked up beside me.

"Ah, it's my second assistant." He made a grand gesture of checking his watch and said, "I see your middle name precedes you."

Brogan Starr: CEO and comedian, ladies and gentleman.

A hot flush started in my neck and worked its way up to my cheeks. Of course he would remember the one—okay, he had quite a few to choose from at this point—stupid thing I'd said yesterday. "Would hate to disappoint."

"Consider me impressed." Brogan was wearing a

charcoal-colored suit today, with an immaculately assembled black tie. His chin and cheeks were covered in stubble, and his lips appeared to be a couple shades darker than the past couple times I'd run into him. As if he'd read my mind, his tongue slid over his bottom lip, and I watched, completely transfixed.

My own mouth dried up faster than my bank account at a Sephora sale. *Focus, Taylor. You do not want him. You like the idea of him. Yes, the idea of a powerful man with amazingly broad shoulders pushing you up against the wall of this elevator and pounding you harder than your head after six glasses of wine.*

Okay, brain, so not helpful.

"I think you have a little something in your hair." He reached to the back of my head and extracted a leaf.

The little glimmer of hope that I'd make it out of the elevator without humiliating myself died a slow and torturous death. I stared at the leaf in his hand and contemplated the possibility that somewhere in the world there was a contest for Most Awkward Girl Ever. I'd hands down win the shit out of that. My acceptance speech would consist of a faceplant on my way to the stage, and end with the contest judge announcing they'd called the wrong name just after I'd finished thanking my mother.

"Thanks. Must have fallen on me on my way to work."

"Of course." He smiled.

There was absolutely no way he could know I was at the park. And I'd play ignorant about that morning until the day I died.

He was merciful enough to steer the conversation in a different direction. "Any big plans for the weekend?" he asked.

"Hanging out with my roommate. We're still getting situated in our apartment." Not to mention I was still living out of boxes. I couldn't help but think this was temporary. Something deep down was preventing me from unpacking, because I knew the second I cozied up to the idea that this was permanent, something would happen with my mom and I'd have to move back at a moment's notice. "You?"

"I'll be here." He sighed and gave a conspiratorial grin. "Sometimes I feel like I'm here more than my own apartment."

"You are."

He quirked a brow.

Err…that didn't sound creepy whatsoever.

Lainey Taylor, your friendly neighborhood stalker.

"Not that I track your every move. That would be slightly disturbing."

He turned to me, a look of concern painted across his face for a quick second. It quickly faded as he resumed his typical easy-going smile. Only a little tenser. "Just slightly?" he asked.

Crap. He thought I was serious. I really wasn't racking up any brownie points with the guy who signed my paychecks.

"Okay, very. And I was kidding. I'm in charge of your schedule, so it's only right I know where you are during business hours."

His look said it all: *Riiiiight.* "Tell me again how you passed the background check?" Even though I assumed he was most likely joking, there held a hint of unease in his voice.

"Would you believe I bribed HR with cookies?"

Must. Stop. Talking.

Joking around with him was the last thing I needed to be doing. He was my boss. And yet, my smart mouth refused to shut for one damn second. It was like the elevator ventilation system was laced with some sort of nerve gas that lifted inhibitions.

I stood there, unsure of what to do, or if I'd gone past the point of no return, and my comedy routine had landed me with a pink slip.

After a moment of painfully awkward silence, his lips cracked into a smile, and he chuckled. "Lainey Taylor, you are quite an interesting addition to my staff."

"Interesting" was not exactly a ringing endorsement, but given the current situation, I wouldn't complain about his choice in adjectives. Color me impressed, because nothing seemed to faze this guy. Calling him the devil? No big deal, rolled off his shoulders. Having a conversation about stalking in the elevator? Brushed it off like a pro. Why would I have assumed any different? I was sure if I'd told him I wanted to dress him up as Thor and lick Nutella off his bare chest (not a half-bad idea…), he'd nod and smile and pretend like I'd just asked him about the weather. This guy was the poster boy for even-keeled.

I nodded and decided it'd be smart not to speak anymore.

"It's comforting to know I have such a dedicated employee who knows where I am," he said, a hint of amusement in his voice.

Heat licked my cheeks, and I held back a groan. This was the part where the oversize anvil fell on my head, right? If only I could just pluck the words out of the air and stuff them back into my mouth and pretend that I did not schedule-stalk my boss, that'd be much appreciated.

The elevator stopped at our floor, and we both exited. He kept walking toward his office as I plopped my purse down on my chair.

Before closing his door, he turned and said, "Have a nice day, Lainey. And if you need me, you know where I'll be." He winked.

I went to my desk and laid my head down for a couple minutes, deciding that I should surgically sew my mouth shut.

By the time lunch rolled around, I'd managed to keep a low profile and avoid any contact with Brogan. As soon as Jackson returned from his lunch break, I grabbed my PB and

J and beelined it toward the staff room. Zelda was already there, along with a few other people that I recognized, but couldn't remember their names.

"How's it going, newbie?" With her, it came out as a term of endearment, unlike Jackson's words laced with malice.

"Better today. Just trying to not put my foot in my mouth."

"You get any more clients?" Zelda was the only other person at the company who seemed interested in my role with the firm. Apparently, it wasn't common that a second assistant received clients (or so she'd told me), but with my thesis focusing on social media, and endorsement from HR, Brogan had decided to take a chance and give me an opportunity to prove myself.

I frowned. "No." Not that I'd complain, because one client was a heck of a lot better than none, but my multi-task-loving self was itching to take on more.

"Don't worry. Brogan will see you're doing a good job and give you more in no time."

That was the plan. Keep my head down. Stop making stupid comments. I could at least manage one of those things. "Do you know much about him?" If anyone did, it would be Zelda. She was friends with everyone in the office and knew all the gossip. Like how the previous second assistant was canned due to the fact that she slurped her tea too loud for Jackson's liking (on the DL, of course).

"Like what? He's here a lot and likes the Seahawks. He sometimes wears a jersey on Friday's during this time of year." Both were things I knew and completely unhelpful in my quest for achieving total Brogan stalker-dom.

"What does he like to do outside the office?"

She looked at me, studying my face. I made sure to keep my expression impassive. "Why? You looking to ask him out?" She quirked a brow.

"No," I stuttered, and heat plumed across my cheeks. Was

it bad that ever since I'd first seen him, I'd had a reoccurring dream of our clothes pooled on the floor and our bodies pressed together on the couch in his office? Yes, very bad. But this question was for research purposes only. Like any business associate, the more I knew about him, the more I'd be able to play to my strengths, win him over, and earn more clients.

"I was just kidding. You saw the tattoos, though, huh?"

I nodded. Those were just one of many reasons why I was drawn to him. But it was more than Brogan's looks that interested me. His mere presence in the same room captivated my attention, a magnetic pull that I couldn't ignore. Kind of like how I felt when I listened to John Legend hit those falsetto notes. Mind-numbing would be the only way to describe it. Brogan turned my mind into a bumbling mass of mush.

"Honestly, I'd climb him like a fucking mountaineer if given the chance, employee manual or not."

"Zelda!" I tore off a piece of my sandwich, not willing to admit that, yes, I wholeheartedly agreed with that sentiment.

"What? He's totally hot."

I nodded. "Okay, yeah."

"To answer your question—other than he's a Seahawks fan and likes cinnamon in his coffee, that's about it. He always loves hearing about everyone else, but keeps his personal life to himself."

"How many years have you worked here?"

"Three."

Wow. If she didn't know anything, I doubted anyone else did—besides Jackson, and I definitely wasn't going to pump *him* for information. How could a man hide everything about himself from people he saw every day? Then again, my dad did the same thing. I shuddered at the thought. Brogan was nothing like my dad. Probably.

"If you're into the tattooed men, I have a few friends I

can hook you up with. You should come out for drinks with us this weekend."

Inside I was doing the happy dance at the fact that Zelda extended the invitation to hang out. Someone besides Zoey — because, let's face it, after years of being best friends, she was obligated to hang out — wanted to spend time with me outside work. The initial high quickly deflated, though. Drinks meant money and money wasn't something I was exactly rolling in at the moment. Fifteen dollar martinis added up pretty quickly in terms of what I could use toward Mom's bills. "I'll think about it," I said.

Zelda nodded and took a bite of her tuna melt. "Just keep me posted. I'll make sure Brent is there. He owns a tattoo shop downtown." She wiggled her brows suggestively.

The thing was, I'd never really been into tattoos. In college, I'd dated clean-cut guys that most people would consider all-American, none of them lasting more than a couple months. In fact, I was pretty sure I was only into Brogan's, which was both stupid and a tad bit problematic. Because how could I focus on work when I was lusting after my boss? Not that I was lusting after him.

If I had a penny for every time I'd lied to myself this week…

Maybe going out with Zelda's friend would be a good thing.

I returned to my desk at twelve thirty on the dot. Jackson was nowhere to be found, so I assumed he was either making copies, filing, or off looking at comics on his phone. When I'd gone over to his desk to ask questions, the past few times he'd been so glued to his phone he didn't see me come up.

At around three, the elevator opened, and a petite guy with a T-shirt that swallowed his thin frame came through the doors with something that I could only describe as a small horse pulling him on a leash. Sweat beaded his face as he tried to contain the animal, and his arms strained as he gripped the leather harness. Jackson was in a meeting with one of our clients, which meant I needed to do damage control ASAP.

I waived my arms, trying to get his attention, which was focused on the door at the end of the hallway—Brogan's office.

"Excuse me," I said to the kid. He couldn't have been older than nineteen, and obviously hadn't hit his growth spurt yet.

The kid ignored me and walked toward the office.

I stood from my desk and said louder, "Excuse me. Dogs aren't allowed at Starr Media."

The baby-faced dog walker continued to ignore my existence, and all my patience disappeared.

"Hey, asshole. I'm talking to you," I shouted.

But I was too late, and the guy and miniature pony of a dog were through Brogan's office door faster than I could get out from behind my desk.

The kid shot me a look and handed the leash to Brogan, then exited the office. I quickly recognized the dog as the one from this morning. Well, crap. I really wasn't having much success with the whole "keeping stupid comments inside" today.

"For someone who says they studied the rule book, you have a knack for breaking them, Lainey," said Brogan. There was a hint of a smile in his voice as he crouched down and the dog licked the side of Brogan's cheek. Yuck. I was all for animals showing love, just not when it involved copious amounts of saliva. "Do that again, and I'll be forced to write you up." He looked up at me, this time his expression dead serious.

Again I wondered why he didn't write me up right here and now, considering my predecessors would have surely been ushered off the premises with a small cardboard box of their belongings if they'd done half the stuff I'd managed to accomplish in the first couple of weeks. Whatever the reason, I considered myself lucky and wouldn't try to push my luck any further.

Brogan's sleeve slid up his arm as he petted the dog, revealing an ellipses tattoo on his wrist along with an intricate swirl of black ink. The fabric slid back down after each stroke, and I stood there, mesmerized. Static interference fuzzed over my coherent thoughts, and replaced them with things like mild jealousy over a canine and strong manicured hands.

It took me a second to process what he'd said, since I was still focused on his arms and there being a dog in an office. The dog's tongue lolled out of his mouth, and drool pooled on the floor in front of him. His tail swished against the floor as Brogan scratched the top of his head.

I shook my head, trying to regain some semblance of higher brain function. He'd said something before I went into my tattoo hypnosis.

Right. Rules. No cussing. "It won't happen again." Yeah, because I really was doing so well at following them as is.

A little daydream scenario crossed my mind of Brogan punishing me for breaking a rule.

That'll be five ass-smacks for your disobedience.

"Oh no, I'm so sorry, Mr. Starr. I've been such a very bad girl. Please punish me with those big, strong hands of yours."

Then he'd bend me over his desk, pull up my skirt and his palm would smack my—

"Lainey."

By the way he was staring at me, I could tell I'd zoned out for a little too long with that fantasy. Is this what long-term dating hiatus did to the body? Maybe I needed to join a dating site, because I'd never meet anyone if I was at work during all of my waking hours.

He cocked his head and looked at me. "Have you been

working on Willington's account today?"

I cleared my throat and snapped back to reality. "Yes. I've made three posts and used the pictures from his vacation."

He nodded. "Good. He'll be pleased."

The dog let out a low woof and began pacing around the room. I still could not get over the fact that this beast was in the building. What was this, take your dog to work day?

"That's an, um, interesting dog you have." Could I have possibly picked a worse adjective?

He smiled and pointed to the dog. "Lainey, this is Bruce. Bruce, Lainey."

I'd never been introduced to a dog before, so I wasn't quite clear on the protocol. Shake a paw? Pat on the head? Doggie etiquette shouldn't be this damn confusing. This would be one of those instances where a special rule in the employee manual might actually prove helpful.

Rule 652: When meeting the boss's dog, hop on one leg and transition into a twerk, followed by a flourish of jazz hands. Allowing a polite butt-sniff is also acceptable.

"Nice to meet you, Bruce." I settled for kneeling down to his level, and reached my hand out to pet him. A set of jagged teeth gleamed as his jowls pulled back. Bruce squinted his demonic doggy eyes and snapped at my hand, but I managed to pull it away before he could make a meal out of my fingers.

"Christ on a cracker." I pushed up to a standing position and planted my hands on my hips.

"Bruce!" His deep voice boomed, and he pointed a finger at him. He turned to me and frowned. "Sorry about that. He has trouble meeting new people sometimes."

The urge to blurt out "Yeah, ya think?" was overwhelming. "No problem." I tucked my hands behind my back just in case the beast decided to take another lunge at me.

Bruce rolled over, and Brogan scratched his belly, the dog's behemoth paws twitching in the air as a sound that I could only describe as a pig snort came out of his mouth.

A photograph of Brogan with a little girl in a blue and white dress hanging on his shoulders sat on Brogan's desk. The girl had to be about five, maybe six. Unlike Brogan, she had massive blond curls and big blue eyes. My mind turned to sleuth autopilot. Daughter? Niece? Hopefully the latter of the two. Our first few conversations hadn't exactly been stellar, and his dog didn't seem to like me, so maybe this was my chance to make it up to him. Nothing like asking about a person's loved ones to jumpstart a good rapport. Plus, I was dying to know.

As soon as my fingers touched the frame, Brogan stiffened. "Don't touch that," he boomed.

The sudden outburst startled me into fumbling with the frame, and I quickly placed it on the desk with a hard *thunk*. "Oh, I'm so sorry, I—" I turned around to face him. Jesus. I could not win with this guy. Everything I said and did managed to either concern him or piss him off.

The barest hint of a scowl disappeared from his face within the time I'd taken a breath, but his shoulders were still bunched together, the muscles coiled. "I didn't mean to raise my voice. I don't like my stuff touched. If it's in my office, it's off-limits. Even pictures of my niece."

Private guy. Got it. Didn't like his stuff touched. Wouldn't be making that mistake again. But I did give a big sigh of relief that Brogan was kid-free. "Okay," I said, filling the silence.

All righty then.

I slowly moved toward the door, not sure if I'd make it there without doing something else to piss him off. "Right. Well, I should get back to work."

"Good idea." He cleared his throat and focused his attention on Bruce. "Tell Jackson that he needs to take Bruce home tonight. I have a meeting and won't be able to feed him dinner." He tossed the leash to me and went back to his work.

Right.

I stood there for a few seconds, irked beyond belief at myself that I couldn't manage to have a single conversation with Brogan that didn't involve me screwing up somehow. Seriously, why was I even still employed here? If I weren't in such dire need of money, I'd fire myself and put us both out of our misery.

Bruce turned to me and let out a loud *woof,* and I clutched the leash to my chest and walked out of Brogan's office, shutting the door behind me.

I chucked the leash onto Jackson's desk and made my way back to my own. I still had a bit of paperwork to fill out, enough to keep me busy until after five. But with one client and Jackson hogging all the tasks, that left me twiddling my thumbs for the rest of the week. How was I supposed to prove myself as an asset to the company if I didn't have anything worth contributing?

Chapter Seven

Starr Media Handbook Rule #425
Any misspelled or grammatically incorrect posts must be taken down immediately. Failure to do so will result in a chain of consequences listed in Appendix A.

The next day, I dedicated the entire morning to the Willington account. Cranking out a tweet for Craig was akin to playing a game of Operation. Every time I thought of using a certain word that was on the list of "words that should never be mentioned" an internal buzzer sounded in my head.

Craig_Willington: *Hey ~~you all~~ y'all. Houston was a blast. Can't wait to ~~be in you~~ meet everyone in St. Louis!*

I spent five minutes staring at the exclamation point at the end of the sentence. Would Craig be the type to use one? Or maybe he was more the laid-back, chill guy on social media. How was this my job to worry about expressive punctuation? I felt like I'd just unlocked some sort of life achievement.

Deleting it and adding a period instead, I then attached a picture of Craig crowd-surfing at the Houston concert, the spotlights shining on his sweat-soaked face. Anything was better than focusing on the dozens of ways I'd made an ass out of myself in front of Brogan during my brief employment. If I was going to make it for the long haul, I really needed to shape up with this whole interaction with the boss thing.

Within minutes, thousands of people had favorited the post. One of the rules from Brogan's book stated that it was our job to like or favorite all replies to the posts. Something about boosting signals and hitting more people. Social media had algorithms that I couldn't even begin to fathom.

By the time lunch hit, I'd spent my morning on tasks pertaining to one tweet. No wonder Craig hired our company. It was a full-time job just to keep up with social media.

Jackson sauntered over from his desk with a stack of files cradled in his arms. A couple of weeks into the job and I was beginning to distinguish between the different arches in his brows. So far, I'd identified three definitive angles:

1. The Cartoon Character: *Ohh, girl, I have so much work I'm passing off on you.*

2. The Squiggle: *Your ignorance amuses me.*

3. The One Brow Shooting up Face While the Other is Aimed Down: *I pity you for making an ass out of yourself.*

I'd only seen the third arch once, after the elevator incident. The second happened whenever I opened my mouth to ask a question. This was definitely the cartoonish, over-exaggerated arch that was only be attained by villains and Jim Carrey.

"How's it going, Lenny?"

I looked down at the computer screen, attempting

to quell the urge to roll my eyes. He didn't need any more ammunition. I didn't get why he had it out for me. I'd made it longer than most of the previous assistants, so the hazing should eventually come to an end. Right?

"Lainey," I said, keeping my tone light. He knew this. I'd corrected him for weeks. But I would not let a dude with a comb over and receding hairline get under my skin. Not to mention I was at least four inches taller than him, and I was only five four on a good day.

Last I checked, my big girl panties were securely in place. I had more pressing things to focus on, like not getting fired before my next paycheck could go toward Mom's chemo.

"I need you to address these envelopes." He threw half the manila folders down on my desk. "And file these in the storage room." He dropped the rest of the files on the other side of my desk, papers spilling out across the surface. "Oh, and I need you to walk Bruce tonight. Here's the key to Starr's condo." He slid the key across the part of my desk not littered with paper he'd just thrown down.

The latte I'd been sipping sputtered across my screen. "Excuse me?" Me. Going to Brogan's place? That sounded like a recipe for disaster. The dude already thought I was a grade A stalker. No need to give him any more ammunition.

"Here's how it works, Lenny. I'm Brogan's assistant. You're second assistant. Brogan commands me. I command you. You comply." He gave brow arch number two and said, "If you have a problem with the pecking order, I can make sure to mention it to Brogan, and you'll be canned before tomorrow's meeting."

A knot formed deep in my stomach. I was essentially being blackmailed into walking a dog, but that didn't mean I was stupid enough to try and defy him this early in my career here. I had zero leverage and my mom to think about. And damned if I'd let Jackson succeed in his attempt to bully me out of the company. I was stronger than the masses of second assistants that came before me. "Fine." I grabbed the leash from his manicured hand.

Brogan was scheduled for meetings until ten tonight, anyway. He wouldn't know I'd even set foot in his condo. I bet he didn't even sleep there half the time, because he was in his office before I came in and left long after I went home.

Jackson smirked and swaggered back to his desk, turning to me before he reached his chair. "Oh, and word of advice: stay in front of Bruce at all times. He has a major flatulence problem."

A dog with fart issues. Jesus, what had I gotten myself into? I clutched the leash a little harder.

"He gets two scoops of kibble and seventeen squares of wet food. You must chop them up in one inch by one inch chunks or else he won't eat it."

My gaze flicked to his. This had to be a sick joke, one that was followed by a "ha ha, just shitting you, loser who now has this horrible responsibility of walking a gassy dog." Except Jackson didn't look like he was joking. His normal air of superiority dissipated, and he looked very serious for once.

"You need to follow that exactly. Do you understand?"

I tilted my head at him, wondering why this was so important. Besides the fact that I was going to be in my boss's house when he most likely—100 percent likely—wouldn't be okay with it. "Yes." He was making this such a bigger deal than it needed to be. It was a dog. Eating dog food. This wasn't business calculus.

Before I went to make copies for Jackson, my phone rang. I picked it up with much less anxiety than during my first week on the job. "Starr Media, Brogan Starr's assistant Lainey speaking. How may I help you?"

A smooth voice caressed my ear. "I'd like to speak to Brogan. Tell him it's his father calling."

After the whole Gizzara incident, I knew better than to deny his dad. "Yes, sir." I put him on hold and buzzed through to Brogan's office. "Mr. Starr?"

His gruff voice came through the intercom. "Yes?"

"Your dad's on the other line. I put him through."

"You *what?*" he growled.

Okay, so family calling work wasn't a good thing. "I'm sorry, I assumed since it was your dad…"

"Have you ever heard the phrase assuming makes an a—"

I scrunched my eyes shut and inwardly cursed myself. Seriously, I could not get this right. "Yes. I'll make sure to ask next time."

Before I said anything else, the red light on my phone disappeared. Even if he was pissed, he at least took the call.

A few seconds later, muffled shouting came from his office. I couldn't make out most of what he was saying, but choice words cut through the walls and streamed into the entryway.

Note to self: Don't put Brogan's dad through if he ever phoned the office again.

I walked to Brogan's apartment building after leaving the office at seven. I stared at the lone silver key in my sweaty palm, the metal catching in the light outside Brogan's door. I had a feeling that Brogan would have a conniption of epic proportions if he knew I had access to his personal sanctuary right now. This went way beyond a picked-up picture frame.

I let out a deep breath and put the key in the door. Before I could tell what was happening, a brown blur leaped from the ground and tackled me to the floor. My back hit the tile with a muffled thud as my boots slipped out beneath me. Drool splattered across my face as Bruce stood on my chest, licking at my hair, pulling strands out of my French braid.

My arms shielded my face, taking the brunt of the tongue assault. "Jesus, Bruce, I need to be wined and dined before making out." Sad truth, this was the most action I'd seen in months. With everything going on, I wasn't left with much time for things like picking up dudes at bars. Although I was still kicking myself for not talking to the guy reading Emerson on the light rail.

Bruce backed off my shirt and sat beside me, tongue still lolling out of his mouth.

"Does this mean we're friends now? Earlier you wanted to bite my head off. I need a man who doesn't go hot and cold."

He let out a loud woof, which I took as an insult because he ripped a fart near my face and then trotted into the apartment with his tail wagging.

I closed the door behind me and glanced down at the gaping hole in my shirt that hadn't been there prior to my opening the door. A piece of fabric was stuck to one of Bruce's nails and flopped around on the floor as he pranced around the kitchen island. A special circle in hell was reserved for this dog.

Bruce trotted over to a set of matching silver bowls. He pawed at the empty one and let out a high-pitched whine.

"Yeah, yeah." I looked around the expanse of the kitchen, all the granite counters clear of anything indicating where Bruce's food might be. "Help me out here a little? I don't know where your food's stored."

Was it possible for a dog to have a condescending glare? Bruce really knew how to channel the "you dumbass" look. Jackson must have been rubbing off on him. He huffed out a sigh and loped over to a cabinet and sat in front of it. He pawed at the door and let out another loud fart.

"Maybe you need to get a different brand of food," I muttered and pinched my nose as the smell assaulted my nostrils.

He growled, and I rolled my eyes and opened the cupboard. Boxes and cans of organic food were stacked with expert precision on the top half of the pantry, and a clear bin with dog food was at the bottom.

I scooped out two cups worth of dry food and Bruce went airborne, dashing toward the bowl. A skittering of puppy paws tap danced across the wood as he impatiently waited for me to drop the food in his dish.

"Sit." I commanded.

Bruce barked in response, his butt not coming any closer to the floor.

"Sit." I repeated.

Bruce huffed—and was that an eye roll? Could dogs even do that? This was exactly why I liked cats. They weren't needy, and they certainly didn't leave puddles of drool that called for a mop and heavy duty rain boots. Zoey's cat Jitters was far superior to this mangy mutt.

I wasn't up for playing games, so I dumped the food in the bowl and almost lost a finger when Bruce lunged at the bowl. This solidified it. I'd never in a million years be a dog person.

My next hurdle was to find the wet food, which Jackson had been kind enough to mention that Brogan kept in the fridge. I unwrapped the neatly packaged dog food and gagged as soon as the scent hit my nose, by far worse than Bruce's gas.

With my nose plugged with one hand, I managed to cut seventeen cubes as per Jackson's instructions and quickly wrapped the rest and shoved it back in the fridge. I didn't even bother walking all the way to Bruce's dish, I just set the plate down on the floor and let him go to town.

As he was in doggy heaven snarfing down food, I finally had a moment to take everything in. To say Brogan's furnishing style was minimalistic was an understatement. If Jackson hadn't told me that he walked the dog every other evening, I wouldn't believe someone lived here. There was a dining room table, a French press, a couch, a basket of dog toys, and a huge television in the living room, but that was the extent of the decor. No family pictures on the wall, no empty glasses sitting in the sink, not even a pile of mail on the kitchen counter. Nothing in here indicated that this apartment was inhabited by my boss. *Did* he even live here? Or was he so rich that his dog got his very own condo? Somehow this wouldn't surprise me. From what I heard, those Silicon Valley zillionaire types were a cupcake short of a baker's dozen when it came to anything outside of work. Why would Brogan be any different?

Well, for one, he made eye contact when we spoke, and had the ability to flip the good old hot and bothered switch with one look from those deep, soulful brown eyes.

Oh boy. Not the best idea to fantasize about the boss's eyes while technically trespassing on his property. Then again, since I was here, I might as well take advantage of getting to know the boss on a deeper level than his Wiki page, right?

Ever since I was a little girl, I had this fascination with Nancy Drew. My earlier years were spent honing my sleuthing skills—though Mom would argue that I was a snoop and just liked going through people's shit. Technicalities aside, I liked knowing more about people, what they chose to keep as opposed to trash. It would annoy my mom to no end when I went through her stuff, but after a while she came to terms with my snooping.

My Nancy Drew itch got the best of me, and I slyly made my way to the fridge for a better look. Just like a man's hair, you could learn a lot about a person by what they kept in their fridge. Organic milk, an industrial size bag of chocolate chips, microbrew beer, and a container of leftovers wrapped in foil made up most of the contents of the fridge. In other words: boring.

Instinct told me I was pushing my luck, that I should close the fridge, but I couldn't help prying a little more and lifting the foil to his leftovers. I realized then this was an all-time low if I was in someone's apartment digging through their food, but the Nancy Drew gene was a force to be reckoned with.

As soon as the foil lifted, the comforting aroma of garlic chicken with a pesto sauce wafted out of the fridge. Aha! Garlic! What a hypocrite. For one second, where I claimed total insanity, I contemplated taking a bite.

Girl, you are not Goldilocks. Drop the garlic and move away while you still have your dignity.

The voice of reason had spoken, and I quickly tucked the foil on the container and backed away from the fridge. Bruce had finished his chow and sat next to my feet, judgment in those devil eyes.

"What? I didn't eat it."

He let out a huff.

"Like you've never thought about eating his food." I scowled.

Not like my sleuthing even worked because besides the fact that Brogan liked chocolate (which, seriously, I'd start to worry about the guy if he didn't) and had quite possibly the grossest dog in the city, I was no closer to finding out anything about him.

Chapter Eight

Never get in-between a girl and *Bachelor* night.

I snuggled into the recliner with my bowl of rocky road ice cream with exactly two minutes to spare. After stripping out of my ripped shirt and exchanging it for a comfy old tee, I made sure to call my mom for our weekly ritual: *Bachelor* co-watching.

"Are you ready? It's almost starting."

I reached for the remote and clicked through until I found the channel. The preview for this week's *Bachelor* was just finishing up. "Rodger that."

"Do you think he's going to let that airhead Vanessa go this week?" Mom asked.

Zoey rushed into the room, toting a bag of microwave popcorn and a bowl. "Did I miss anything?"

"Mom thinks Vanessa is going to get voted off this week."

Zoey had been an addition to our house ever since she lost her mom to a car accident in middle school. Soon after we started weekly rituals, movie nights, pajama parties, and it'd stuck even ten years later.

"No, he likes her boobs too much. I'm guessing it's Jill," said Zoey.

Mom let out a loud sigh that blasted through the speaker in my phone. "But Jill is so sweet."

I eyed the phone while Zoey smirked. "Mom. Since when did that earn points with Derek?"

The line went silent for a moment, then she added, "Good point."

"Okay, shh, it's starting!" Zoey whisper-yelled.

The most sacred of all Taylor family traditions was *Bachelor* night. I'd only missed it once, and that was when I'd been in the ER with appendicitis. And even then, my mom had DVRed it, and we watched it as soon as I got home from the surgery.

"How was Dictator Jackson today?"

I shot Zoey a look. I hadn't told my mom about the incidents at work because I didn't want her to worry. She had enough on her plate. She didn't need to hear about another man with control issues. She'd already had enough of that with Dad. When he wasn't off, you know, having a secret life on the side. Although Jackson had one up on my dad because I highly doubted Mr. Comb Over was living a double life with two separate families. The guy probably didn't even have a girlfriend.

In some ways, though, Brogan (barring the obvious attraction) reminded me a lot of my father. He had all the rules and hardcore policies. He was charismatic, just like my father had been...to one too many women, apparently. I'd just like to understand what made a person like that tick. Then again, if he really was anything like my dad, I should stay far, far away. Nothing but pain could come from that type of man.

My mom chuckled. "Who's Dictator Jackson? Does he

have a handlebar mustache?"

I eyed Zoey, signaling to keep her mouth shut. "My coworker. Complete d-bag."

"Eh, screw him. If he's that much of a jerk, he probably won't last long in the company," said Mom.

Yeah, not so sure about that. Jackson seemed so far up Brogan's ass, he could be medically diagnosed as a polyp. "Mm-hmm."

Zoey got up and made her way to the kitchen while Mom fired more questions my way. "Is your boss nice? You haven't talked much about him these past couple weeks."

Did it count as nice that he said nothing when I stared at his crotch? Or that, in fact, he was very nice, both on the eyes and personality-wise. So much so, that my shower head was getting a lot more action lately.

Mom didn't need to hear about my boss and coworker woes, though. I needed her to be as stress free as possible, and I had Zoey to vent to in the meantime while she went through chemo.

Before I could answer, Derek just promised Jill she was getting a rose in tonight's ceremony. "What a rat bastard. He's so lying through his teeth," I said.

We managed to make it through the whole episode without Mom needing an emergency bathroom break. Her intense nausea seemed to taper off a few days after chemo treatments, thankfully. As soon as the episode ended, I promised to call her after her chemo appointment in a few days, and hung up.

Zoey turned to me, almost tipping the bowl of popcorn sitting between us on the couch. "What was up with that earlier?"

"With what?" I popped a piece of popcorn in my mouth and stared at the TV.

"You not wanting to talk about Mr. Epic Douchebag.

Mama Taylor is usually privy to those juicy details."

"You know how Mom gets. One whiff that I'm having trouble at work and then there's a million questions. She's already stressed enough with her treatments."

"Secret's safe with me." Zoey pretended to zip her lips and throw away the key. "But what are you going to do about him?"

"What can I do? I just need to not screw up long enough to prove my worth there."

She nodded.

"Is that dog hair?" She picked a hair off my knee and examined it.

I rolled my eyes. "Bruce hair. Don't even get me started."

"Bruce isn't a coworker is he?"

I huffed out a laugh. "No. Bruce is half horse, half leaky faucet."

"Jitters will be jealous that you're fraternizing with other species."

Zoey's cat was currently curled up on the windowsill, looking at the city skyline. She'd promptly ignored me when I walked in, but I attributed that to her usual lack of shits given about anyone but Zoey.

Zoey pulled out her laptop from her leather satchel and opened an Excel spreadsheet with a rainbow of colors and formulas. It dawned on me that I hadn't even bothered to ask about her day. As soon as I breezed through the door, it had been the Lainey Show. Really, I was winning in the friendship category this week. "How's your workload? Any new clients?"

She shrugged. "I have a new client meeting next week. Getting used to all the logistics. Lots of paperwork. Nothing like I thought it'd be."

"Right? The real world is so anticlimactic." I pushed my head into the back of the couch and repositioned my feet on the coffee table.

Zoey rolled her eyes. "Not everything can be like the movies."

"If it were, I'd have to do some major snooping in Brogan's apartment for a torture room."

"Hey, I saw those arms. I wouldn't mind being the subject of his torture."

"I'll give you one of the employee manuals. That should have you screaming the safe word in no time."

"Point taken," she said, and went back to eating popcorn and checking social media.

I decided to open up my email and make sure I didn't have any pressing issues that needed to be handled before the morning. A deluge of CC'd interoffice memos flooded my inbox as I scrolled down the list. Just as I was about to close down my email, a new message pinged. My heart stuttered as my eyes scanned the sender. Brogan.

My first thought was *crap, I should not have snooped in his fridge; he totally knows I almost ate his garlic chicken*. It was followed by the realization that the email was only addressed to me, something that had never happened before.

FROM: BROGAN STARR
TO: LAINEY TAYLOR
SUBJECT: MEETING TOMORROW

Lainey,

Jackson will be out of the building tomorrow. Can you schedule a phone conference with Patrick Duvall tomorrow at 8pm. Tell him we'll be discussing his client's growth in media following.

-B
Brogan Starr, *CEO Starr Media*

Antichrist

My heart tapped tiny staccato beats against my ribcage. He'd emailed *me*—okay, because Jackson was off tomorrow, but still!—to handle someone as important as Patrick Duvall, and he'd snuck in a joke about being the devil. I quickly clicked the reply button and pondered how to respond. The appropriate reply would be a short *On it, boss,* but when in the past few weeks had I been appropriate around Brogan Starr? No sense in starting now.

FROM: LAINEY TAYLOR
TO: BROGAN STARR
SUBJECT: RE: MEETING TOMORROW

I will call him first thing in the morning. Hope you get to leave the office soon.

Lainey Taylor
Second Assistant to Anti-Antichrist
Person Suffering from Chronic Foot in Mouth Syndrome

Yes, this email was fishing—and slightly unprofessional. Except he totally started it. I couldn't help wondering, though, where he was right now. In his office? Back in his barren apartment with Bruce slobbering on his leg? I didn't even want to delve into the reasons why he might be thinking of me at such a late hour—because *Ah!* Brogan Starr was thinking about me after ten!

Good thing he couldn't see that I had the mentality of a middle schooler when it came to my interest in him…which would surely go away sometime soon. Right as soon as I gave up dark chocolate and free samples from Sephora.

A reply came back almost immediately.

FROM: BROGAN STARR
TO: LAINEY TAYLOR
SUBJECT: RE: MEETING TOMORROW

Who says I'm at the office? For someone who claims to know my whereabouts at all times, you're doing a poor job.

Brogan Starr, CEO Starr Media
Employer of uninformed 2nd assistants

This definitely counted as flirting, right? I wasn't just imagining it. What did it say about me that I wanted to flirt back? *That you're a normal, red-blooded American girl with a Kindle overloaded (never!) with office romances.* I stretched my neck and gave myself a moment to come up with another reply. This was not flirting, this was Brogan being nice, as always, in his witty, typical way.

FROM: LAINEY TAYLOR
TO: BROGAN STARR
SUBJECT: RE: MEETING TOMORROW

I'll try to hone my schedule-stalking skills by next month's meeting.

Lainey Taylor
Non-stalker Second Assistant

FROM: BROGAN STARR
TO: LAINEY TAYLOR
SUBJECT: RE: MEETING TOMORROW

Good. You'll know where to find me. Good night,

Lainey.

Brogan Starr*, CEO Starr Media*

"Good night, Mr. Starr," I said. There'd be no sleeping any time soon on my end. Not with thoughts of rolled-up sleeves, strong hands, and a set of irresistible dimples to keep me up. What had changed his mind about me? Maybe, just maybe, I was finally fitting in to the company. I closed my laptop and smiled. What had I gotten myself into?

Chapter Nine

Lainey Taylor Rule of Life #77:
If you decide to trespass into your boss's place, make sure he's not home first.

I grabbed the leash off Jackson's desk at the end of the workday a week later. I hadn't seen Brogan the rest of the week after the email exchange, and there hadn't been any other email interactions, which made me think that a) I'd imagined the whole thing, which would be entirely possible if I didn't have the emails as evidence, or b) He really was just being friendly, nothing more. Which was entirely more plausible.

Jackson had already headed home and instructed me to walk and feed Bruce. This being the fourth time in the matter of a few weeks, I'd stopped getting that smarmy feeling whenever I stepped into Brogan's condo.

The ten-minute trek to the apartment chilled me to the bone, and by the time I entered the building, every muscle in my body was tightened in on itself, trying to conserve heat and energy. In concept, I was a huge fan of cold weather. Pumpkin spice lattes, boots, and skinny jeans? Sign me up. But stick me in sub-sixty-degree weather for more than two minutes, and I was shivering more than a teacup Chihuahua. For a Portland girl, I was a wimp.

Bruce was sitting in the entryway, tail thumping against the floor, when I entered the posh apartment.

Before he could jump up, I put my hand out in front of me, standing my ground. I'd read a few online dog obedience articles during lunch today, and was willing to try anything to preserve my clothes. So here I stood in Brogan's entryway, having a showdown at the O.K. Corral with this slobbery heathen.

There was only room for one alpha in the room, and it sure as heck wasn't going to be Bruce. "Sit, boy." I'd made the mistake of wearing tights with my boots this morning and did not want to walk ten blocks with holes running down the expanse of my thighs.

Bruce licked his chops and gave an exaggerated huff, but followed my command and plopped his butt down on the slate tile.

I smiled, relieved that I didn't have to go through another round of chasing him down the hall, or dusting paw prints off my shirt. "Good boy." Maybe he wasn't too bad. We'd just gotten off to a rocky start.

I worked my way into the kitchen and picked up his food bowl, then moved over to the pantry to scoop some kibbles into the bowl. We'd found a good routine, Bruce not jumping all over me, and me getting as little dog saliva on my skin and clothing as possible. It's not that I hated dogs. I mean come on, who didn't love a cute Yorkie? But Bruce was, to put it in the best terms possible, a disgusting, slobbery dog. Drool pooled on the floor, slopping from his jowls as he waited for me to get two scoops of food from the pantry.

My lips curled in disgust. "We need to get you a bib, dude."

Bruce huffed in response. Apparently he didn't like my dig at his leaky mouth problem.

The food scoop had disappeared into the quicksand of kibble, and I had to dig to get it. As I was stooped over, sifting through the food, one inhalation shy of keeling over from the toxic fumes, there was a tug at my sweater. I ignored it as my fingers hit the metal scoop.

I measured out two cups and turned to drop it in Bruce's food bowl, but was immediately thrown off balance. I turned and found a large chunk of my sweater in his mouth, his jaw working a hole in the thin fabric.

"What the hell? Your nasty food probably doesn't taste great, but neither do my clothes." I tugged my sweater out of his mouth, pulling it close to my body, and the soppy wet end wacked against my thigh.

He abandoned my sweater for dog food, not caring that he had, again, annihilated another sweater.

"What is with you and ruining my stuff?"

I'd decided to hold off on the wet food until after our walk, since that was what seemed to give him the most gas. A less gassy Bruce equaled a happier Lainey.

I pulled my sweater tighter around me and grabbed his leash off the counter. The wet spot Bruce had used as a chew toy sopped against my leg, and I glared down at him.

He just wagged his tail in response. Monster. Hope the sweater gave him extra gas tonight—after I left.

I leashed him up, and we strode out to the elevators, his toenails clicking against the tile. I looked down at the mutt and shook my head. What was the story with Bruce anyway? Everything else in Brogan's life seemed so clinical, clean, organized. This dog was a mess. What neat freak who couldn't handle garlic in the workplace wanted a dog that farted non-stop and left a trail of drool like a slug along the slate floor? It didn't make sense.

It wasn't my job to speculate, though. It was my job to make enough money to not drown in health insurance debt for the rest of my life.

As soon as Bruce and I entered the street, I pulled my phone out of my purse and dialed home. Mom had just gone through another chemo treatment today, and I wanted to check on her. She picked up after the fourth ring, her voice weak.

"Hello?"

"Hey, Mom."

She took a deep breath, exhaling into the phone. "How are you, sweetie?" Her voice trailed off, barely carrying through to my end of the call.

Dang, she'd sounded more tired than I'd heard her after prior treatments. "I'm okay. How are you? How did treatment go today?"

She paused for a moment, the silence saying more than anything else. I imagined her hunched over the toilet, all alone in the house, no one to take care of her. What if she passed out? What if she had a bad reaction and no one was there to take her to the hospital? All the what-ifs washed over me and my gut twisted.

"It was tough."

A cold sweat broke out on my back and everything suddenly felt too warm, too much. For her to admit this meant things were way worse than I'd originally envisioned. This was the same woman who shot a nail through her finger during a kitchen DIY project, and instead of freaking out, took a picture first and laughed the whole way to the emergency room. "The doctors don't think these meds are working as well as they should be. I'm going on a new cocktail next week."

My heart lodged itself in my throat, and I pinched my lips together to keep from letting out a sob. Obsessing over worst-case scenarios really wasn't how I tended to live my life, but this was a living, breathing incarnation of my worst nightmare. In fact, nothing else was on the same playing field.

How many other treatment options were there? What if this next one didn't work well either? Tight tendrils of fear gripped my chest, and it took me a second to work away the stiffness and realize I was the one who needed to be strong here. *I* wasn't the one who was fighting cancer, because I refused to believe she was dy—I couldn't even bring myself to *think* the word.

"Do you need me to come home? I can drive back this weekend." If I actually had PTO, I'd leave right that second with the damn dog riding shotgun in my car. My voice warbled, and I blinked away the fresh sting in my eyes. Nope, I would keep it together. This was a setback, not a catastrophe.

She sighed, and her voice took on this breathy quality that I'd never quite heard from her before, like someone who was breathing through their mouth to keep from vomiting. "No. I'd like to be alone for a few days."

I was a three-hour car ride away, and I felt completely and utterly helpless.

"Mom, it's no problem. I'm here for you." I had to offer at least once more, because in all honestly, I'd lasso the moon for this woman if there was a remote possibility of that making her feel better.

"I know, sweetie. But give me a few days, okay?"

I was twenty-four years old, and I didn't care who knew it—I needed my mommy, and I wanted to comfort her, but I wasn't about to go against her wishes. If she wanted to be alone, I had to respect that. Tears pricked at the corners of my eyes, and I quickly wiped them away with my jacket sleeve.

Bruce whimpered softly and brushed against my leg, looking up at me with those big black eyes.

Right then, I knew in my heart it was a mistake coming to Washington, being this far away from Mom. Money meant crap if she didn't make it past chemo. I hung up and squinted my eyes shut, the air magically vanishing from my lungs. My legs buckled and I fell to my knees in the middle of the park walkway as tears began to stream down my face. I tried to calm my breathing, acutely aware that I was in public and people were probably starting to stare. Bruce licked my cheek, and I hugged his neck, crying into his fur. He put his paw on my arm and I got the distinct sense that he was trying to protect me.

Breathe. You can't give up or else she gives up.

I gave myself a few more moments to compose myself, wiping at my eyes, and then straightened. This was not the Lainey Taylor I'd worked so hard to become. Crying didn't solve things, and if I was anything, I was a fixer. So I'd suck it up and do the right thing, because I was *not* losing her. I couldn't. She was my best friend. Life without her wouldn't be living.

I wiped the tears from my cheeks and looked down at Bruce's sad face. "Don't tell anyone about this, okay?"

He wagged his tail and gave a *toot toot toot* of flatulent reassurance.

I rolled my eyes and tugged at his leash. "You're still gross."

By the time I got back to Brogan's apartment, I was in no mood to deal with Bruce's antics. If he so much as looked at my jacket or shoes the wrong way, I was just going to dump the wet food on the floor and book it out of there.

I fished Brogan's key out of the jacket pocket and looked down at the dog, who, for the first time in our interactions, looked down in the dumps. I squatted down to his level and gave his thick head a scratch. "Don't you know, Bruce? Ladies like men with a proper drool to butt sniffing ratio. You're not going to have any luck with them at the rate you're going."

I stood, still feeling the weight of the day heavy in my shoulders, and turned the key. Pushing the door closed with my foot, I unhooked Bruce and placed the leash on the counter.

I leaned against the granite and pulled out my phone once again to see if my mom had changed her mind and wanted me to come down to Portland tonight. When the screen lit up, I frowned, my phone empty of messages.

"What the hell are you doing here?" a loud, very unhappy Brogan Starr bellowed from across the room.

Chapter Ten

My head snapped up and my phone clattered to the ground. Brogan stood in the middle of his condo, wrapped in a towel. Hung very low. Droplets of water beaded down his chest, rolling over the taught muscles.

The towel lay flush against his body, outlining a bulge. On a scale of *aww…how cute* to *there's no way that's fitting*, it was the Goldilocks of bulges. Just right.

I swallowed hard and realized a few seconds too late that I was staring at his lower half and the trail of hair leading to parts hidden by the towel. What was with me and thinking about his damn dick? It had been a while since I'd seen any action with a real-life one, but this was getting ridiculous. A silicone one did the same thing and didn't come attached to a person who decided my financial fate. Okay, this really wasn't the appropriate time to debate the pros and cons of dildos versus my boss's dick, standing in his kitchen while he was half naked. And I was still staring.

My head shot up, and I met his eyes. "You're home." *Real smooth there, slick.*

"And you're as observant as ever," he said drily. "That doesn't answer my question, though. What are you doing in my house?"

He wasn't supposed to be home. I'd checked the schedule—he had a phone conference with Japan until nine tonight. Shit, was I going to lose my job because of this?

All that came to mind was *durrrrrr*—I'd been hypnotized into a state of Brogan Starr Bulge Mind Melt. (It's totally a thing, okay?) Yeah, because that response would go over well. Once I gained the use of my voice, I said, "Jackson sent me to take Bruce on a walk." I left out the part where I'd been doing this for the better part of two weeks.

His eyes narrowed. "You aren't supposed to be here. Only Jackson is allowed in my apartment."

"I'm so sorry. Jackson was…" *Think.* Even though I disliked Jackson, I'd never put his job in the crosshairs intentionally. Though I could safely bet the feeling wasn't reciprocal. "Sick."

The weight of everything that had happened in the last hour slammed into me like a semi truck. Seriously, did all this shit have to happen today? I wasn't one to be a woe-is-me girl, but really, when all roads pointed to Rome, well, it was happening.

He raised a brow, and his mouth worked. I knew this was it, he was about to fire my ass for something Jackson made me do. And then I wouldn't be able to pay any flippin' healthcare bills. And if I couldn't pay bills, then would my mom receive treatment? My pulse throbbed in my temples, and I couldn't tamp down the temper bubbling to the surface. A girl could only have so much shit flung on her Jimmy Choos before she went into rage mode.

His voice was cool and matter-of-fact as he said, "I don't care if Jackson promises you the damn Taj Mahal. I don't want you in my apartment. This is my personal space. Bruce only responds well to people he knows. To trustworthy people." This was the first time I'd seen him be uncharacteristically uncharismatic.

Hell. No. What a condescending prick. Screw this totally hot man standing painfully naked in front of me. Screw the fact that he insinuated I wasn't trustworthy enough for his damn dog. Heat pooled at the base of my neck, and I narrowed my eyes. "You know what? I have bigger things to focus on than your damn rules. I mean, who the hell cares if there's a semi-colon in a tweet? Nobody! Or how about the whole leggings aren't pants thing dress code, because I have a pair in my closet that begs to differ." I threw my hands in the air. Who did he think he was trying to make everyone abide by his stupid manual that made zero sense? "And you're welcome for walking your slobbering mutt in freezing weather while he pisses on my shoes, and tries to hump a poodle that's way out of his league."

He took a step back, his annoyance quickly morphing into shock. "Excuse me?"

I took a step toward him, not backing down from what I'd started. If I was going to get fired, dammit, I was going to lay it all out on the table because tonight I really gave zero shits about Brogan and this stupid job two hundred miles away from the person who needed me most.

"You heard me. I've been dealing with my mom who has cancer and who's dy—" I paused to collect myself, my throat tight. "Bills keep piling up, collectors keep calling. The last thing I need is for you to treat me like I'm some asshole." My breaths came out in heavy pants, but I kept going. "I walk your damn dog for you. One who uses my sweaters as kibble, because the small horse probably isn't getting enough food.

Seriously, you need to feed him more, because he can't survive on my cashmere sweaters."

Brogan went to speak, and I put a finger up, signaling I wasn't quite done giving him a piece of my mind.

"And another thing. The garlic rule is totally stupid. Everyone knows Luigi's is the best place to eat, and your office rule is a total buzz kill. On a side note, it is really hard to rant when you're standing there in a towel." I'd at least managed to keep my gaze from meandering below chest-level. Okay, maybe my eyes wandered a couple times, but that just proved my herculean restraint, because it could have been much worse.

He blinked hard, and the corners of his mouth twitched in amusement. "Are you done?"

I crossed my arms and looked down at Bruce, who was wagging his tail, looking from me to Brogan. Damn dog. "Yes."

His gaze softened. "Sit down." The two words were quiet, but still held the authority of a man who ran a Fortune 500 company.

I shifted my eyes to his, not understanding. Surely he should have called security by now, or at the very least had Bruce chase me out the door. "What?"

"I said sit down." He pointed to the leather sofa in the living room.

I was still fuming and feeling a bit sassy, heavy on the *assy*, when I said, "You know, for a boss, you're awfully bossy."

He shot me a look. "I'm going to let that slide because you're having a shitty day." As he led me to the living room, he motioned for me to sit on the sofa. "Do you like tea?"

"Coffee."

He nodded. "Okay."

I sat there alone in the living room, staring at the mantle. There were no pictures hung, just abstract art. A fire crackled in the hearth, and Bruce snuggled next to the heat, belly up on the white shag rug. I shifted on the sofa, feeling suddenly self-conscious that I'd just told my boss off while he was half-naked, and he hadn't kicked me out.

He came back a few minutes later, fully clothed in a black T-shirt and gray sweats, carrying two steaming mugs and handing me one.

"Thank you." I cleared the last bit of sniffles out of my nose and cupped the coffee with both hands.

Brogan cleared his throat and shifted restlessly on the couch. "I'm sorry to hear about your mom."

I frowned, staring into the coffee. "Me, too. She's my best friend." I blinked back a few rogue tears that were trying their best to escape. What would I do if she didn't make it through? I'd have Zoey, but my father was living his own life now, and my grandparents were long passed. I'd be a twenty-four-year-old orphan. Did that even count if you were past eighteen? "I don't know what I'd do without her."

He cut his eyes to me and said, "I hope it doesn't come to that, but if it did, you'd be fine." A small, comforting smile formed at the edge of his lips, and without the expensive business suits and corporate environment, he seemed so much younger than his work persona. His gaze softened, and for the first time since I'd met him, Brogan didn't look like he minded being in the same room as me.

I smoothed my thumb over the rim of the coffee mug, wisps of steam curling into the air. How could he be so sure when I felt like the life I'd built was being ripped out like the pages of a story. "How do you know that? You don't even know me."

He placed his mug down on the coffee table and turned to me, his expression serious.

"Because if you were the type to give up, you wouldn't come to work for me, and you certainly wouldn't put up with a bunch of *rules.*" He used air quotes for emphasis.

Damn me putting my foot in my mouth. I really had no self-preservation whatsoever when it came to keeping this job. "That came out a little harsh, didn't it?"

He smiled. "Yeah, but I understand. I know it's not easy on a lot of people, but it's how Starr Media runs."

"Then why do you put all these ridiculous rules into effect?"

He let out a heavy sigh, and for a split second I could feel the weight of Brogan's world heavy in my chest. The hundreds of calls every day. The thousands of questions. I loved working at a big corporation, but I would never want to run one. "Because if I didn't, I leave myself open to the possibility of hurting my company. Starr Media means everything to me, and I'd never do anything to risk that."

I tilted my head and did my best to hold back the sarcasm in my question. "How is a garlic breadstick going to hurt Starr Media?"

"You obviously haven't been on the receiving end of a garlic-eating mouth-breather client."

I blanched. "Can't say I have."

He leaned back and spread his arms across the top of the couch, making himself comfortable. "I used to play racquetball with a client who would eat Italian before playing, and he'd literally sweat garlic." He shuddered.

"Gotcha. Personal vendetta against Italian."

"My cross to bear. Although, I really do love Italian food. Just not on other people."

I decided not to share that I knew this little tidbit from my perusal of his fridge the other week.

"Nice to know you get out of the office at some point. It's good to get exercise and fresh air."

"I usually run along the waterfront. Racquetball is only for clients."

"Me, too. Funny we haven't run into each other." Besides

the bush-hiding incident that I'd take to my grave.

"You mean besides that one time a few weeks ago?" His voice held a playfulness that I'd never heard in the office. Brogan was always congenial and charismatic at work, but this felt different, slightly more intimate. "Or was I not supposed to bring that one up?" He winked.

My jaw dropped. Was there anything this guy didn't know? I swore I'd hidden before he even had the chance to notice I was in the vicinity. "How did you—"

"Can't say many people jump into bushes when they see me coming. Or have leaves in their hair when they come to work. You leave quite a lasting impression, Taylor, I'll give you that."

Heat trickled to my neck and cheeks, and if the sofa happened to swallow me up, I'd be thankful right about now. "Yeah, I don't even want to try to explain that one."

He nodded and a smile played at his lips, but after a few moments his expression turned serious. "All joking aside, this company is my life, and the first few years are always the toughest with any business. I know these rules may seem a little"—he searched for the right word—"tough, but I have to do whatever it takes."

"But you need to get out and have fun once in a while. You'll drive yourself mad if you're in your office twenty-four seven."

"Aren't I supposed to be the one trying to make *you* feel better, not the other way around?"

"Giving life advice to people older than me does the trick." In fact, talking with Brogan, along with the cathartic rage, was a welcome distraction from worrying over my mom.

He shook his head and smiled, probably reassessing his decision not to call security when he had the chance. "I'm supposed to take advice from someone who hangs out in bushes?"

I swatted him in the arm and immediately retracted my hand. Smacking my boss probably wasn't the smartest route to go, especially if it was flirtatious. Crap, I wasn't just hitting Brogan, I was hitting *on* him.

"Fine." He put his hands up in defense but still had a smile etched on his face. "What do you suggest I do?"

"I don't know. Go out to movies? Clubs? Do you like dancing?"

"Negative on the dancing. My mom signed me up for ballet when I was seven, and I got kicked out when I spit in my teacher's bun."

"Okay, dancing is officially crossed off the list. I'm surprised that's not in the manual."

He side-eyed me. "Pushing it, Taylor."

I stuck out my tongue. "Pushing the limits is what I do best. It's why you hired me."

He raised a brow. "Is it?"

"Judging that I've made it past the one-month mark, I think so." In fact, on Monday, it'd be two months, as long as I didn't manage to get canned within the next few hours.

"Yes, you have. An impressive feat. And if you really must know, I like to stay in and read. Sometimes I play online chess."

I cupped my hand to my ear. "Do you hear that?"

His brows furrowed in confusion as his eyes darted around his condo. "Hear what?"

I picked up my phone and pretended to take a call. "Hello?" I put my hand over the receiver and whispered, "It's AARP, calling about your membership."

He chuckled and shook his head. The dimples made a quick appearance, and my mind fuzzed to static for a split second before hearing his question. "Okay, fine, what do *you* do for fun?"

"I usually watch Netflix with my roomie, *Bachelor*

every Monday with my mom, and I like hiking and farmer's markets."

He smiled and sat back against the couch again, his arms spreading across the top and his left leg propped up on his right knee. This was the most casual I'd ever seen Brogan, and I had to admit, the look was particularly appealing tonight.

"What were your plans tonight, after you were done breaking into my house?"

"I was *not* breaking into your house. I was taking care of your dog while you were supposed to be in a meeting. But if you must know, I was going to go home and bake."

His eyes darted to mine with newfound interest. "What do you like to bake?"

"The Taylor specialty is chocolate chip cookies. My mom's recipe is awarded the blue ribbon each year at the state fair."

Brogan groaned. "That sounds amazing. I haven't had cookies in forever."

"What? They don't go well with your prune juice and Tums?"

His lips pressed into a thin line, but I could tell he was trying his best to suppress a smile. "I'm still your boss, you know."

"What were you planning on doing tonight, since you've mysteriously come home early from your meeting?"

"Watch a movie. Maybe a documentary," he said matter-of-factly.

"A documentary? Oh, boss, we need to get you in the twenty-first century. Where's the remote?"

He handed me the remote, and I clicked into Netflix.

"Have you seen *The Breakfast Club*?"

He shook his head. "No. Does it involve bacon, because I could get behind that."

I looked at him with wide eyes and a serious concern that he'd grown up in some cult in the middle of nowhere. "Jesus.

You're worse off than I thought. How have you not seen this? It's a classic." Even though I wasn't even born when most of the classics came out, my mom and I watched them all the time when I was younger.

He shrugged. "Didn't watch a lot of movies growing up."

"What *did* you do?" Movies were a quintessential part of my childhood. Each movie marked a different stage in my life. My first date watching *Fast and the Furious* on my Mom's couch. Watching *The Notebook* after every breakup. Or kicking it old school, binging on *Ferris Bueller's Day Off* and wishing I could be Sloane.

"I was busy with school and studying. My parents were…" He trailed off. I would have prompted him to explain further, but a stormy expression bloomed across his face, darkening his features. From the way he reacted during the phone call to his father, I knew their relationship must be less than amicable.

I clicked on the movie and cued it up. We both sat in the middle of the couch, nothing but a few inches between our hands as they rested at our sides. It occurred to me that I'd just invited myself over to watch movies with my boss. Who I'd just seen in a towel not thirty minutes prior. I so deserved to be canned.

I hadn't been on a first date in a long time. Being in Brogan's house—uninvited, no less—was a far cry from a first date, but the whole fizzling situation going on in my stomach didn't care about this tiny detail.

We nestled in just as people in the movie started arriving for mandated detention, and I found it a little ironic that I was sitting next to someone who was a polar opposite to me—like Penny and Leonard from *The Big Bang Theory*. Wait, did that make me the science geek or the failed actress in that scenario? I guess if I lost my job, I was one step closer to working at the Cheesecake Factory. And I could probably pull off a dress better than Brogan.

I folded my hands together in my lap and forced myself to stare at the movie, fighting the urge to glance over at Brogan. Which went about as well as trying to rein in my one-click finger while perusing Amazon. Even I didn't have that kind of self-control.

You ever get those déjà vu moments where you're transported back to the horrible hellhole of seventh grade, and Lenny McCafferty, the star quarterback, is sitting on your couch in the basement, watching a movie with you? Except you're not really watching the movie, more like not-so-discreetly checking this person out, and your eyes are burning because you're overusing your peripheral vision? And instead of enjoying the movie, you wonder why you suddenly have turned into the world's loudest breather, and you're sweating in spots that you didn't even know perspired? Yeah, that was me as I settled in on Brogan's leather sofa.

Except this time, I didn't have braces or a horrible case of bacne, but the sudden worry of that tacos for lunch mixed with coffee sounded very unappetizing in terms of the breath department.

Much like with my middle school crush, I'd been struck by a severe case of what I liked to call The Self-Awares. It was the perfect setup for a medical commercial.

Hey you! Yeah, you, the one sitting on the couch like an antisocial dimwit. Are you suffering from a bad case of the self-awares? Unsure? Symptoms include:

*1. **Awareness of how many freckles are on your skin.** As a fair-skinned person spending a lot of time in the sun, this was inevitable, but since when did I have so many?*

*2. **Reduced resistance to environmental smells.** They were hard to ignore when Brogan was fresh from the shower. A mixture of cologne and body wash wafted my direction, and my body instinctively leaned toward the smell.*

*3. **Poor body placement.** I'd chosen the worst possible spot of the couch—the crack. Now my ass was sandwiched in between the cushions and vice grips might be required to excavate me. It was past the time of opportunity to move to either side of the crack because either Brogan would think I was trying to hit on him if I inched closer, or if I moved farther away, he might wonder my motivations.*

*4. **Peripheral vision overuse.** Because, is he watching the movie or me?*

I had a truly severe case of the Self-Awares if I was over-thinking couch placement. Every time I was in Brogan's vicinity this feeling would pop up, everything was so fresh, so new. Maybe it was the dry spell. Maybe it was his tattooed arms and muscular chest that discombobulated my damn neurons. Whatever it was, it took everything in me to hold on to my composure and keep my ass planted on my side of the couch.

He put his arm on the top of the sofa, and from what I could see out of my burning eyes (Self-Awares Syndrome Symptom #4 at work) his fingers curled naturally into a fist near my shoulder. If I moved a couple of inches to my right, he'd technically be putting his arm around me. With this realization, the hairs on the back of my neck stood on end, and my pulse picked up a few notches. I closed my eyes and inhaled Brogan's clean scent and idly wondered what body wash he used because I'd never smelled anything so masculine and delicious in my life.

He shifted toward me, and my pulse ticked against my temple in rapid rhythm. "Let me get this straight. They send all these people to detention and then leave them alone? That sounds like a lawsuit waiting to happen."

"It was the eighties, what do you expect?" Okay, so I wasn't even a blip on my parents' radar in that decade, but I'd heard stories from my mom. And, according to her, the movies weren't too far from the truth. I used this opportunity to reposition myself, making sure to put myself a little farther from Brogan and out of the dreaded crack. His gaze focused on the spot I'd just moved from, and I'd give up every couch make out session from my past to know what he was thinking at this exact moment. "Plus, what kind of story would it be if they couldn't conspire against the principal?"

"Did anyone ever tell you that you have horrible taste in movies?"

"Quite the contrary. I always picked the flicks for movie night when I was in college. People trusted me with this important decision."

A wry smile twisted his lips, and he sat back against the couch. "Under duress? Or did you break into their house and take over their living room, too?" He bumped his knee into mine and let out a low chuckle that rumbled in my chest.

I stared down at his sweats where they'd just connected with my leg, then took a quick glance up his chest, finally ending at his strong stubbled jaw. His tongue slid over his lips and his eyes twinkled with playfulness when he looked at me. He cracked an easy smile and his dimples made a reappearance.

Hello, lady parts? Are you there? Nope, no answer, most likely due to the fact the rubble of my ovaries was scattered over a ten-mile radius. Seriously, how was this guy single?

A 180 pound wall of pure muscle sat next to me with a few shreds of clothing in the way. Was it getting hot in here? The coffee from his French press must be giving me hallucinations. Brogan Starr actually loosening up and…flirting?

I decided the best thing to do was to ignore it and keep my cool. "Ha. Ha." I gave my best eye roll and focused my gaze back to the movie. "Just keep watching. I assure you, you'll change your mind."

He folded his arms, putting his tattoos on full display, although from my non-obvious peripheral ogling, I couldn't make out any specifics, just swirls of black ink against his skin. Teen me would high-five present-day me for this moment, aside from the fact that it was my boss and we were in this weird pity-Netflix time warp.

"Wait, now they're just toking up in school? What about the essay?"

"Loosen up, Starr. They'll get there. They have to realize how pigheaded they've been toward each other first." Because if this movie taught me one thing as a teen, it was that people were more than the front they put on for other people. Just like there was more to Brogan than his hundreds of rules and CEO title.

"That Andy dude's father deserves to be punched in the face." He scowled. Brogan leaned forward, his forearms resting on his legs as he watched, transfixed. Crappy movie choice, my ass. He was totally into it.

I smiled. "That he does."

The last few minutes of the film played on the big screen, and I sighed. This movie never got old, no matter how many times I watched it.

"Isn't that the best?" Claire had just given John her earring, and all was right in the world of the best detention ever known to mankind.

"I…have no words." He said, still staring at the TV in

what looked to be horror.

I crossed my arms over my chest. "I don't think we can be friends anymore," I joked.

His gaze flicked to mine, and my breath caught in my throat at the intensity of his eyes. "We aren't friends. I'm your boss." I couldn't ignore the heat in his expression, the same flicker I saw the day my sweater fell victim to Betsy. I'd give anything for him to push me down on the couch and make me forget my name.

"Right. It was just an expression." I cleared my throat and shook off thoughts of couch fornication.

He nodded. "Tonight was nice. It's been a long time since I've hung out at home."

Something about that statement jogged me out of my little bubble of bliss. This guy lived and breathed his job. Not that I didn't work unhealthy hours, too, but this cut way too close to home. It was bad enough I was infatuated with him, but I saw firsthand what happened with relationships with workaholics. Secret families weren't a high risk with Brogan, but he was kind of married to his job. The experience with my dad was enough to give me pause. But I was getting *way* ahead of myself, because this wasn't heading that direction. Not that I wouldn't enjoy doing a personal inventory of every muscle on his body.

"Anytime." I backtracked. "I mean…" I sighed. I really needed to work on thinking before I spoke in front of him. "Oh, you know what I mean."

"Yeah." He smiled. "I do."

"I should be going. Thanks for listening. I feel a lot better." Even though the stress of everything going on with my mom would likely flood back as soon as I got back to my apartment, it was nice to have a short reprieve.

Just as I stood, he cleared his throat and held up a hand. "I'll walk you out." He pushed up from the couch, and the muscles in his biceps bunched together in the most delicious of ways. It took a moment of channeled concentration to fight back the urge to violate at least ten rules in his damn employee manual.

He ushered me to the elevator, locking Bruce in the apartment. I turned to face him after I hit the down button. Just inches apart from him, I had to crane my neck to look at his face. If I took one step forward, our bodies would press flush against each other, and my hands would be forced to splay against his chest. Something that I'd like. A lot.

His eyes searched mine with a softness that stole the air from my lungs. This new side of Brogan, with the joking and laughing…I wanted it to continue. But starting at seven on Monday, things would go back to normal—professional colleagues. Ones that nodded in the hallways and said a polite hello as they passed. The way it was supposed to be.

"I—" He breathed the word, like an exhale. He lifted his hand, inches from my cheek when the elevator dinged and the doors slid open. His hand dropped to his side, and he pressed his lips together.

What?? I wanted to scream. He couldn't just leave me hanging like that. Surely he had something insightful to say. Such as *I want to throw you over my shoulder and take you back to my condo and do unspeakable, delicious things to your body,* or *I think your excessive babbling and breaking into my apartment is sort of cute and am glad I hired you.*

"I'll see you Monday." He gave a nod and then proceeded to pat me on the shoulder.

What the hell just happened? Did I…just get rejected?

I did a quick mental inventory of the various types.

Levels of rejection*:*

> *Full-on rejection: dude swiping left on your Tinder pic. Burn.*

Semi-rejection: guy suddenly going dark on social media after a date. Rude.

Quasi-rejection: trespassing into your boss's apartment, forcing him to watch your favorite movie, and ending the night with a friendly pat on the shoulder in the same manner as someone consoling a kid who lost a t-ball game. Off-putting but understandable. Right?

I stepped into the elevator, ignoring this odd sting of quasi-rejection. "Bright and early."

The elevator doors shut, and I leaned against the rail and stared at my flushed face in the mirrored panel. I was in so much trouble.

Chapter Eleven

<u>Lainey Taylor Rule of Life #32</u>
***If you don't want to board a train to Crazy Town, stop
trying to read into things. Seriously, stop.***

Zoey was in the middle of the living room on a yoga mat,
posing in a sun salutation when I woke up. Jitters was belly-up
on the couch, waiting for me to scratch his tummy as I passed
him to grab my laptop.

"How's your upward froggy pose?"

"This is cobra. And it wouldn't hurt you to try this, you
know." She curved her spine and splayed her arms straight
out on the mat, going into what I thought was a child's pose.
In college, I'd joined her in a yoga class and ended up falling
asleep in that very position. Best sleep I ever had. Which was
quickly interrupted by the instructor telling me to *Namaste*
the hell out of her class. "Did you know that people in desk
jobs are eighty percent more likely to get blood clots?"

I moved toward the kitchen, grabbed my cuddle mug and
poured a full cup of coffee. "And did you know that I'm 100

percent closer to dying each day I live?"

She let out a deep belly breath and shook her head. "I really adore your stubbornness sometimes."

"It's one of my many endearing qualities." I smiled sweetly at her.

"Yeah, yeah." She continued with her yoga poses as Jitters eyed her, his tail playfully swatting the couch cushion.

"I'm going home this weekend to see my mom. You able to hold down the fort?"

"Yeah, I need to catch up on my paperwork. I'll also be at the center," she said.

In Zoey's spare time, she enjoyed working with kids at the youth center. All were from at-risk homes, and I didn't doubt she would be the Michelle Pfeiffer those kids needed to stay out of trouble.

"Where were you last night? I didn't hear you come in."

I smothered a smile, trying my best to contain my excitement "Brogan's."

Her eyes widened. "Like, with Brogan?"

"Not *with* him with him, just spent the evening on his couch."

"I need all the details, woman. Did he remove the stick out of his ass before he entered his home, or is that a twenty-four seven accessory?"

"I kind of walked in on him as he got out of the shower."

Her brows disappeared under her bangs. "The plot thickens."

"That's what she said," I interjected. I could never pass up a good *that's what she said* joke.

She gave me a look. "The pun was totally intended. Okay, hold on—was he naked?"

"In a towel, but I saw things."

"Things," she repeated and gave a quizzical look.

I raised my brow. "Things."

"And how did these *things* measure up?" She put her hands out, using them as a makeshift ruler. I shook my head, and she spread them wider. I shook my head again, and she gaped. "Dear God, woman. That just sounds unhealthy."

A delicious heat pulsed between my legs just thinking about his lean chest. The water droplets that clung to his skin. The edges where tanned skin met intricate tattoos. "I didn't actually see it, so it might have been a mirage."

"And you just watched movies…on his couch? Or are we talking, like, Netflix and chill?"

"Just a movie." I frowned. Did it still count as friendly if I'd *wished* more had happened? I didn't quite know how to feel about that yet. It had been a long time since I'd saddled back up for dating, and in terms of horses, Brogan was an Arabian. Wild, untouchable, not meant to be ridden by employees in any capacity. Why couldn't I set my sights on a nice Paint. Or a show pony? Something safe.

Not only was it against company policy, but if I went for him (which I totally wouldn't, because I liked to think my hormones didn't make me stupid), what happened if it ended badly? I couldn't afford to lose this job.

A cashmere scarf and riding boots were perfect accessories to pump up a dreary fall day. Red and yellow trees lined the sidewalks, and mist hung in the air, coating my clothing in a light sheen of raindrops. Like most of those living in the Pacific Northwest, I tugged my hood over my head tighter, opting out of an umbrella. Nobody but transplants used umbrellas, and I wasn't going to start now.

As soon as I got in the building, I removed my coat and shook off the water beading on the fabric. I smiled to myself as I pushed the button to the fortieth floor, thinking back to the other night. The Brogan cold front had passed and was now turning into a major heat wave.

Jackson was at his desk, typing away, when I breezed through the elevator doors, this time keeping my coat tightly fixed to my sides. A coffee cup was sitting in the middle of my desk, and I cut my gaze to Jackson.

"Who left this here?" In a moment of weakness, I hoped it was Brogan, like a secret "I had so much fun the other night, here's a cup of coffee because I think you're awesome" kind of treat.

"Zelda."

Relief and disappointment flooded over me. Of course it would be from my only friend in the company and not the man who I walked in on naked. Okay, almost naked. Wishful thinking. What dream world did I live in where CEOs of multi-billion dollar corporations doted on assistants? I really needed to lay off the office romances for a little bit because, much like Disney princesses, they were planting unrealistic ideas in my head, like the possibility that my boss could be smitten over me. Because in real life, if I screwed things up, it wasn't just my life that would be ruined. "Oh? Do you know why?"

He pointed to his pinched face and said, "Does this look like a face that cares enough to ask?"

"No," I said under my breath. "No, it doesn't."

I gave a tentative smile as I tore open the note left under my coffee.

Happy two-month anniversary at Starr Media. Here's to many, many more!
-Z

Six weeks longer than my last two predecessors.

I took a sip and groaned. My absolute favorite drink.

"Double caramel mocha. Light on the whip," said Zelda

as she rounded the corner to the front of the office.

"How did you know?"

She put her hands on her hips, and her dangly earrings jingled as she talked. "Girl, it's my job to know everything."

"Right." I took another sip. "And thank you. This is really nice."

"My pleasure. Nice to have some new blood in here who actually appreciates people." She tossed a glare at Jackson, and he grimaced back. Most of the other coworkers seemed to tolerate Jackson, but Zelda openly showed her complete and utter disdain.

"Anyway, I have to get back to work. Congrats on the big milestone."

"Thanks." She pulled me into a quick hug and her corkscrew curls tickled my nose.

As soon as Zelda disappeared down the hallway, I turned to Jackson and said, "I ran into Brogan on Friday."

"Where?" he whispered, like this was some top-secret meeting.

"At his apartment."

His beady little eyes popped open, and he slammed his hands down on his desk with enough force to rattle his coffee mug. "What did you tell him? I swear if you threw me under the bus—"

"Relax." Maybe it was the milestone coffee giving me that extra sense of security, but I propped my hands on my hips and leveled him with the same condescending look he so often used on me. "I saved your precious hide."

As if to contradict me, Brogan's voice boomed through the speaker. "Lainey?"

I pressed the button on the receiver. "Yes?"

"In my office. Now."

Jackson's pasty complexion paled to a nice shade of Vampire White, and his eyes pleaded with me as I moved toward Brogan's office.

Good. Let him sweat. He'd made my life hell for the past two months and deserved a little taste of his own medicine.

The glass door closed behind me with a soft hiss. I held my hands behind my back, not sure what to do in this situation. We'd spent a fun night together, but we were in our work environment now, and I didn't know what, if anything, carried over. Or there was always the possibility he'd decided to pull out the rule book, tell me exactly how many rules I'd violated, and send me packing.

A smile played at his lips as he watched me fidgeting obviously. His demeanor, even from last week in the office, had taken a complete one-eighty. "How is your sweater doing today?"

Relief ebbed through me as I realized I hadn't been called in here to be fired — or if I had, he was a seriously sick individual for joking with me first. I thumbed the material, pretending to inspect it. "Untouched and unslobbered."

"Good to hear. Sit down." He motioned toward the chair across from him.

As I sat down, I crossed my legs and smoothed out my pencil skirt.

He steepled his hands together on the desk, tapping the pads of each neatly-manicured finger together. "I was thinking. Bruce really likes having you around, and so I thought I'd pass off walking duties to you instead of Jackson."

I went to uncross and re-cross my legs, and in the process the toe of my boot brushed against his leg under the desk. We both froze, his eyes locking with mine. If I'd looked away for even a second, I would have missed the dilation in his pupils, and the way his Adam's apple slid down his throat as he swallowed hard. A shudder started at the base of my spine and splintered through my back.

I cleared my throat and decided to focus my gaze on

something safer, opting for the picture of Brogan with Bruce on his desk. Much like the other night, the heat of self-awareness—mainly the awareness of how elated I was to come into contact with any portion of his body—prickled the skin from my elbows to my toes.

Note to self: start an eHarmony account, because this is treading dangerously close to the pathetic category.

"That's fine. I can handle you." I choked, realizing what I'd just said. "*That.* I mean I can handle that, not you." I ran a hand through my hair and resisted the urge to groan.

Schoolgirl crush. That was the only way I could explain this feeling. Back in high school, there was the demigod of all science teachers—Mr. Chandler. He was young for a teacher, wore his T-shirts tight across his broad chest, sported tattoos much like Brogan, and the taboo of liking someone so forbidden had played a key role in my infatuation with him. That was all this was—an infatuation. Because Brogan had the *S* trifecta: Sexy, Smart, and SO out of my league.

His warm brown eyes studied me. His teeth nipped at his bottom lip, and I imagined what they'd feel like dragging over my neck, my arms, my—

He cleared his throat and unbuttoned his blazer. "As long as this won't be a problem, I think you're a better fit."

Wait. What? Better fit for what? I was jostled out of my Brogan stupor in time to see a wicked grin playing at his lips. I backtracked through our conversation and realized my mind had gone ten steps beyond dog walking. While he was focused on a proper caregiver for his pooch—seriously, Jackson's nurturing ability would emotionally stunt a pet rock; what had Brogan been thinking?—I was focusing on whether he was a giver or taker in the bedroom. Most definitely a giver.

That settled it—dating site would happen tonight. And under personality traits would be: delusional, fantasizes about the wrong people at the wrong times, and "dog people need not apply."

I crossed and uncrossed my legs again, this time making sure I wouldn't bump Brogan. "I guess I'll be over tonight?"

"Yes. I have a conference until nine. No impromptu towel meetings again."

"Probably for the best." My subconscious side-eyed me. *Oh, I'm sorry, did an alien suck your brain through a swizzle straw?* In what universe was this a good thing?

He nodded, his expression turning businesslike, sliding back into our roles as they'd been before the other night. Amicable acquaintances. The shift in his demeanor was palpable, the room suddenly stuffier than a sauna. "I think so, too." He tapped his pen against his desk, but kept his gaze on me. "I'm sorry if I gave you the wrong impression. I stand firm on *all* my policies in the handbook." That one word said everything I needed to know.

Laymen's terms: Not dating you.

"Of course." I kept my face impassive. The guy was doing me a huge favor. This was exactly what I needed to crush this annoying—okay, so it wasn't annoying, but lying to myself felt so much better—fantasy of being with him. So what if I'd do unspeakable things, worse things than I'd commit for a Klondike Bar, to catch a glimpse of his dripping wet body in a towel again? Hell, no need to be wasteful with laundry, forget the towel.

I blinked away that thought. He gave me a job, and with it, an opportunity to break into a cutthroat business. Throwing that away for a chance at a weekend romp was both stupid and juvenile. Now if only that memo would hurry up and arrive at the other parts of my body.

The key to his condo was already on my desk when I got back outside. Jackson sure wasn't in any hurry to relinquish his dog walking duties or anything. Bruce wasn't *that* bad. Slobbery and gassy, yes. But any dog who let me hold him while going through a quarter life crisis was okay in my book. Now we just needed to work on him not making a meal out my very expensive wardrobe that I couldn't afford to replenish any time soon.

Okay, maybe it still sucked, but I didn't care because that night with Brogan, worrying about my breath and if I'd applied enough deodorant, was a bright spot in the suckage of the past few days.

By the time lunch rolled around, I had scheduled my posts for the week and managed to book a few appointments for Brogan. As a treat to myself, I went to the dollar taco stand a few blocks away, and since the rain had let up for a little bit, I decided to stroll around the park. After shoveling the tacos down, I pulled out my phone and dialed my mom's number. I hadn't spoken to her over the weekend because I was trying to give her space, but anything past three days was pushing it. We'd planned for me to head home this weekend, and I wanted to make sure we were still on for a junk food and movie fest.

She picked up on the third ring, her voice sounding way more chipper than it had on Friday. "Hello, love bug."

"Feeling better?" I said, hopeful for any improvement since last week.

"Much. Just went in for an appointment to finalize the drug combination for the new treatment."

I smiled, a weight lifting off my chest. "That's great. When do you start?"

"Wednesday. Are you still coming home this weekend?"

"I was thinking about it. If that's okay with you." This would be a much needed distraction from the fact that I wanted my boss and the feelings weren't mutual.

"Of course. Sorry I needed my space. But nothing a Greasy Guy's burger couldn't fix."

I groaned. "I miss Greasy Guy's." I missed eating good

food from home. In fact, I missed everything about home.

"Then it's settled. Saturday, you, me, and Guy's takeout."

"It's a date."

Anything to keep myself distracted.

Chapter Twelve

Never piss off your mom. The wrath is far worse than any shit storm you can possibly imagine.

"I, Lainey Taylor, am a successful, smart, independent woman." I gave a nod to my reflection in the rearview mirror.

"Men do not dictate my thoughts. Especially men with tattoos and dimples." If I could magically cash in all the lies I'd told myself in the past few weeks, I'd have enough to pay for Mom's treatments and still have money leftover to fill an in-ground pool with coins and swim around in my wealth.

"I will not be a Lapdog Dean. I am a Jess. Completely cool and unfazed." I wrung my hands on the steering wheel, and an overwhelming sense of relief washed over me as I crossed the bridge into Oregon. This was my opportunity to press the reset button on life and get back to square one, remembering what was really important in life—family and love. Not a boss who flirted with me—maybe? Sort of?—but was completely off-limits.

By the time I pulled into my old driveway, my mood had lifted, much like the early morning fog blanketing Portland.

All of the sunflowers and dahlias had closed up in the piercing late autumn chill. The oak trees in the yard were holding on to their last leaves, brown and dull, waiting their turn to float down to the rain-soaked walkway. I pulled open the creaky wooden door to our downtown bungalow and wiped my boots on the mat.

"Mom," I called, unwinding my scarf and laying it on the coat rack, shucking off my jacket as well. A toasty warmth wrapped around me as I breathed in the familiar scents of home—something baking in the oven, a fire in the fireplace, and fresh laundry.

"In here." Her voice carried from the living room to the hall. I made my way down the entryway and turned left before the stairs. Mom lay sprawled across the couch, two blankets tucked over her. She sat up when I entered the room, and a smile spread over her face. "There's my love bug." She held out her arms, and it took every ounce of restraint not to barrel into her.

Since starting chemo, she'd lost about ten pounds. She'd already been fit from her marathon training and Crossfit, so the loss was a more substantial hit to her slender frame than it would be on others. Her collarbone jutted out sharply, and her cheeks had sunken in. The sight formed an automatic knot in the back of my throat.

I sat on the couch beside her and leaned on her shoulder, breathing in her comforting smell. My mom's signature scent hadn't changed since I was a child: a hint of ginger, peppermint, and vanilla, like a complex latte that you can't help but want to bury your nose in because it smells so good.

"You look tired," she said, smoothing her thumb over my cheek.

I cocked my head and did the smart thing, keeping my

mouth shut. The irony did not escape me.

In fact, "you're tired" ranked right up there with one word answers to texts—both annoyed the ever-loving crap out of me. Because, really, it was a socially acceptable way for someone to tell you that you looked like shit. Then again, with the long hours I'd been putting in at work, there was no denying that I'd be adding wrinkles instead of tan lines for the unforeseeable future. A few years in the job and I'd look like the before and after on a D.A.R.E. poster. *This is you on four hours of sleep, deadlines, and 100 milligrams over the Recommended Daily Allowance of caffeine.*

"Long drive." I didn't need her worrying about my work schedule. She had to focus on her health, solely.

She gave me another once-over, but didn't say anything else on that subject. "How is work? Is that obnoxious twit Jackson still giving you a hard time?"

The name elicited a Pavlovian eye roll and the sudden urge to bang my head against something hard. "He's gotten better. I think he's finally accepting me into the company."

"Well, that was inevitable. You're sweet. How could he not like you?"

"Not everyone has to like me, Mom. This isn't kindergarten."

She pursed her lips and patted my thigh. "How is your boss?"

Besides the fact that he turned me down, great. I was still deciding which was more mortifying—the fact that he'd made it clear nothing would happen between us or the fact that I hadn't even been coming on to him in the first place. "He's good. Giving me more projects to work on."

A grin spread across her face. Her smile was a welcome breath of fresh air. If she was smiling, then the world couldn't possibly be that bad of a place. "Sounds like you're doing really great. One of these days, when I'm feeling better, I'd love to come to your building and see where you work."

I smiled. Any talk about the future was both comforting and welcome, and the constant vice grip around my lungs loosened the tiniest bit. "I'd love that, too."

She grabbed the takeout menu for Greasy Guy's from the coffee table and raised a brow. "Ready to destroy our girlish figures and ingest a few gut bombs?"

"Always." The Taylor metabolism hadn't failed me yet, and I was going to use it to its full advantage for as long as possible.

"I bookmarked a few movies on Netflix that I thought would be good," she said, pulling up the number for the restaurant on her phone.

I lay my head on Mom's shoulder and everything else seemed to dissipate. "Sounds perfect."

The food came forty minutes later, and while I demolished the entire half-pound burger with caramelized onions and enough pickles to be classified as a biohazard, she'd barely taken three bites of hers.

"You okay?" I asked, piling another fry into my mouth.

She frowned down at the burger. "I think my eyes are bigger than my stomach."

She was looking a little queasy, most likely from the new chemo treatment. A wave of unease settled in my gut, and I pushed the remainder of my food across the coffee table, out of reach, no longer in the mood to carbo-load. My hope was that after a few more months of this new medication, Mom would be on the mend and getting back to normal life. I pushed back the what-ifs and focused on what I could control—spending time with her right now, because that was all I really could do.

Just as Mom cued up a movie on the TV, my phone buzzed, jumping along the wood of the coffee table. I ignored it and snuggled closer into her, the blanket pulled over my arms and chest. The transition into a carb coma was well underway, and I was ready to hibernate on the couch until Sunday evening.

My phone vibrated again, then two more times before I decided to pick it up.

Jackson's nickname flashed across the screen, and the primal urge to Hulk-smash the phone coursed strong through my soy-latte-run-hating veins. During the weekends, I'd *maybe* inferred to Jackson that my apartment had horrible cell service just to get a few hours to myself. And if it were any other weekend, I'd claim just that, but we'd happened to have been working on one of Jonathan Gizzara's clients' accounts this week, and I had a sinking feeling that the texts were directly related to this. The last thing I wanted was something to go wrong with an account that I'd personally worked on.

Grinch: *Can you come in this weekend?*

The proper response to this: *Screw off, tiny dictator.*
But, since I valued my job, I replied: *What's going on?*

Grinch: *It's the Gizzara account. Brogan wants us to share our findings in the presentation on Monday. You can help me present.*

Shut the front door. I stared at the text and read it five times just to make sure I wasn't imagining it.

Jackson was willing to work with me on a project and share credit in a meeting? This was huge. I could finally contribute something essential to the team and solidify myself as a functioning member of this company. Maybe this would lead to a different position. Okay, I was getting a little ahead of myself, but this was a huge step forward. A Bigfoot-size step.

I glanced at my mom who was flipping through Netflix to find a show, and my heart sank. To give up this opportunity would set me back at least a month, because who knew when

I'd have another chance to work on such a high-profile client case.

Lainey: *I'm in Portland. Can I work from here and send you slides?*

The second the text sent, my guilt-meter teetered in *crappy daughter* zone. To analyze the data we'd discussed in meetings this week—that would take me at least ten hours of work, if not more. I mentally calculated, and with traveling back to Seattle at a reasonable time, there was no possible way to watch all the movies Mom wanted to catch up on and get this presentation finished in time, too.

Grinch: *Yes. Send me your data on Tegan Jackson and Elliot Hurr.*

Lainey: *Thanks, Jackson. I'll have it to you by tomorrow night.*

Grinch: *Whatever. Don't screw up.*

I sighed and chucked my phone on the couch cushion next to me.

"What's the matter, honey?"

I took a steadying, self-loathing breath. "Work."

She frowned. "On the weekend? Is this why you've been so tired?"

"It's one of our multi-million dollar clients. He needs projections for next year by Monday." That phrase felt foreign and douchey coming out of my mouth. It went right along with "I drive a Lincoln," and "I only buy T-shirts that cost more than a laptop." Coming from a Portland girl with chickens in her backyard, who preferred Oktoberfest to a wine tour in Sonoma, it was unexpected, to say the least.

"Do what you need to do. I'll be right here." She gave a weak smile and the stab of letting her down speared through me.

"You're sure?" The hollowness of my question made me want to punch myself in the face. "I can wait until I get back home."

"No. This sounds really important." She gave a reassuring pat to my thigh.

I pulled my laptop out of my bag and cued it up, while Mom watched a movie. Her mood shifted from jovial to something I'd describe as *Mommy Faking It* mode. Ever since I was old enough to really read my mom's emotions, or anyone's really, she'd get this look on her face—her smile a little tighter, her eyes taking on a harsher edge, a faint sigh that she thought no one could hear, maybe even an utterance of *for fuck's sake* when she thought I wasn't in the room.

Times this look made an appearance:

1. Four-hour dance recitals

2. When I told my kindergarten teacher that my mom had special toys just for her bedroom that she wouldn't let me play with.

3. Any time I asked her to sit through an episode of *Toddlers in Tiaras*

4. When my first boyfriend picked me up for a date in a '77 Chevy truck with a mattress in the bed of the pickup.

So, for the record, *I, Lainey Taylor, am officially the world's worst daughter for choosing work over my sick mom.* Now that we had that straight, I could push guilt aside (sort of, maybe) and dig in to my slides. Spreadsheet after spreadsheet, I worked out an algorithm that projected the potential growth based off their followings and social media history.

By the time nine rolled around, I had completed a quarter

of the slides I needed to finish before tomorrow evening. I flexed my stiff legs and stretched my arms above my head.

"Coffee break?" Mom asked, her tone hopeful.

"Is that even a question?"

She smiled, this time more genuine. "I'll make some." She patted my knee and leaned forward to get up from the couch.

I waved her to sit back down. "Seriously, I can get it myself. You need your rest."

I went to tuck the blankets back around her feet, but she pushed them away and uprooted herself from the couch. A hurt that I'd never seen before was etched across her features. "I'm not a brittle old lady. I'm just as competent as I was before treatments, and I'd appreciate if you acted that way."

For a second, my speech failed me. I guess I had been treating her different since her diagnosis, but how was everything supposed to go back to normal when something inside her was trying to take her away from me? "I didn't mean anything by it. I know you're tired, and I was just trying to help."

"I know you mean well, but I want to take care of my daughter, so let me do my job, and you can do yours, okay?" She leveled a look at me that gave the clear vibe not to contradict her, or else.

"Okay." No use arguing with the woman I'd inherited my stubborn streak from.

She disappeared into the kitchen and came out a few minutes later brandishing two mugs of black coffee. She placed the red mug on the end table next to me, and then she rejoined me on the couch.

A soft sigh came from her end of the couch, and if I wasn't so engrossed in numbers and patterns, I'd have noticed her stare burning a hole through the side of my head sooner.

"I don't like how hard they're working you," she said, not bothering to hide her lack of enthusiasm toward Starr Media.

I shifted and put my laptop on the coffee table. "It's part of the job. Can't really help it."

"I just don't want you to turn out like…" Her voice trailed off, but the meaning was there, whether she said the words or not.

I smoothed a hand through my hair. Under any other circumstances, I'd let the comment slide, but I was ten PowerPoint slides past irritable and sure as heck didn't like being lumped into the same category as my father just because I was overworked.

I blinked hard and looked up at her. "Like what, Mom? Like Dad? Just because I work hard doesn't mean I'm going to end up running off with someone and leaving my family." As if I weren't already medaling in the Shitty Daughter Olympics, this jab really put me in solid gold medal standing.

The *Faking It* smile faded, replaced with a wobbly frown that wrung out my insides. She stared down at her coffee mug. "You're right. I shouldn't have even brought it up." Her expression crumbled, right along with my spirit.

"Mom, I didn't mean that. I'm sorry."

"It's okay, love bug." She took another deep breath and closed her eyes, looking as if she was fighting to center herself. "I'm going to head to bed now. I'm pretty tired." She gave my calf a squeeze, and left with another fake smile.

I stared from her retreating figure to my laptop and knocked my head back against the couch. I swallowed past the tightness in my throat and mashed my quivering lips together. Damn, I really hoped this presentation was worth souring what could have been an awesome weekend with my mom.

• • •

On Sunday, I drove home in the early misty morning. The

feeling of disappointing my mom and the unpleasantness of getting in a fight for the first time since ninth grade when she wouldn't let me shave the side of my head — *Thank you, Mom, you were so right* — hung heavy over me like the blanketing fog on I-5.

A little past ten, I pulled into the parking garage of my apartment and rested my head against the back of my seat. Was it possible to have more than two places to call home? This was the first time since I'd moved to Seattle that I felt overwhelming relief to be at the apartment — a refuge in the chaotic whirlwind of work, dog walking, boss fantasizing, and mother disappointing.

Zoey's door was closed when I walked in. I lightened my tread, not wanting to wake her if she was still asleep, and when I got to my room, I dropped my duffel bag and flopped on my bed. Rarely was she still asleep at this hour, but maybe she had a late night with paperwork. I scrubbed my hands over my eyes, willing my aching body to find some energy so I could do a few last minute tweaks to Jackson's presentation before I sent it off.

I frowned, thinking about the weekend that was supposed to be filled with horrible movies and junk food. Instead, I'd ignored my mom, solidifying my standing as douchiest daughter on the west coast. The only plus side was that I'd had zero time to focus on Brogan.

A knock came from my door a few seconds later, and it took every ounce of strength to pry my eyes open. Zoey stood in the doorway in a set of matching pink pajamas, her hair pulled back into a messy bun.

"Never thought I'd see the day where I was up hours before you," I said.

"Yeah, well…" She wrung her hands together, and for the first time since she dropped my flatiron in the toilet in college, looked a little nervous.

I sat up on my elbows, and a chill ran down my spine. "Is everything okay?"

"Yes." She moved over to my bed and sat down. "If I tell you something, you have to promise not freak out, okay?"

"Of course." Few things could possibly freak me out, just clowns, walking over a wet spot on the floor while wearing socks, and fetal pig dissection (still scarred from tenth grade. Thanks a lot, Mr. Ellington). Doubtful she'd be doing any of these things in the next few minutes.

"There's a guy."

I lifted my brows. "I like the start of this story."

"And he's kind of here right now."

As if her words summoned him, a tall guy with a square jaw, mussed hair, wearing sweatpants slung low on his hips and no shirt—for good reasons, because *holy* abs—appeared in my doorway. "Zoey, I'm gonna take off." He shook his hair off his forehead in a way that rivaled Sean Hunter from *Boy Meets World*, and if there weren't Zoey's feelings to consider, I'd stand up and break into a slow clap for that perfect little move.

She sucked in her bottom lip and shot a sheepish look in my direction.

"Please, take it off," I muttered. Okay, so I couldn't fully hold back.

She smacked my leg and turned to me, "I'll be right back."

"Take all the time you need. Bye, Shirtless Dude," I called to the retreating guy.

He smiled. "Bye, Roommate Whose Name I Don't Know." His deep voice rattled down my chest, and I had zero questions as to why Zoey had picked this guy. He was a walking, talking lady boner on a stick.

She walked over to him, and he put his arm around her as they made their way across the hall, disappearing into her room.

At least someone in this apartment was getting some.

Chapter Thirteen

Coworkers can be assholes.

So that rule wasn't in the rulebook, but I had every intention of adding it to the *comments and suggestions* box. If we actually had one, anyway. It wasn't so much that I was mad Jackson assigned me work on my one weekend off. Oh, no. It was what tiny dictator grinch did afterward that reinforced the sentiment of my newly minted rule.

Brogan had called an all-employee meeting Monday morning.

After everyone took their seats at the boardroom table, Jackson set up the projector and pulled up the presentation we'd made. I should have known something was off when I glanced over to his computer and noticed my name had been left off the title page, with only Jackson's name appearing in bold black letters.

Jackson shifted uncomfortably and grimaced, which on his face looked like he maybe had one too many of those soy lattes and was auditioning for a starring role on a Pepto commercial. I rolled my eyes. Whatever. Once we got to my portion of the slides, I'd take over and get my five minutes of presenting and proper brownnosing, and move one step further toward solidifying my position in the company. Badda-bing Badda-boom, Brogan wouldn't know what hit him.

Marta and Eric from accounting started off the meeting, and staff members worked their way around the table with news each person brought from their specific division. Since Jackson sat next to Brogan, we were the last two to present our information.

I shuffled my notecards in my hands and the damp edges started to curl around the curve of my palm. Okay, so I was a few steps beyond a little bout of stage fright. This was the first time I'd done a presentation not talking out of my ass, and at this point, the notecards were merely just a security blanket in case I fumbled over my wording. Zoey would truly be proud of my preparation, except for the fact that these technically were her notecards. She was too busy talking on the phone to Shirtless Dude for me to ask to borrow some, but the girl was an office supply junkie—I doubted three notecards would really put her out. Just in case, I'd buy her an extra pack next time we were at Costco.

As soon as Zelda sat down, Brogan pointed to Jackson. "Go ahead," he said. He drummed his fingers along the edge of the table, almost seeming to tap out a tune. If I were to bet, I'd guess it was a song from one of his thousands of records lining the walls in his office. Is that what he did when everyone left for the night? I could picture him leaning back in his chair, closing his eyes while the pop and crackle of some sweet baroque melody on the record player flooded the corner office. That delicious mouth would be slack and completely kissable.

I shook my head, erasing those thoughts. *Game time,*

Lainey. Focus that sixty-thousand-dollar education on these next few minutes and make the impending doom of paying off your student debt worth something.

Jackson started the presentation, giving all the facts and data to suggest that we were behind on our quarterly quota and a few ways to improve on our losses. He pressed the clicker and moved to the next slide, which was the Gizzara account—my slides. I pushed my seat out to stand next to him, but he continued on with the presentation, not giving me a chance to take over.

"As I was saying"—he paused and glared at me, as if daring me to say something—"Gizzara's clients are not using our services to the full extent." He continued, but all I could hear was *I, world's tenth worst human being* (there had to be a couple handfuls worth of assholes worse than him, I prayed) *can't think of any good ideas on my own, so I must steal them from my smart, sweet, innocent coworker who currently wants to throat-punch the crap out of me, the insufferable first assistant.*

I was still frozen in a pre-standing half-crouched position. I waited a few more seconds, thinking maybe Jackson was going to intro me, to somehow make up for this. Because even I had a hard time believing the "*Et tu, Brute*" level that he'd just stooped to. Was that a knife sticking out of my back or just the stab of cold hard betrayal? Either way, I could officially mark him off my list of people to catch me during a trust fall exercise.

Brogan shifted his attention to me, and his eyebrows pushed together as he took in my hunchback position. I sunk back into my seat and chewed on the inside of my cheek to keep from both verbally and physically maiming Jackson. What a frigging jerk.

The point about adding more services than just social media management to the company to diversify was one that

I was proudest of. I glanced over at Brogan as Jackson said this and a thrill shot through me as he nodded along, clearly pleased. Pleased at *my* work, I internally screamed. My work that was being passed off as someone else's, unfortunately.

As Jackson got to the end of the slides, Brogan stood up, his chair cutting through the silence of the room. "This is excellent work, Jackson. I'm impressed."

"Thank you." Jackson beamed.

I clenched my jaw and kept waiting for the *Yes, and Lainey came up with everything, and yes, I do hide my bald spot by combing my hair to one side!*—something to redeem what he'd just done to me, because under all that Dolce and Gabbana cologne, I'd like to believe his heart wasn't two sizes too small—but it never came. My eyes narrowed as I turned toward Jackson, and he gave a shrug and apologetic smile.

Current list of most hated things:

　　3. Mildew on my shower wall

　　2. Uber rides with sketch drivers

　　1. Jackson friggin' Wells

I shot him a look and rolled my shoulders back. Maybe if I stared hard enough I might actually burn a hole through his skull.

"We'll start implementing those ideas tomorrow." Brogan turned to me. "Lainey."

My heart floated in my chest. Maybe he'd realize that this was my work. Not that he had any reason to, because he'd never seen a project from me cross his desk, but one could hope.

I stopped grimacing at Jackson and turned to our boss. "Yes?"

"Do you think you can set all this up? I'll have Jackson walk you through the steps."

My eye twitched. "I think I can handle that," I said, slow

and measured.

What was that about a side order of spit to go along with Jackson's next soy latte?

Unlike some people, I wasn't about to be a rat in front of the whole office. My hands curled into fists, and I chewed on the inside of my lip until I was sure a WWE style death fight wouldn't ensue in the conference room, complete with spandex and death metal music.

What reality was I living in where I assumed my name would be on that presentation? *Wake up and smell the coffee, Lainey Taylor. You're not in the goodie gumdrop forest, you're in the big leagues.* And big leagues meant bigger pricks. There'd be no making this mistake again.

Brogan adjourned the meeting, and everyone filed out into the lobby. The only people left were Brogan, the Grinch, and me.

"You didn't have anything you wanted to add?" Brogan prompted me, expectant.

Um, yeah, your second in command is a fink who deserves a million paper cuts on his tongue as penance. "I agreed with the presentation. I didn't really have anything to add to it."

Brogan turned to me and frowned, a look of true disappointment etched on his face. "You can really learn a lot from him. I suggest spending more time together on projects so you can see what it takes to get ahead in this company."

I nodded. "Oh, yes, I'm learning so much." I turned my gaze to Jackson, and he looked away, much like a dog who'd disobeyed his owner and gotten caught. Then again, Bruce had the decency to look me in the eye when he peed on my shoes. Bottom of the barrel in terms of the pecking order in the company or not, my name deserved to be on that presentation and Jackson knew it.

Brogan joined the rest of the staff in the lobby to celebrate Tonya's birthday. I sat back down at the conference table and laid my palms on the surface, staring at the grain in the cherry wood. I didn't trust myself not to climb over the table and hit Jackson over the head with his damn laptop. I stared him down, not moving from my position.

The silence that spanned between us was charged with the anger that was now freely flowing from every inch of my skin.

"Listen, I'm sorry about that, but Brogan's really been breathing down my neck lately."

I blinked at him. "You're sorry." That was the first time he'd ever uttered that word in my direction. I laughed because a) the apology fit him as well as a cheap Men's Warehouse suit and b) it was much better than the alternative—throwing my chair at him, or worse, giving him any clue that it had, in fact, hurt me. My gaze narrowed into a glare. "Save it for someone who cares."

I packed up my laptop and brushed past him, and as soon as I crossed the threshold into the main office, I let it go. No good could come from holding a grudge. As my mom always said, *While you're carrying a grudge, the other guy's out dancing.* Jackson was doing the frickin' Mambo Number Five, and I wasn't going to spend another minute sulking. Time to come up with a plan.

Chapter Fourteen

Cookies do solve all problems.

Brogan was sitting on the couch, his feet propped on the coffee table, when I brought Bruce back from his walk on Wednesday. It had been two days since the infamous Meeting of Betrayal and I'd had time to cool down.

"I thought you had a meeting until nine?"

"I don't want to talk about it," he grumbled and continued to sift through the paperwork spread across the cushions.

"That good, huh?"

He closed his eyes and leaned his head back against the couch, his arms behind his head for support. The fabric of his shirt stretched over his chest, and for a split second my breath hitched. Even when he wasn't trying, it was like his body pulled me under a spell. A brain power outage spell. "Worse," he said. "So, so much worse," he muttered to himself.

This made me pause. Over the past two months, he'd never shown this side, one that I was only privy to because I was in his personal sanctuary.

Brogan never broke a sweat at the office, always happy, joking around, the life of the party. But seeing him so vulnerable in his home, where he didn't need to put on an act, made me realize how much I didn't know about him. How he seemed so perfect at work, but it was all just for show.

Even Superman had his kryptonite.

"You know what makes it better?" Whenever I had a bad day at school, Mom and I would bake together. Sometimes it would be cookies, other times elaborate cakes. Somehow she was able to get my mind off whatever had bummed me out that day. With as many bad days I had in middle and high school, I was shocked I wasn't diagnosed with childhood diabetes, or at the very least hadn't ended up the size of a humpback whale. *Thank you, Taylor genetics.*

"A new job?" he deadpanned.

I rolled my eyes. "Right, because this company isn't your baby or anything."

"A parent needs a break from his kid every once in a while," he grunted, but his tone held a little less irritation than a minute ago. He didn't bother opening his eyes. "What's your proposition to make this shitty day better?"

"Cookies."

"Cookies?" He repeated it like I'd just told him the answer to the question of life was three. This man was a poor, deprived individual if he didn't indulge in my one—okay, one of many vices.

"You know, the magical food not made with prunes or anything remotely healthy, but tastes amazing?"

He blinked slowly, his long eyelashes fanning over his face. "I know what a damn cookie is, Taylor. I just don't see how it's going to solve my problems with this possible merger."

"You obviously haven't had my world famous chocolate chip."

"World famous? What makes these cookies stand out from the rest?" He shot a skeptical look in my direction.

"I have a few secret ingredients. But it's the unicorn tears that really push it over the edge." When he didn't look convinced, I added, "C'mon. how can you pass up ooey-gooey chocolate chips nestled in an array of ingredients that will blow your goddamn mind?"

"You're really building yourself up, Taylor. But damn…" He groaned, and the sound vibrated deep in my chest. "Cookies do sound kind of good."

"Well, boss. I think we could both use some. You have chocolate chips, flour, butter, baking soda, eggs, and sugar?"

He nodded. "Think so."

"Good. Prepare to be wowed."

I could have sworn that I'd heard him mumble "I already am," but decided that it was my imagination and the overflow of emotions swirling around in my head at the moment. I had to hand it to Brogan, he'd succeeded at taking my mind off the fact that I'd been screwed over by my coworker and my relationship with my mom was strained for the first time in years. It was much easier to focus on the mundane task of measuring and mixing. And eating. Always eating. Because when I was stuffing my face, I couldn't possibly say anything stupid.

A few minutes later, all the ingredients for the cookies were laid out across the granite countertops, along with a red KitchenAid mixer. For someone who consistently spent more time in his office than at home, he kept his kitchen well-stocked.

Once the wet and dry ingredients were mixed together, I began balling up cookie dough and placing it on a baking sheet. Scoop. Roll. Smash. Scoop. Roll. Smash. Three very easy tasks that took all my focus. By the time I lined up enough to cover an entire sheet, the worries of today seemed to fade to background noise. It was a long way away, but I couldn't wait until I had a kid of my own to share this tradition with.

Brogan joined me at the counter, the evidence of a long day etched into his face.

"Have you had a chance to watch any of the other movies I recommended?" I asked, trying to get his mind off whatever was bugging him from work.

He drummed his fingers along the granite countertop. "No, but they're queued up on my Netflix account."

"I think you'll really like *Mean Girls*. It's a classic."

"Obviously we have a much different definition of what a classic is."

"Okay, tough guy, what would you deem worthy of the label?"

"*Casablanca. Gone with the Wind*." He waved a hand with a flourish. "Movies that have stood the test of time."

I continued balling up cookie dough onto the baking sheet. "You do know they make movies in this thing called color now, right?"

"Is that right up there with—what do you call it"—he paused—"a 'cellular phone'?"

I opened the oven, popped in the sheet, and set the timer. "I'm shocked there's not a rotary phone in your apartment."

"There's one in my office," he winked.

I tsked. "You really were a deprived child."

He huffed out a laugh. "Look at Miss Big City getting all high and mighty."

"I'm not from here. Born and raised in downtown Portland, thank you very much." I sat on a barstool at the breakfast bar, and Brogan joined me.

"That explains so much." He smirked, and his dimples made an appearance for the first time tonight.

I crossed my arms over my chest. "Excuse me, but what does that mean?" Only Portlanders were allowed to call our people weird. Same way I could complain about something my mom did that annoyed the crap out of me, but if someone even thought about saying a less than flattering comment about her, I'd go full on Hulk-smash.

"Portland's just full of weird people. Pink chickens, people walking around topless, penis doughnuts."

I ticked off numbers on my fingers. "First off, the shirtless thing is all Eugene. And only during the Country Fair." I winked. "Second, everyone should enjoy a Cock-N-Balls at least once in their life." I held up my hand with three fingers out. "Third, my mom has two chickens — Betty and Horace."

"Is it even legal to own those in the city?" He looked at me as if I'd said I was from a traveling circus troupe and performed on the trapeze.

"Yes. Seriously, have you had fresh eggs? They're the best." I settled back on my stool, thinking of Saturday mornings when Mom would go into the chicken coup and come back with the most beautiful blue and brown eggs. She'd cook them, along with bacon and hash browns, while we discussed who was going to be voted off our favorite reality shows.

After Dad left, this became our weekend ritual when I'd come home from college. I frowned, thinking about how I'd totally blown my mom off and declined her offer of breakfast during my visit, and instead bought us doughnuts from the coffee cart a few blocks from her house. Yep, I deserved the title of Shit Daughter.

"The closest I've come to fresh eggs is buying cartons with pictures of farms on them." He smirked when he saw my grimace. "Did you see her this weekend?"

The timer beeped, and I busied myself with extracting cookies from the oven. "How did you know that?"

"You looked happier than usual on Friday."

My breath caught and I frantically searched for a spatula in the drawers, needing something for my hands to be doing.

Brogan noticed *me*. And not just me, but my mood before the weekend from hell and Jackson crushing part of my soul.

"Yeah, I did. She started a new treatment a few days ago. We'll see how it goes."

"Good. I hear that it can take a few cocktails before they get the right mixture."

After a few minutes of letting the cookies cool, I scooped them onto a plate and brought them back to the counter. Something felt right about being in his condo, having a normal conversation. I talked with Zoey all the time, but sharing things about my life with Brogan felt…special. When I was ready to get back on the dating horse, I'd want the guy to be like Brogan. Smart, successful, sexy as hell. Yes, that killer combo would be the death of me. No other guy seemed to even be on the same playing field as him.

I cleared my throat, extinguishing those thoughts. They wouldn't help in my already pitiful dating life. "Seems like you know a lot about cancer."

He shrugged. "I may have done some research after you left the other night." Brogan grabbed a cookie off the plate and took a tentative bite. His eyes closed and he moaned, and my mouth suddenly went dry. His lashes fanned over the tops of his cheeks as he squeezed his eyes shut, and my heart went sideways in my chest. I'd give up ice cream for a year to hear that sound come out of his mouth again. "Holy shit. These are amazing."

"I told you—blue ribbon cookies reign supreme."

I took a bite of cookie, keeping my mouth busy because, holy crap. He'd done research. Because of something affecting my life. If my mouth wasn't full of chocolate chips, I'd probably say something like *could you be any more perfect?* Or, *please keep making those cookie moaning sounds.*

"You got a little something…" He swept his thumb over the corner of my mouth. "Right here." He brought his thumb to his lips and sucked the chocolate off his finger.

A sound, something between a gasp and a deflating balloon, came out of my mouth. My pulse kicked up to a strong gallop, hammering against my temples. Heat radiated through the space between my thighs, and words drained from my mind. Not a single coherent thought formed as I watched his finger edge along the seam of his mouth.

I stared at his bottom lip and the stubble that ran across his chin. My tongue ran across my lips. If I leaned over a few inches, my lips would sweep across his. I gripped the counter, not trusting my hands to keep to themselves.

Before I made a complete fool out of myself, I pushed back from the counter and began piling dishes into his sink. "I'd better clean up."

Looking around the high-end kitchen, the thought of me and Brogan existing together in the house was a joke.

I hadn't grown up wealthy. Everything I needed, I had, but there were no extraneous gadgets, definitely not a dishwasher or a fridge that talked to me. Brogan and I came from two opposite ends of the spectrum. He had a maid that did his laundry and dusted his immaculate house. I had week-old soda cans scattered on my nightstand and managed to throw a load of clothes in the washer when the bra and panty situation was at Code Red. The thought of him setting foot in my mom's nineteen-fifties bungalow was almost laughable. Two people from two separate worlds had no place being together. Not that I was even considering this. I was there as his dog walker and second assistant, purely in a professional capacity.

That didn't derail the incessant crash of my heart against my ribs. Or the fact that I had the worst case of sweaty palms I'd ever experienced in my life. And that was saying something, because teenage Lainey had palms sweaty enough for it to be considered a chronic disease.

"I was just about to sit down and watch some Netflix

after I finished up my paperwork. Do you want to join?" He motioned toward the couch where Bruce was currently belly-up, snoring.

I hesitated. Everything in me yelled, *Yes! I want to Netflix and chill with you so hard.* But I had the proposal to work on for the Gizarra account and the slime of a twelve-hour work day to wash off. "I should really be going."

"Oh." His lips turned into a pout which was almost as adorable as his dimples. "Well, at least let my driver take you home."

I waved him off. "It's no big deal. I can take the light rail."

"Listen, I'm not in charge of you—" A devious smile twisted his lips, and his eyes brightened. "Wait, yes I am." He scrubbed his chin and regarded me. "And as your boss, I'm giving you direct orders to use my driver."

I rolled my eyes. "Anything else I can do for you, boss?" I made an exaggerated curtsy.

"Take some cookies with you. I can't possibly eat this many." He motioned toward the dozens of cookies spread on cooling racks along the counter.

Now that was something that I could get behind. "Okay. I'm sure my roommate will appreciate that." No way was Zoey getting any of these.

We stood in the doorway for a few moments. I made the mistake of glancing up at Brogan's face. More specific, his eyes. Those brown eyes raked down my body with a heat I wasn't prepared for.

Play it cool. This is your boss, and he just wants you to get home safe.

Bull-freaking-crap. I clenched the cookies, definitely trying to push away thoughts of him in a flimsy, bulge-showcasing towel, of that broad chest that would crush me if he were on top, pinning me into his bed. Heat licked up the inside of my legs, and a smattering of goose bumps crept down my arms.

To say I was affected by him was the understatement of the twenty-first century. In fact, affected didn't even seem like a strong enough word. I doubted there was one in the English language that could completely encompass what I was feeling. I bet there was an obscure Russian word for this emotion. One that screamed: *I want to jump my boss's bones, but that's a really bad idea to even be considering it in the first place.* Yes, a seventeen syllable Russian word for that. Something like *I-vanna-hump-my-bosses-leg-cshvogh.*

"I hope you enjoy your cookies." I held up the container of my portion, which I would be stress eating in T-minus thirty minutes.

"It was a pleasure eating your cookies." His lips twitched in amusement.

I giggled. "Is that what I should put on the sexual harassment report that's going on my boss's desk in the morning?"

"Yes. Right under breaking into his condo and dognapping."

"Hey, I always bring him back. That has to count for something, right?"

Bruce showed his assent by letting out a loud fart.

I bent down to scratch behind Bruce's ears and said, "This is why you don't have a girlfriend, Bruce. We'll work on the bodily functions, and maybe I'll let you near the poodle in Twenty-Seven A."

Brogan chuckled, and a smile broke out across his face. My heart stuttered in response. "Don't get the poor guy's hopes up. He has a long way to go."

I said, "You're right. Maybe you should sign him up for etiquette classes."

Bruce huffed in response and rolled on his back, snorting while rubbing his back on the rug.

"Maybe not. I think he's a lost cause," I mused.

"Never too late to teach an old dog new tricks, is it, boy?" Brogan bent down to where I was crouched and gave Bruce's belly a rubdown. Lucky dog. Bruce let out an even louder fart in response.

I stood and plugged my nose. "On that note, I'll go meet your driver in the garage."

We walked down the hallway toward the elevator, and I jammed my finger onto the down button with a little more force than intended, anything to not feel this need pulsing through my body.

"Lainey." He grabbed my arm, and I desperately wanted to be the type of girl who could ignore the obstacles between us and push him toward his condo and into his bedroom and remove each and every article of clothing until I got exactly what the ache between my thighs begged for.

Instead, I said, "Yeah?" My voice came out strangled. Definitely did not go along with my "keeping it cool" facade.

"Thanks for tonight." His hand brushed my cheek and tangled with my curls. I leaned into his touch, staring into those melted-chocolate-chip-brown eyes. His gaze shifted from my eyes, down to my lips, and then back to my eyes again. His tongue darted across his lower lip, and my eyes fluttered shut, anticipating how soft his lips would feel pressed against my own.

His breath fanned across my cheek as he closed the distance between us. His stubble grazed along the side of my jaw as he inched closer, taking the fleshy part of my ear between his teeth. I couldn't resist him any longer. This pull between us was too much to ignore, and just this once I had to let myself give in and lose myself in the moment. A breathy moan whispered past my lips, and I tilted my head to give him better access.

The elevator door dinged open, and we suddenly weren't the only people in the hallway.

Balls.

Seriously, what was with me and my perpetual bad luck with elevators?

He pulled back a fraction of an inch, and his expression took on a pained quality, almost like he was warring with himself. He groaned and muttered something under his breath. Our gazes met, and a swirl of hesitation and raw desire flickered in his eyes. Enough to send a shiver trickling down my spine, because those dilated pupils told me everything I needed to know in that moment—I wasn't going crazy. Brogan was fighting this urge, just like me.

An old lady with a walker clomped her way out of the elevator. A muffled swishing sound filled the hallways as the tennis balls on the bottom of her walker slid along the floor. She glared at us the entire time she passed, which was a good ten seconds, since she was moving at the pace of a slow-motion replay.

Brogan cleared his throat. "Good evening, Mrs. Ellingson." He nodded at her and smiled.

"Damn kids don't even have the decency to use the privacy of their own home anymore," she muttered. She pointed a finger at him and jabbed him in the chest. "I have HBO if I want to see that kind of smutty stuff." She continued to scowl at Brogan, even though she had inched past us.

"Right. Have a nice evening," he said as she shuffled her way to what I assumed was her condo and disappeared through the door.

As soon as it closed, we looked at each other. We both erupted in laughter. I doubled over, unable to catch my breath, tears streaming down my face.

After finally finding my composure, I said, "Your neighbor's a real peach,"

"She has her moments. Can't say this was one of them," he said, still chuckling.

He smiled and grabbed my hand, his large calloused one encompassing mine. My whole body tensed in response to the unexpected touch. His eyes were devoid of the heat that was there a few minutes prior, but still managed make my knees buckle. He leaned down and whispered, "Let's do this again." He pulled back slowly, his jaw brushing along mine.

I nodded, not looking him in the eyes this time. Because those brown eyes were doing things to my resolve that I wasn't proud of. How the hell was I supposed to function in the office when he was less than twenty feet away, the only thing between us a door and a set of unforgiving rules?

Chapter Fifteen

<u>Lainey Taylor Rule of Life #76</u>
Good girls don't kiss and tell.

A week had passed since the meeting and my awkward cookie interaction with Brogan. He hadn't been home the rest of the week when I walked Bruce. It had also been a week since I'd talked to my mom, the longest stretch since, well, I couldn't remember the last time it'd been that long.

I spent the rest of the day huddled over my laptop, finalizing figures to present to my boss in hopes that I could somehow get into his good graces again in terms of my work performance. By the time I looked at the clock in the corner of my screen, it was well past time to go, and Jackson had fled the building, probably retreating to his home in the sewer.

The interoffice messenger dinged on my computer, and a flashing message from Brogan popped up on the screen.

Brogan: *Are you still here?*

It didn't surprise me he was here this late, but it left me

wondering how often this happened. Twenty feet. One door. One man I couldn't seem to shake out of my mind. Ever since *The Infamous Cookie Baking Night* I was left wondering where the hell I stood with him. There was only one way to find out.

Lainey: *Yes*

Brogan: *Come in my office, please.*

I pushed back from my desk and rushed to Brogan's office. The emptiness of the building, and lack of ambient noise carrying through the halls, amplified the clicking of my heels against the tile.

The door was unlocked when I jiggled the handle, and Brogan was sitting at his desk, his brows furrowed as he had an intense stare off with his computer.

"What do you need, Mr. Starr?" Using his formal name felt like Nutella on my tongue—rich, savory, and foreign. His eyes dilated, and he sat up straighter in his chair. A chill ran down my spine at the total déjà vu moment this was. Except this time, I didn't have an alarm to interrupt.

"You're here really late," he said.

I leaned against the doorframe, not trusting myself to go in any further. "I wanted to get ahead on the project."

He nodded. "I'm impressed with your work ethic."

"Thank you, sir." It felt odd addressing someone who was just a few years older than me so formally, but he hadn't corrected me thus far.

He paused and tapped his pen against his desk, looking like he was choosing his words carefully. "I know you helped with the presentation last week."

My breath caught in my throat. If he knew this whole time, why hadn't he said anything—or put Jackson in his place? "You did?"

He gave his pen a couple of quick clicks and said, "Jackson has never come up with material like that. Plus, when I asked him about the numbers this morning, he fumbled through it."

I nodded, not quite sure what to say to this.

"Why didn't you say anything after the meeting?" he demanded. If I didn't know any better, his expression held an air of disappointment.

"I didn't want to humiliate him." I could send mental eye-stabs from across the room to him all week, but I wouldn't be able to live with myself if I'd taken it too far.

His lips pursed, and he squinted his eyes at me, as if finding the right words to say. "This is a cutthroat business. You need to speak up if someone takes your idea."

Somehow I decided that I would look like an ass if I'd done that in last week's meeting, not Jackson. "You'd want me to humiliate your second in command in a company meeting?"

"If you didn't feel comfortable saying something during the meeting, at least tell me afterward. You even had a chance to say something at my place." He paused and swallowed hard, then looked up at me, his gaze pulling me under. "I didn't get to where I am today by letting people stomp all over me."

I'd never met a boss like him—not that I had the vast knowledge or network of CEOs, but to imagine Brogan raising his voice above a kind remark (other than when someone was touching his stuff) was a little hard to fathom. "But you're so…"

He arched a brow. "Nice?" He smiled. "I've learned to pick my battles."

I nodded. "Next time I'll make sure to bring the cold hard hammer of Thor down on him."

"You'll take over the Alexander Freeland account tomorrow."

"But that's Jackson's." Anyone who was represented by Gizzara was automatically shoved in Jackson's caseload, no questions asked.

"And he'll learn the hard lesson of what happens when he takes what's not his. I was waiting for him to come and tell me after the meeting, gave him a week even, but it never happened. So it's yours." He looked at me through long lashes. "Unless you don't want it."

"I want it," I said a little too quickly. I was equal parts thrilled and terrified. How would Jackson handle this news? An eye for an eye didn't seem to be a great idea in this scenario, but Brogan was the boss, and like hell I'd say no to getting more clients. "Thank you."

"Great. I guess we can both get back to work then," he said, frowning at his computer screen.

"What are you working on?" Like I could pass up this opportunity to be nosy.

"I'm stumped as to what to do with the Travers account. His social media growth has gone down since he's been here and I don't know what to make of it. Nothing seems offensive on his account, and yet fans are abandoning him."

The heavy frosted glass door slid closed behind me as I walked over to his desk. Data sheets and graphs splattered his screen, and I scanned the information for any possible trend. I leaned against the edge of the desk and crossed my ankles. Inches away, Brogan's shampoo was hard to ignore. The delicious scent tugged at something inside of me, and I had this desperate need to move closer to him. I gripped my fingers on his desk to keep myself planted here. A professional I would remain, even if it was becoming physically painful. "What happened in January of this year?" I took a look at the graph in the left-hand corner of his screen and spotted the mistake almost immediately.

"Why?"

"It seems his followers start leaving around then, and then they level off as the month continues."

"Interesting." His gaze shifted from his computer to my legs and slowly, much too slowly to be deemed appropriate or within his rules, worked his way up my body. "Good catch."

I had a hard time believing that an MIT alum who graduated the top of his class couldn't spot something this simple. Unless…

Our eyes met, and I stood frozen, clutching the desk for support. I finally understood what it meant when books said that anticipation hung heavy in the air. It meant a shaking that started so deep it rattled my bones. It meant internal organs mysteriously shifting to places they have no right being. It meant my skin burning up and turning to ice simultaneously. So, apparently my brand of anticipation felt like a fifty-year-old menopausal woman.

"Thank you," I whispered.

He cleared his throat, and the moment came to a screeching halt.

Right. Rules. Job. Money. *Stop thinking about his lips, Lainey.*

"You heading out?" he asked.

I stood and smoothed the wrinkles from my skirt, and I didn't fail to notice his eyes followed my fingers the entire time. "No, I have a bit of paperwork I need to finish."

His stomach let out a growl, and we smiled at each other.

"Have you eaten? Had a prune shake?" I asked.

His lips twitched in the corners. "Prunes are great for the digestive tract."

I blanched. "If you're eighty or a plugged up toddler."

"Real food would be nice," he agreed.

"Coming right up, boss." I left the room, only able to breathe when the glass door slid shut.

After leaving to get sushi, I brought the food back into

his office and plopped down in the chair across from his. An assortment of sashimi lay across the table in a rainbow of raw fish. His face brightened "You're the best."

"It wasn't totally altruistic. I hadn't eaten dinner either," I said while grabbing a pair of chopsticks from the bag. "Want me to help fill out some of that paperwork?"

He nodded and slid a few files across to me. I'd moved my chair next to his while we were eating so we could talk numbers on his computer while scarfing down sushi. As he hunched over his desk, studying the information, he kept stretching his neck side to side, rolling his shoulders and grimacing. "Can you call my masseuse tomorrow and set up an appointment?"

"First thing tomorrow."

He rubbed his shoulder and grumbled a few choice words under his breath.

"Bruce pull your arm out of the socket on a walk?" Seventy pounds of wrinkly dog was no joke, and I might as well have been made of papier-mâché with the way he dragged me around downtown.

"Messed up my shoulder doing deadlifts." He gave another wince as he gingerly kneaded his fingers into his shoulder. His collared shirt was rolled up to his elbows, and the ink on his skin was on full display.

Images of Brogan's muscles bunching together as he lifted weights, sweat trickling down each notch of grooved skin crossed my mind. Before I took time to process what a bad idea it was, I asked, "Do you need a massage now?"

His shoulders stiffened, and his voice grew wary. "I… don't think that's a good idea."

Oh, Brogan, you are so right. So very right.

And yet, I never had a knack for going with the consensus. Instead, I dug myself a deeper hole. I blamed this boldness on wasabi, dimples, and lack of sleep. "It's something you'd pay a complete stranger to do. I really don't mind." I'd like to say that my selfless tendencies were firing on all four cylinders tonight, but let's be honest here—I'd take any excuse to be near Brogan, in any capacity. Because my masochistic streak was the size of the Space Needle.

"I mind." His voice lowered an octave and hit me square between the thighs when he said, "Being this close to you makes me forget why I wrote the rules in the first place."

Air magically dissipated from my lungs, and words jumbled up into nonsensical groupings. Because, holy hell in a hand basket, it was one thing to have a flirty moment at the elevator. An entirely different one when he said this aloud. What had changed in the span of a week? And more importantly, did I want this? If I pushed further, I was clearly violating the employee handbook, therefore jeopardizing my spot in this company, and then where would I be with helping Mom? I had more than myself to think about here.

The smart thing to do would be to apologize, slink out of the office, and return to the Ben and Jerry's Cherry Garcia pint I'd been working on last night. The spoon was still in the container, ready and raring to go.

Something in his expression kept me from rescinding my offer, though. His eyes were filled with heat, wanting, and they were aimed at me. Frankly, I'd be an idiot to pass up this opportunity.

"What does it say in your manual about massages?"

He mashed his lips together, his hooded eyes focusing on my mouth. "I don't think there is anything listed about it."

I stood and placed a hesitant palm over his shoulder. "And what about touching the boss? Does it say anything about that?"

He stiffened momentarily and then melted into my touch. "Not specifically."

"Then I don't see anything wrong with a friendly

massage." I swallowed hard. Maybe friendly was the wrong term, because my *I want to jump your bones,* and, *does this massage come with a happy ending?* thoughts were not of the friend variety.

He swiveled his chair to face me, and my hands fell to his chest. Charcoal gray dress slacks boxed in either side of my legs, and I gave in to my need to move closer. Brogan's Adam's apple bobbed as his gaze lazily traced down my body.

"I won't take it as friendly." His gravely voice caressed my skin and goose bumps followed in its wake.

Even though he was sitting, I'd only have to bend down a couple inches to reach his face. A silence spread between us, eyes tracked eyes, breaths and the hum of his computer the only thing cracking our little bubble of office-rule-breaking.

"What are we doing?" I whispered as his strong hands found my hips and pulled me closer so that my legs were flush against his chair.

His gaze dipped to my mouth and he said, "I'm tired of playing by the rules. I've wanted you since that first day in the break room. Your smart mouth drives me insane. In fact, I haven't thought about anything besides your lips all night."

I stopped breathing altogether as he moved a fraction of an inch closer, his grip on my hips tightening.

"This is a bad idea, right?" This was the proper thing to say, when one occasionally sexually harassed one's boss, but for the life of me I couldn't come up with a reason to stop. The only things running through my mind were flashes of Brogan in a towel, the weight of his body against mine, the need for there to be way less clothes in this current equation.

"Yes." His hand skimmed up my arm and caressed my cheek. He lightly tugged on the back of my neck, and I leaned down, my hands clutching the armrests. A few inches spanned between us, close enough that his exhale was my next breath. His deep brown eyes darkened with a hunger, a need that pulsed straight to my core. His lips parted, and he closed another inch of the gap between us.

"Should we stop?" My voice came out barely above a whisper.

His lips skated along the side of my neck. "No."

And with that, his hands were in my hair, pulling me closer until our mouths connected. Soft lips swept over mine, and a sigh escaped my mouth. A lulling warmth spread from where our skin met, trailing to every muscle, every bit of skin, turning my limbs to jelly. His tongue traced along the seam of my lips, and I parted them, welcoming his touch. I melted into him, spiraling to a place of deep desperation to be closer to him.

His hands slid down the back of my shirt, down until they reached the top of my pencil skirt. My knees buckled, and I all but fell into his lap as our kiss deepened. He pulled back, heat and desire evident in his gaze, and he worked his way along the side of my jaw, finding my neck, kissing his way down my collarbone.

My hands were in his hair, across his shoulders, memorizing every inch of him. My fingers molded against Brogan's taught muscles, and he groaned as my hands skimmed lower and lower. I'd wondered for over a month what this exact moment would feel like, and I finally had an answer. He felt like everything—a stolen breath, soft lips, a mouth that demanded all I had to give.

A sound cut through the chaos, pulling me out of the moment. The phone. The frigging phone. We both froze, hands mid-grope, lips brushing lightly, when the gravity of the situation hit harder than a foul ball to the face.

The phone continued ringing, and we just stared at each other. The panic seeping into his eyes matched the horror pounding in my chest.

Because at that moment a few things became apparent:

a) Holy crap, my imagination paled in comparison to reality.

b) I'd just taken a flying leap over the line labeled DO NOT CROSS.

c) *Holy crap*, this was my boss. Abort! Abort!

What had we just done? And what did this mean in terms of my job? Oh my God, did he think I was one of those people that tried to sleep their way up the company ladder, because most likely anyone that didn't share a brain with me would view it that way. Did that make me the office floozy? Did people even use that word anymore?

The phone was still ringing, each shrill *ding* making me flinch. "You should probably get that."

His Adam's apple bobbed as his gaze raked over my face. "I should."

I awkwardly extricated myself from his lap and backed toward the door. "I'm just going to head out now." I put my hands on my hips and rocked back and forth on my heels, fighting for something intelligent to say. All that came out was, "Uh, thanks for that."

And before he could respond, I was out the door, grabbing my purse and keys from my desk, and beelining it for the elevator with the taste of Brogan still on my lips. Going back wasn't an option, so where did that leave us? Where did that leave my job?

Chapter Sixteen

"He gave you *what*?" Jackson shrieked. The vein in the middle of his forehead visibly throbbed from across the room. He'd come in this morning to a memo from Brogan ordering him to send all the information he had on the Alexander Freeland account to me.

There came a time in someone's life when they had an opportunity to take some variation of a personality test. Between fashion magazines and Buzzfeed quizzes that asked me which Harry Potter character I'd be (Ginny, obviously) this was a monthly occurrence. And in each one, they'd have a question that went a little something like this:

Your enemy gets his ass handed to him, how do you feel?

a) Jazz hands it up, yo

b) I have the emotional stance of Switzerland on this topic

c) Aww, I have the sudden urge to console them

While I'd always circled *C* (did anyone ever fully tell the truth on those things? I mean, seriously), right now I was breaking out the inner spirit fingers, dancing the "Cell Block Tango," because really, *he had it coming*.

I kept the gloat out of my voice when I said, "The Gizzara account." Well, one of his clients, at least. The rest were safety in the talons of Jackson's nubby little man-child hands.

"I can't believe this. You don't deserve Alexander Freeland." His voice pitched into a petulant whine. He pulled the files from his drawer and flounced over to my desk, dropping them in an avalanche of manila folders on my keyboard.

I straightened the files and placed them in my inbox. "Toughen up, Jackson. I'm here to stay, so you might as well get used to it." Or at least, I hoped.

I could have sworn I heard "we'll see about that" muttered under his breath, but I decided to be the bigger person and let it go.

My false confidence began to flag, though, when I glanced over at Brogan's office. After what happened last night, I wasn't so sure Jackson's grumblings weren't a smidge warranted. I crossed the line majorly, and that left me in limbo in terms of my job. If Brogan was one thing, he was a stickler for his damn rules.

Brogan hadn't bothered to stop me before I left, and if he wasn't going to bring it up again, I would chalk it up to a one-time loss of sanity and pretend it never happened. Because, let's face it, a sane Lainey wouldn't have risked her job like that. Even if his lips were enough to ruin me for all other men for the next decade at least.

By the time I went on my lunch break, Jackson was back to his normal self, pushing more filing my way and sending me on two coffee runs (a brave thing to trust a woman scorned with your coffee). But I didn't care—I'd earned a new client on my own merit, and damn did it feel good.

After saying hi to Zelda on my way out, I took my peanut butter and jelly out to the park a few blocks from work, planning to call my mom. We hadn't spoken since my less than amicable departure last Sunday, and my guilt-meter was teetering in the red.

As soon as I sat down on my usual bench, I pulled out my phone and dialed her number.

"Hey, Mom."

"How are you?" Her voice lacked her normal cheer. I couldn't tell if it was from the treatments or if she was pissed off at me still—rightfully so.

I sighed and scooped up enough courage to face the facts. I'd screwed up, and I needed to fix whatever I'd done to throw our relationship off kilter. "I'm sorry about last weekend. I didn't mean to upset you."

A heavy rush of air came through the receiver, and she was quiet for a moment. "Honey, I'm glad you care that much about your career. It's important, and I handled it in the wrong way."

I frowned, feeling even worse. Why the hell was she apologizing to me when I'd acted like an ass? "You don't ever have to apologize, Mom. I was a jerk and ruined our weekend." After the way Dad treated her, choosing his work over her ninety percent of the time, and by "work" I mean his secretary, I didn't blame her for being a little bitter toward the career-obsessed.

"Let's forget last weekend ever happened, sound good?" she said.

"Promise?"

"Yes." I could hear the smile in her response.

I grinned, and a weight lifted off my chest. No matter how good my life was going, if things with my mom were strained, it sucked the beauty out of every other aspect, because nothing felt quite complete unless we were on good terms.

"How did your presentation go?"

I explained what had happened, and then how Brogan knew that it had been my work—minus the whole making out in his office detail. Somehow I didn't think my mom would be as stoked as I was about my after-hour escapades. In fact, as much as I loved every second of his lips on my skin, even I was starting to question my choices. Because I wasn't a kid in college anymore. This was my career, and I could have put it in jeopardy.

"I can't believe that guy," she said, appalled at Jackson's behavior.

I tore the corner off my sandwich and shoved it into my mouth. "I honestly can't either." He'd always been a jerk, but I didn't think he'd stoop to that level. Just went to show, people were like a fresh pint of Rocky Road ice cream: Smooth on top, but once you dug deeper, there was an overwhelming number of bumps and nuts.

"I'll be back down to visit within the next few weeks. And I promise, this time I won't bring work with me."

"Sounds like a plan."

"Love you."

"You too, love bug."

I hung up the phone and felt ten times lighter. Once I returned to the office, my email was full of new client information, and one message in particular that slapped a stupid smile on my face.

To: Lainey Taylor
From: Brogan Starr

SUBJECT: DOG WALKING

Are you free tonight? Bruce would love to see you. He'd also enjoy if you'd have homemade pasta with him and a bottle of wine.

-B
Brogan Starr, *CEO Starr Media*
CEO in need of a dog walker

Okay, breathe, he's not firing you or exiling you to the mail room. Although, with the bottle of wine suggested in the email, the mail room wouldn't be a bad place to sort some— *ahem*—mail. We hadn't discussed the specifics of whatever this was. A fling? Office tryst? That sounded so cheesy, yet delightfully dirty. Whatever it was, it was going to stay on the down low, as evidenced from this email…as long as Bruce didn't actually mean Bruce, because having wine with a dog was a little too country song for me. We'd hash out the details about this tonight, because vagaries wouldn't cut it when we worked together every day.

I clicked on the reply button and began typing.

TO: BROGAN STARR
FROM: LAINEY TAYLOR
SUBJECT: RE: DOG WALKING

Maybe Bruce will appreciate garlic more than his owner.

Lainey Taylor, *Second Assistant to Brogan Starr, Starr Media*
Professional dog walker and wine drinker

TO: LAINEY TAYLOR

FROM: BROGAN STARR
SUBJECT: RE: DOG WALKING

Garlic, yes, but the owner might be better company.

Brogan Starr, *CEO Starr Media.*
Great conversationalist

TO: BROGAN STARR
FROM: LAINEY TAYLOR
SUBJECT: RE: DOG WALKING

But who can resist Bruce's sloppy kisses?

Lainey Taylor, *Second Assistant to Brogan Starr, Starr Media*
Walker of a very kissable dog

TO: LAINEY TAYLOR
FROM: BROGAN STARR
SUBJECT: RE: DOG WALKING

Is it okay to be jealous of a dog?

Brogan Starr, *CEO Starr Media.*
Owner of a lady-stealing dog

. . .

Brogan was standing in the kitchen stirring a saucepan when I returned with Bruce to the apartment at seven. I'd done the usual trek to the park downtown, and I made sure to put his doggy bag in the dumpster outside the building two blocks away. While Brogan's eccentricities had bothered me the first few weeks, they'd become something cute, something that made him stand out. What was it in a young CEO's mind that made him tick a little differently than the men I was used to? And had he really bent all his rules for me from day one because he wanted me? I didn't know how to feel about that—except that I didn't like the thought of having special privileges because of his attraction to me.

After I unhooked the leash, Bruce padded to his doggy bed in the living room and flopped down with a huff, rolling around on his back, doing his pig snort deal. I shook my head and smiled. A nice alliance had formed, one where he didn't eat my clothes, and I let him sniff eighty percent of the hydrants and bike racks along the city blocks. I drew the line at dry humping the neighbor's poodle, who was way out of his league, because it was no use getting the poor guy's hopes up.

The savory aroma of homemade marinara sauce floated through the apartment, and my mouth watered. I only had a chance to scarf down a granola bar on my way out of work, and anything that was warm and didn't come from a box sounded particularly mind-blowing.

"That smells amazing." I dropped my purse and keys on the counter and sidled up next to Brogan at the stove. Just being near him, the warmth of his body washing over me, was enough to frazzle my mind like ten too many tabs open on my internet browser.

"My grandmother's recipe. She lives in Italy, and I gain about ten pounds every time I visit her."

"Does she adopt?" Because my Top Ramen diet wouldn't cut it for much longer. I could pull that off when I lived in the dorms in college, but eleven-hour work days left me needing more sustenance than broth and noodles. Every penny of the two paychecks I'd earned, except for my portion of the rent and a bare minimum in food, had been sent to my mom's crap insurance that didn't even begin to cover half her treatments. Sure, Mom wasn't happy that I was spending my hard-earned cash on her, but what was I supposed to do? Indulge my purse and leggings addiction while she was too sick to work and the bills piled up? Nope. Not a chance. She tried sending my checks back a few times, and I ended up getting around that by directly depositing the money in the online billing account. Besides, blowing it on luxuries like silk scarves, Italian leather handbags, or steaks and chicken meant more that she'd have to pay off later down the road. I couldn't let that happen. So Ramen and off-brand mac and cheese were it for the unforeseeable future.

He laughed and continued stirring the sauce. I unwound my scarf, and Brogan took his attention off the cooking, his jaw going slack for a moment as his gaze worked over my low-cut top. "I'm glad you came." The formality we'd used with each other during office hours fell away as he ran his fingers along the curve of my spine, pulling me in for a long, slow kiss that simmered my insides. His lips had this uncanny ability to take me down to seven brain cells—just enough to keep my mouth functioning and air coming to my lungs. When he pulled away to continue stirring the sauce, I was left with swollen lips and an early onset heart arrhythmia.

He ran his thumb over my lower lip. "Best part of my day, by far." Both his hands found their way to my hips, and he tugged me in for another kiss. This one held the urgency of someone who knew what he wanted, someone who *always* got what he wanted. And when it came to Brogan, I was willing to give just that.

The sauce simmering on the stove picked up to a roaring boil, and Brogan broke away from the kiss to turn down the heat. In that split second of reprieve, I was able to remember my mission for tonight: figure out what the hell *this* was. As soon as I found the right moment.

I looked around the kitchen, unsure of what to do with my hands…besides manhandle Brogan, obviously. "Can I help you with anything?" I asked. The whole workplace fling was new to me, and I didn't really know how it worked in terms of hook-up etiquette. Did we just get to the good stuff, or did I help out like a girlfriend would? Shove my hands in the butt pockets of his *very* well-fitting dress pants? Or remove his collared shirt, one button at a time? Decisions, decisions.

An embarrassingly loud growl erupted from my stomach, and Brogan quirked his brow. "You can be my taste tester for the sauce."

"I like that idea," I said. He gently guided the spoon toward my lips, and the flavor exploded on my tongue, a rich mixture of tomatoes and garlic and spices. I groaned, and my eyes fluttered shut. "Oh my God. That's amazing." Quite possibly the best thing that I'd eaten in a month.

I opened my eyes, and Brogan stood frozen, his gaze fixed on my mouth. His brown eyes dilated, holding a different type of hunger than the one rolling around in my stomach. That look transported me back to last night—the feel of his fingers running through my hair, the softness of his lips as they devoured mine. The sauce spoon still hovered inches from my lips, shaking ever so slightly in Brogan's grip. For the first time, he looked unsure of himself. The boardroom persona had been stripped, leaving him open, vulnerable.

He must have realized the shift in his own demeanor, because he quickly deposited the spoon on the counter, clearing his throat. "I'll make sure to relay the message to Nona." We stood there in silence for a few moments, both staring at each other. He opened his mouth and closed it, as if he were debating what to say. Maybe, *Meet me in my bed in thirty seconds,* or, *Please, let me help you out of these clothes and take total advantage of you and christen this leather couch.*

Instead, he said, "Will you set the table? Plates are over

there." He pointed to a cupboard above the long expanse of granite. Okay, so no clothes would be coming off yet, but dinner was a step in the right direction.

"Sure." I made my way to the cabinet and grabbed two plates. I set them on the table, along with utensils and napkins. The motions felt so comfortable, like we'd been doing this for years, almost like I belonged here. This was the second time feeling this way at his place…a dangerous thought when I didn't know what this was between us. I barely knew the guy. He was my boss, and he was cooking me dinner. We'd kissed a whopping two times, and suddenly everything in my world was feeling a little topsy-turvy. Was this a typical occurrence in his household? With Brogan's good looks and money, I doubted his bed stayed vacant for long.

"Everything okay?" He gave me a sideways glance as he poured the sauce in a bowl and extracted meatballs from the oven.

"Yeah." Maybe? I didn't know.

I sat down across from him at the table, tapping my fingers against the edge of the glass.

He cleared his throat again, this time shifting restlessly in his seat. "I don't do this very often. Usually, it's just me and Bruce."

It made sense. Even if he could easily make anyone's "Most Eligible Bachelor" list, he didn't make it out of his office enough to even go on a date.

I snorted. "The conversation must be stimulating."

"Bruce is good company. Excellent table manners." He reached down and scratched Bruce's pudgy head.

"My disappearing wardrobe is clear evidence." I rolled my eyes.

Brogan's mouth pulled into an attractive smile that set my pulse into an unsteady tailspin. "We're still working on manners." He looked down at Bruce and said, "I think we have a long way to go. I'd like to reimburse you for your ruined clothes."

I thought about saying no to this, but when would be the next time I could afford nice clothes? Plus, I wouldn't *need* new clothes if it weren't for Bruce. "You can add it to my paycheck."

"I'll let Tony know first thing in the morning."

I nodded and bit into the tender meatball with the perfect amount of garlic and seasonings. Juice dripped down my lips, and I quickly blotted the mess with my napkin. "These are amazing balls." *Oh my God, did that really just come out of my mouth?* My eyes widened, and if there was a beach nearby, I'd have gladly shoved my head in the sand right about now. "Meatballs. I meant meatballs."

"Your way with words never ceases to amaze me, Taylor." He had the audacity to smirk. "I'm glad you like my meat*balls*."

I cleared my throat and tried to steer the conversation back on track. "Is it another recipe from your grandma?"

This time a genuine smile crossed his face, one that made the corners of his eyes crinkle. "Yes. I made a few alterations to the recipe, though."

I took another bite and rolled it around on my tongue, trying to place the flavor. "Nutmeg?"

He nodded, impressed. "Yes."

We went back to eating, and as I stared at him from across the expanse of the table, I wondered how this could possibly work out. Flirting and kissing were one thing, but what did this mean? I couldn't possibly go to work and pretend nothing was going on between us and then come over in the evenings while he cooked me amazing Italian food, could I?

Umm, yes, I totally could if it involved these meatballs.

My normal go with the flow mentality had been thrown severely off-kilter by last night's events, and the lull in conversation posed perfect timing for the question that had gnawed at me the entire day.

"Brogan?" I finally said, not able to contemplate these thoughts one more minute like a damn lunatic.

"Yeah?"

"I don't want this"—I pointed between us—"to affect my job." I couldn't move forward with this if it put my job in jeopardy, no matter how much I liked his sweet mouth on mine. "I have my mom to think about."

His expression turned serious, and he dragged the tines of his fork over the edge of his plate. "Nothing that happens outside the office will influence my opinion of you at work."

"Good." Right, one element of my neuroses out of the way. Now I could focus on the big question. "Then what is it that you want out of this? I want things to be clear." Because we all knew where ambiguities went. A straight course to crazyville, and I sure as hell wasn't boarding that train.

He sighed and pushed around the spaghetti on his plate. "You're smart and beautiful and I like spending time with you—I don't know if I can put a label on that. I haven't done this in a really long time, so I'm out of practice with the whole dating thing."

"I like spending time with you, too. And I don't need a label—I'm not in high school." Praise Jesus, hallelujah. "But I think we need to have some rules."

His brow lifted a fraction, but a smile still played at his lips. "The rule breaker is opting for rules? I think I'm having a stroke over here."

"Quick, where's your Life Alert button?"

His lips twitched. "Maybe I should invest in one. Wouldn't want to be left stranded if I broke a hip."

"You could wear it around like Flavor Flav's clock necklace."

"I…" He paused shaking his head. "I have no clue who

that is."

I groaned and rolled my eyes. "I have so much to teach you, Mr. Starr."

His nostrils flared at the use of his name, and he sucked in a deep, jagged breath. "Is that so?" He liked when I called him that, it was clear. Maybe I took a little too much satisfaction in knowing this.

He swiped his thumb across the expanse of his lower lip and gave me an appraising look. "You're right. Rules are probably a good thing."

I motioned to him. "You're the rule master. What do you propose?"

He paused for a minute, taking a sip of his wine and dabbing his mouth with his napkin. "I've never done anything like this—I really don't know the proper protocol. But let's keep it simple. One: no one in the office can know. Two: we can't be *together* at work again. It's too risky. And three: no attachments."

"No attachments?"

"I can't commit to anything serious. Not with the company still early in its creation." He looked up from his plate, and his eyes took on this sad quality that I'd never quite seen before. "If you can't handle that, we can pretend last night never happened. I don't want to pressure you."

"I appreciate you being upfront." This was a lot to take in. For a split second, my thoughts flickered to my dad. Was this how it started with his mistress? Just an office fling that turned into a brand new family? I shook away that idea. This was a completely different situation—there was no other woman. But was this arrangement something I wanted? For once, I would give anything to be as meticulous as Zoey, equipped with lists and spreadsheets of pros and cons for every minute detail of life.

If I were to create one right now, it'd look something like

this:

Pro: Brogan Starr wanted me.

My inner fourteen-year-old self, who practiced kissing on my JTT poster, was majorly fist-pumping at the moment.

Con: this was essentially a fling.

I mean, the word was off-putting enough. I wasn't a disposable coffee cup to be tossed in the garbage as soon as someone had their fill. Plus, people had different expectations when it came to flings—someone got more attached than the other, and someone always got hurt. Something told me I wouldn't come out on the winning end of this deal.

Pro: A fling with Brogan was way better than not having him at all.

That was self-explanatory.

Con: an expiration date already in place with the person who gave my paycheck.

No money meant no chemo payments. And even though Brogan promised that this wouldn't get in the way of work—I didn't see how this wouldn't bleed into everyday interaction in the office.

Pro: Brogan

Again, self-explanatory. Because come on—hot, smart, tattooed man who could command a board room did something to me. There weren't that many times where I could say that my ovaries took the front seat in decision making, but this rare occurrence wasn't something I could ignore.

Con: Brogan was a nice guy (normally an excellent thing).

A lot of girls underestimated the effect of a nice guy. Sure, bad boys were appealing—who didn't like a dangerous guy that would promise nothing but sin and heartbreak on the back of their Harley? But a nice guy, that was dangerous. Those were the guys that you'd *want* to bring home to mom. The type to bring you breakfast in bed and pick up tampons from the supermarket on his way home from work because you're busy stuffing your face with ice cream and crying over the unfairness of Rose losing Jack in *Titanic* (there was totally room on that piece of driftwood for the both of them). Yes, the nice guys were the real danger, because something told me Brogan wouldn't be someone I could recover from quickly, if and when this ended.

Okay, I was sick of coming up with negative aspects. Yes, he was my boss. Yes, this was probably really stupid, maybe more stupid than my teenage near-head-shaving incident, but dammit, if I couldn't make poor choices with my money, I might as well dabble in dating suicide.

I realized I'd left him hanging as I lost myself in my mental pro and con list. When I looked up from my plate, Brogan sat staring, brows furrowed, swirling patterns with his fork into the marinara sauce on his plate. "I think this arrangement might work," I said.

Brogan set his fork on the table and looked visibly relieved at my response. "Me, too."

We'd both finished dinner at this point and worked our way to the kitchen to rinse our dishes and put them in the dishwasher.

The last bits of marinara drizzled into the sink as I rinsed the plate. If I'd been alone, I totally would have licked the plate clean, because that sauce was out of this world. "I don't want any preferential treatment at work," I added, remembering the sinking feeling in my stomach at the thought of Brogan letting me be the exception to his rules.

His lips pulled into a smile. "I wasn't planning on it." He grabbed my plate and handed me his dirty one to wash.

I leaned my hip against the counter and crossed my arms. "And if I screw up, I need to be held accountable, just like everyone else." I paused, and my voice took on a harder edge. "I want my success to be earned, and don't want anyone to mistakenly think that it's because we're hooking up." Because right now I was in the trenches, working my way up doing menial tasks, but someday I'd be putting my degree to use, and I didn't want anyone to question why.

He leveled an equally intense gaze at me. "I wouldn't dream of it. You'll work just as hard for your success as everyone else."

"I think that settles it." I smiled. "I'm in."

He smiled and pulled me into a hug. My hands ran along his biceps, along the strong ridge of muscles that wound down his arms. "Me, too."

Chapter Seventeen

Starr Media Handbook Rule #322
Emails will remain professional and polite.

Jackson had resumed his role as uninterested coworker by the time I came back to work the next day. He sat at his desk, slouched in his chair, tapping on his computer with one hand.

"More clients on your desk this morning."

I looked up at him, trying to decipher his motives. Did he give these to me, feeling bad for giving me the shaft yesterday? Pity clients. Heck, I'd take them. The more clients I took on, the more job security I garnered.

"If you're wondering why, it's because I find them lackluster, and they bring down the rest of my portfolio." He glared at me over the top of his computer and then went back to work.

Right. He was all sugar and spice today.

Two manila folders sat on my desk, and I pushed them aside while I booted up my computer.

My email pinged as soon as the programs loaded.

FROM: BROGAN STARR
TO: LAINEY TAYLOR
SUBJECT: MEATBALLS

I hope you didn't bring the meatballs in the office. They have garlic and you might be meeting with a client today at 1:30. Don't be late.

Brogan Starr, *CEO Starr Media*

I quickly replied:

FROM: LAINEY TAYLOR
TO: BROGAN STARR
SUBJECT: RE: MEATBALLS

I wouldn't dream of eating your balls at work. I look forward to the meeting.

P.S.—I plan to eat them with garlic bread and garlic tater tots later tonight.

Lainey Taylor, *Second assistant to Brogan Starr, Starr Media*
Garlic lover

I smirked, thinking maybe I needed to tone it down on the next email, because that *may* have toed the line a bit.

A new event popped up on my schedule—a meeting with JD Sigmund, a news anchor that recently transferred over to MTV. I bounced in my seat as I stared at the notification. Four new clients within a month. At this rate, I'd have a full caseload by the end of next year.

I giggled as I read Brogan's email for the fourth time.

"Please, by all means, share with the class what is so damn

funny, newbie." Jackson gave brow arch number two with a little splash of indignation to mix it up a bit.

"Just a funny email."

"Did you get the YouTube one of that cat that logrolls a watermelon? Janice sent that this morning."

"No." And I felt oddly left out if everyone on the staff was getting goofy cat videos while my inbox remained empty.

Another email pinged in my inbox a few minutes later.

FROM: BROGAN STARR
TO: LAINEY TAYLOR
SUBJECT: RE: MEATBALLS

Trying to ward off vampires, huh? Rumor has it the garlic thing is a myth, though holy water and a salt circle will do the trick. Are you free on Thursday?

-B

FROM: LAINEY TAYLOR
TO: BROGAN STARR
SUBJECT: RE: MEATBALLS

Did you just make a Supernatural reference? I see the Netflix is paying off.

I'll have to check my schedule. My boss runs a tight ship, and I might have a lot of work to do that night.

-L

FROM: BROGAN STARR
TO: LAINEY TAYLOR

SUBJECT: RE: MEATBALLS

I'll put in a good word to your boss.

-B

I smothered my grin with my hand and bounced my legs against the rung of my chair. Oh lordy, was I in trouble.

• • •

Brogan was on his computer when I finished walking Bruce the following night. He had a pair of black-rimmed reading glasses on as he focused on a spreadsheet. The glasses gave a cute geeky edge to his muscled exterior, something that was deliciously adorable.

"How's the Henderson account coming?" I asked, plopping a tote and my purse on the coffee table.

"It's going. Just finishing up." He hit a few keys on the computer and then closed the laptop. He scrubbed his hands over his face, removing his glasses and propping them on the end table. His look of irritation dissipated when his gaze slid over me, replaced with a soft smile. "Damn, you are a much-needed sight for sore eyes. Come here, beautiful." He grabbed my hand and pulled me onto the couch. My fingers ran along the stubble of his jaw as our lips brushed together.

"What's in the bag?" He jutted his chin to the large sack on the table.

"Tonight's festivities." I grabbed the bag and set it on the couch next to him.

As he peered in the tote, his brows furrowed. "Is that a plastic gun?" He put his pinky through the trigger hole and picked it up, examining it.

"Is that a gun?" I scoffed. "It's only the best gun known to man. The Zapper NES."

He shook his head, but a smile played at his lips. "You lost me."

"Have you never played Duck Hunt in your life?"

He just stared at me.

"Did you seriously live under a rock in the nineties?"

"Might as well have," he muttered, and his smile fell momentarily. It quickly reappeared, though, and he said, "The gun's part of the game, I assume? My parents believed that video games and television rotted brains, so the most I got was thirty minutes of PBS. Don't worry, I've made up for it since then." He nodded toward three different gaming consoles nestled in his entertainment system.

"Well, get ready to lose a few brain cells tonight, because we're having an official Duck Hunt throw down." I unearthed the Nintendo console from the bag and hooked up the cords to his TV.

"Can I at least pour us some wine?"

"Is that even a question? Wine goes with everything. Including…" I grabbed a bag of gummy worms from the bag and tossed them in Brogan's lap.

He grimaced at the package and picked it up carefully, like it contained hazardous waste. "Wasn't there something in our arrangement saying you're not allowed to poison me?"

"It's candy, not arsenic."

He lifted a finger and said, "Ever hear that a clean system is a healthy system?"

Right of course. Mr. Organic wouldn't eat a gummy worm. "Then mine must look like the inside of a garbage dump. You can't knock 'em unless you try first."

He rolled his eyes but opened the package. He squished the worm between his fingers and shuddered, looking like he was going to throw up right there on the spot. "This is just disgusting."

I put my hands on my hips and gave an exaggerated sigh.

"Just try it."

"Wasn't peer pressure supposed to end in high school?" he mused, his hand sliding up my thigh, momentarily making me forget what we were talking about. His lips kissed along my neck and goose bumps pebbled my flesh. Something told me I'd never get used to his touch.

He threw the bag of gummy worms to the side and continued working along my collarbone, then lower. "This is a much better alternative to candy," he said, his hands slipping up my shirt.

If he thought he could get away with distracting me with his mouth and hands, well, he was right. But he wouldn't win this time. I could muster up *some* self-restraint. "Did you hear that? I think there's a chicken in your condo."

He let out sigh and said, "I take back everything I said about admiring your determination."

"It's an endearing quality that you'll learn to embrace with time."

"Fine. But for the record, I'm only trying this so you stop giving me those puppy dog eyes. I can't say no to anything when you give me looks like that."

"I'll keep that useful nugget of information tucked away."

His hand caressed my cheek, and he gave me a smile that set my insides ablaze. "Use those powers for good, okay?" He looked at the candy in his hand and took a tentative bite. His expression went from disgust to revulsion in the span of a few seconds. "This tastes like shit."

"It tastes like my childhood." I picked up the bag and shoved a worm in my mouth.

His eyes widened as he watched me chew and swallow the candy. "Well, your childhood should have put you in a hyperglycemic coma by now."

I couldn't help the laughter that bubbled up, because Brogan freaking out about a gummy worm was the funniest thing I'd seen in at least a week.

"Excuse me, I need to wash the taste of shit down with something." He moved his laptop from the couch cushion to the end table and disappeared into the kitchen. A couple minutes later, he came back, brandishing two glasses of red wine. He handed me the long-stemmed crystal, and I took a deep sip. This was a far cry from my three dollar beers. My taste buds would be weeping next time I went to a bar.

I placed my glass on a coaster on the coffee table and strode over to the console and turned it on. The good old hunter and dog flashed on the screen, accompanied by the pesky ducks. I hadn't played this game in years. Ever since the newer gaming systems came out, this one had collected dust under my bed. But when Brogan said he hadn't indulged in good ol' nineties technology, I had to share something that was near and dear to my childhood.

After handing Brogan the controller, I instructed him on how the game worked. "Aim it at the ducks. The goal is to kill each one and you move to the next level."

"Sounds simple enough." He shrugged and pointed his controller at the television.

I smirked. "Mm-hmm." Right. Only a novice would say that. Anyone well-versed in the Nintendo-sphere would know that getting each duck took a certain amount of skill and luck, and positioning the controller a quarter inch to the side of the duck because sometimes the screen was a little off with the laser.

I watched him as the loud *cling* of the trigger rapid-fired, and Brogan continued to miss the ducks flying across the screen. He cussed under his breath, and his brows pinched together in concentration. "What the hell? I had them!"

"It helps if you look through the sight instead of going all G-unit on them. Be one with the gun, boss."

"Right." He shook his head and plopped down on the

couch, holding up the gun to me. "How about you show me how it's done."

I grabbed the controller from his hand and stuck out my tongue. "Gladly."

The round started again and I shot each duck before they were able to fly off the screen.

"I don't know how you just did that but I definitely like watching you with a gun in your hands."

"Yeah?" I pretended to blow smoke from the plastic barrel. "You should see me play Mortal Combat then. I'm proficient with all sorts of weapons." I wiggled my brows.

"I don't know whether to be scared of you or turned on."

A wave of heat licked through me. "Maybe a little bit of both."

I tossed the controller onto the table and climbed on top of him, my legs on either side of his thighs. His fingers wrapped around my sides as he pulled me closer to him. Nothing beat the feel of his skin, the way his eyes softened when he looked at me... The way everything else slid away, my one reprieve during the toughest months of my life.

My palms cupped either side of his face, my hands slipping into his hair. He groaned and leaned into my touch as I massaged my fingers over his scalp.

"Scared is the last word I'd use when you're on top of me." His soft mouth met mine, and a sigh escaped my parted lips. A searing heat spread from where my mouth met his and cascaded down my spine as I arched my body into his. Even though we were close enough that the only barrier left was clothes, I needed more. How could someone so different from me elicit such a reaction? I didn't even begin to understand him, but his willingness to try something that meant a lot to me was heartwarming. If we'd met in college, he'd be a best friend. Someone to share secrets and desires with. Someone I'd want to be around because I liked him as a person first and foremost. Because Brogan was a nice guy, and nice guys were always the most trouble.

His tongue slid across my lips at the same time his hands worked over my back. Any thoughts bumping around in my head quickly dissolved as our kiss deepened, and my grip on reality slipped into a haze of feather light touches, skin, and contented sighs.

Chapter Eighteen

A sure way to a man's heart is through his stomach.

"And, to make it worse, he live-tweeted the whole date. The guy forgot that we followed each other, and that I could see his status updates."

Zoey and I were bent over in a fit of laughter on our bar stools, listening to Zelda's account of her date from hell. I'd finally taken her up on her offer for a girls' night and dragged Zoey along. Luckily, they were hitting it off, just as I'd hoped.

"How did it end?" Zoey asked, while I checked my phone for the tenth time since we sat down thirty minutes ago.

My persistence paid off, because a text sat in my inbox.

Brogan: *I went down the cookie aisle and thought of you.*

A smile plastered itself to my face, and I quickly texted back while trying to listen to Zelda's story.

Lainey: *I don't know whether to be flattered or offended.*

I focused back on the conversation between Zoey and Zelda just in time for Zelda's lips to pull into a shit-eating grin.

"I tweeted him from the cab that he was stuck with the bill, and my lipstick wasn't 'ho red' it was 'guess you're only getting your hand tonight' red."

"Oh my God. Did he tweet back?" Zoey asked.

She shrugged. "Who knows, I blocked his ass and got a free dinner out of the deal. I wasn't too heartbroken over it."

I tipped my beer bottle in her direction. "I want to be you when I grow up."

"It takes a lot of practice on bad kissers, but I think you can handle the job." She winked.

I took a sip of my beer and glanced at my phone again. My heart beat quickened when I saw another text.

Brogan: *Definitely flattered. I bought 7 boxes and none of them tasted as good as the ones you made.*

Lainey: *I told you they're out of this world.*

Brogan: *Does that mean you'll come over and bake for me this week?*

Lainey: *Hmm…what's in it for me?*

Baking cookies for Brogan? Um, where was the signup sheet?

Zelda turned to me and asked, "How about you? Seeing anyone, Lainey?"

I looked up from my phone and tapped out of my message

app. Not that anyone could see while I typed out texts under the table, but no sense in being careless.

"I don't really know yet. It's still in the early stages. Still waiting to see if it's going to work out."

Zelda raised her brow and leaned in closer, leaning her chin on her hand. "Oh? Anyone I know? There are a few cuties in the office."

I felt myself go into deer in the headlights, "how do I answer this" mode. "You know that isn't allowed. No, someone outside of work." Technically this was the truth because I was seeing him out of the confines of work hours.

She sipped her martini and said, "You'll have to bring him around."

Oh, if she only knew. "We'll see. He's kind of shy about relationship stuff."

"I can still hook you up with my tattooed friend if this guy doesn't work out. Not a shy bone in that dude's body, if you know what I mean." She arched a brow.

"Sounds good." Yeah, there was no chance in hell that was happening.

Zoey smiled at me, and I was thankful we were on the same wavelength about keeping the Brogan news under wraps. Even though I liked Zelda, I respected Brogan enough to not say anything to anyone who worked in the office. The worst that could happen to me was being fired—well, and blacklisted from any media company on the west coast—but I had a feeling the consequences would be worse for Brogan, like headlines in the tabloids and lost clientele, especially when our firm had the utmost discretion for clients. If we couldn't keep our private lives private, what did that say in terms of our services?

My phone buzzed in my lap, and I picked it back up.

Brogan: *Hmm... You'll get a happy boss?*

Lainey: *I'll think about it. Not really a good enough incentive as is.*

I put my phone back down and tried not to smile like a sap. Flirting with Brogan was like a good latte or bowl of ice cream—utterly satisfying, but with zero calorie guilt.

"What about you, Zoey?" Zelda asked.

Zoey had been uncharacteristically quiet about this shirtless dude from the other day. I was dying to know what was up with them because it'd been a while since she'd been in a relationship as well. But when it came to her personal life, Zoey didn't like when people pried—she'd tell me when she was ready.

She stirred the straw in her Tom Collins and stared absently at the drink. "It's complicated."

"Does this have anything to do with Shirtless Dude?"

"His name is Ryder," she muttered, a note of annoyance in her voice.

While Brogan had the lean build of a swimmer, Ryder had muscles on his muscles. The dude was a walking, talking Chippendales advertisement.

"Ryder the Shirtless, that's quite a name." Zelda said.

I couldn't help it. Curiosity got the best of me, and I broke our sacred rule and started to pry. "How did you two meet, anyway?"

She cast her gaze to her drink. "Through work."

"Work?" If interior designers looked like that, I obviously went into the wrong profession because, besides Brogan, everyone in the office had a severe case of pancake ass from sitting all day.

Her eyes glazed over, and I could tell she was off in her own head, probably thinking about Ryder. As it was, it took every bit of restraint to stay present in our girl's night and not check my phone every two seconds. "He works for a firm I'm contracted with. I'm redesigning their offices," she said.

"And I'm sure you were just doing a little bit of Feng Shui furniture rearrangement when he came over the other night?" I mused.

She plunged her straw into her drink, and the ice rattled against the glass. "I'd rather not talk about it. Unless you want to share about your love life." She leveled me with a look that said I'd gone too far.

I swallowed hard and tried to catch her eye to say that I was sorry. "I'm good."

On cue, my phone buzzed again. I discreetly checked it while Zoey and Zelda were arguing over the difference between male dancers and strippers.

Brogan: *You drive a hard bargain. I could think of other things to give as payment.*

Suddenly parched, I reached for my beer, guzzling it down.

Lainey: *All I hear is your mouth running. Full of empty promises, Starr.*

Brogan: *I'm sure my mouth could be of use.*

Um, yes, please and thank you.

Lainey: *Consider the cookies a done deal.*

Chapter Nineteen

<u>Starr Media Handbook Rule #7</u>
Change your password often to prevent security breaches.

The office was in complete mayhem when I arrived at seven the next morning. Or to put it better, Brogan was in a complete frenzy, with everyone around him trying to accommodate. Jackson glanced over his computer monitor and let out a low whistle.

"What?" I said, tossing my bag into the bottom drawer of my desk.

"I heard you're in a lot of trouble."

"Trouble?" My brows slid together. What the hell was he talking about? What could I have possibly done in the twelve hours I'd been away from work?

"Didn't you see what Craig Willington messaged out this morning?" Someone really needed to wipe that smug smirk off his face.

Oh crap. *My* account? That just couldn't be possible… could it? The hair rose on the back of my neck. "No." I hadn't even scheduled any posts. That was on my to-do list for this morning, in fact, because I hadn't touched his account since Monday. I pulled up the social media site and clicked on Craig's profile. My fingers froze on the mouse as I stared at his latest post.

> Craig_Willington: *Hey, Gordy, I hope your momma enjoyed being bent over last night. Tell her to give me a call if she wants to ride on my big blue combine with her hayfield again anytime soon.*

A middle finger emoji concluded the spiteful message.

I froze, my mouse hovering over the post. Holy crap buckets. Did Craig just call out one of country music's biggest stars? Craig didn't even know how to work anything past the camera function on his smart phone. No way could he navigate social media and use an emoji—so what the hell was going on? I looked at the time stamp—fifteen minutes before I'd arrived.

Under his offensive message, where he actually tagged Gordy in the post (lord have mercy), hundreds of people commented things like:

OHHHH DO YOU NEED SOME ICE FOR THAT BURN?

LOLOLOLOL HELLA FUNNY DUDE.

FUCK YOU, CRAIG! LEAVE GORDY'S MAMA ALONE.

U LOST RESPECT FROM ME, BUDDY.

Topping it off was a comment from Gordy himself saying, "What the hell, man?"

To make it worse, a few celebrity gossip sites had made note of Craig's dig at Gordy's mother and speculated as to why. I quickly deleted the message, but the damage had already been done. The internet was forever, and even if Craig hadn't written this, people would forever think he rammed his combine into Mama Gordy's hayfield.

Before I could say anything more to Jackson, my intercom buzzed.

"In my office. Now." Anger bubbled over Brogan's voice, and my pulse hummed against my temples as I tried to collect myself and decide what I was going to tell him. I didn't even know what to say, not when I'd just found out about a mistake I wasn't sure I made until two seconds ago.

Something told me there would be no cookie making in the near future.

Jackson's brows rose, and a wicked smile played at his lips as I strode toward Brogan's office. "Oh, how the mighty have fallen."

As I stood in front of the glass doors, I took a deep breath and steeled myself. How had I managed to mess up a post without even trying? Major damage control would be needed to fix this, starting with a few apology posts as soon as I left Brogan's office.

"Sit down." Brogan's gaze was focused on his computer as I walked into the room. Just the other night, we'd been doing the same thing, although when he'd previously asked me into his office, it was under much different circumstances. I much preferred those right about now.

I made my way over to the swivel chair across from him and gingerly sat on the cushion, waiting for him to go off on me.

I tapped my foot nervously as I waited for him to speak. After a few long moments of silence, he finally looked up, his angry gaze lighting a fire under my skin. Even under all that anger, his eyes softened the slightest bit when he regarded me. Keeping my feelings for him under lockdown was hard enough, and it looked like he was struggling with this as well. Sweat beaded at my hairline and behind my knees, and I shifted uncomfortably.

"What was that post all about?" he demanded. He pointed to his computer. I didn't need to look at the screen to know what he was talking about.

Somehow I didn't think *um, I don't remember writing this* would fly in terms of an explanation. "I don't know yet, but it shouldn't have happened. I deleted it as soon as I got into the office."

He pinched the bridge of his nose and closed his eyes. "We never allow celebrities to humiliate other celebrities—especially when they are both our clients." His tone was clipped and cold, devoid of any feeling.

I took a deep breath and pushed away the urge to cower. I was a big girl, and I needed to handle this mess like one. "I know."

He tapped his fingers on his desk in a quick, staccato rhythm. His pained expression was a swift kick to my gut. "Give me one reason I shouldn't fire you right this second," he said. A war of anger and betrayal battled in his eyes. For all intents and purposes, my ass should have been kicked to the curb five minutes ago.

My cheeks flamed, and I tugged at my shirt, trying to get cool airflow to my burning skin. What the heck was I supposed to do about this when I didn't even know about it until a few minutes ago? I'd managed to screw up my client's account without even trying.

No. This wasn't my fault. I'd earned this damn job, and I wasn't about to lose it because of a rogue post I wasn't even responsible for. I'd worked too hard, put up with so much, missed so many moments with my mom when she was at her worst. My pulse hammered in my temples, and the room blurred at the thought that all I'd built in these months of working my ass off, advancing my career, could crumble in a matter of seconds.

Now was not the time to let emotions get the best of me. I

pushed my hurt and anger at being wrongfully accused aside for a second to contemplate what had happened. Technology-inept Craig sure as hell didn't write the post, which begged the question—who, then? "Because I didn't write it."

He cocked his head. "Well, then who did?"

My hands flew up as I said, "I don't know." I frowned. "Which bothers me. Obviously, Craig's account got hacked. I don't know why, but I don't think it was random." I caught his gaze and tried to convey how sincerely sorry I was that this happened, and to let him know that it hurt me that he'd even think I'd do something like this to a client. I didn't have the tech savvy to find out who was responsible for this. The person sitting across the desk staring daggers at me did, though. "Can you look into it for me?"

"Yes, I'll have someone investigate." He swallowed hard and I could tell he wanted to believe what I was saying. "Have you changed your password weekly?"

"No."

His shoulders tensed, and he splayed his hands flat on the desk. "Lainey, that's in the manual. I'll do work on my end, but you need to find a way to fix this by the end of the day." The *or else* at the end of the sentence was definitely implied, his voice as sharp as a broken glass.

The anger I'd pushed aside tugged me under so quickly that I thought I might drown in it. Yes, I understood he was pissed the account got hacked, but if he believed me, he should direct that attitude somewhere else. I tamped down my temper and took a deep breath. There was no use making the situation worse by calling him out. "I will."

"And for God's sake, change your password." His eyes searched mine, and after a few moments he let out a deep breath and sat back in his chair. "Next time I can't let it go. No matter how I feel about you. Are we clear?"

I nodded. "Crystal." *But I didn't even do it,* I wanted to

scream. How had all my strikes been used up when I hadn't even made it to bat? The real world sucked ass.

"Contact Craig's agent and tell him to issue a formal apology. You clean up the social media mess in the meantime."

"Right. On it." I stuck to simple words. Ones that wouldn't allow me to elaborate or somehow get myself into more trouble. Ones that wouldn't show how close to tears I was.

By the time I got back to my desk, Jackson was nowhere in sight, and I'd formulated a plan to issue a public apology on Craig's account. The best way to go about it, I figured, was to tell the truth. The account was hacked, and then hopefully all would be forgiven.

I frowned and sat down in my chair, trying to not let what just happened rattle me. After changing my password, I pulled up Craig's profile and tapped out a quick response to this morning's events.

@craig_willington: *So sorry to Gordy and everyone who saw that horrible post this morning. My account was hacked. I have nothing but respect for Gordy and his family.*

Jackson strode through the elevator doors as I hit send on the message, and he swaggered over to my desk.

"Figured I'd do you a favor and grab a box from the mail room. This should be enough for all your *worldly* possessions." He shoved an empty one over my keyboard.

I glared at him and pushed it back against his chest. "You're not getting rid of me that easily."

He tossed the box at the end of his desk and plopped down in his chair. "What the hell happened, anyway? You get a little text-happy with the social media?"

I threw my hands in the air. Enough was enough. This guy had his lunch money stolen as a kid? I got it, it sucked, but I didn't need to be brought down because of his insecurity issues. "You know what? I don't have time for your crap today. Save it for someone who cares."

I really hoped Brogan found out who hacked Craig's account, because I had a sinking feeling that I might already know who it was. And I'd love to see him kicked off his high horse.

He hesitated for a second, sucking in his cheeks and staring off into space. "Funny, all the sudden I'm feeling very *thirsty*. I could really go for a soy latte."

I stared at him, blinking slowly, not quite believing what I was hearing. Oh, he really was just the icing on top of this shittastic day. Everything in me screamed to tell him just where he ought to shove his latte. Instead, I pushed back from my chair and stalked over to his desk. I leaned over his computer and whispered, "It wouldn't hurt to be nice to someone for once. Maybe you'd actually make friends."

He looked up at me, his mouth gaping like a fish out of water before he finally fixed his face into his normal sneer. "Extra hot—"

"Yes, 'and don't forget the soy or you'll be fired.' Got it." This guy just didn't let up. I wondered if the rod up his ass needed to be surgically removed and maybe he was irritable twenty-four-seven due to anal chaffing. I sped to the elevator and jammed my thumb on the down button.

By the time I returned with Jackson's pristine, untouched soy *extra hot* latte, I'd managed to cool off a bit about this morning. "Well, I guess I need to face the music," I muttered. I'd seen people torn apart online for less, but I was hoping they'd spare Craig this once.

I pulled up Craig's social media account and stared. Thousands of new followers. Fans leaving supportive comments. Even Gordy responded with a "No worries, man."

Well, crap. This couldn't have turned out any better if I'd tried. Not that I particularly liked being hacked. Hopefully

Brogan found out who did it soon. But with Craig's new followers, I might as well make the best out of the situation. It was time to post something to keep them reading.

I opened a blank post, the cursor blinking over the text box. *Think.* Coming up with social media posts for someone I only knew through his iCloud was tougher than I'd have thought before being hired. I wanted him to come off warm, keeping his southern charm—which, as a Portland girl, I had none of. I'd pulled up a few other country stars' accounts this past week and studied which posts were the most popular with viewers. Shirtless pics won by a landslide, followed by sweat-soaked shirts from performances. Definitely not posts involving the word *moist.* That would land me jobless in a matter of minutes at the rate I was going.

If my life this week could be summed up by a hashtag, it'd be #headdesk or #epicfail. Fortunately, I had a chance to redeem myself in Brogan's eyes, and I would do so by continuing to build Craig's following this week.

I spent the remainder of the morning and early afternoon creating posts for Craig and two of my other clients.

By lunchtime, I'd pounded out four posts and had a migraine looming in the periphery of my frazzled brain. Zoey had called two times this morning, but my phone was on silent. I listened to my messages and fought the urge to let out a scream.

Zelda stopped by my desk before going into the lunchroom. "You coming?"

"Can't. I have to make some calls. Apparently there was an emergency with my roommate."

"Oh." She frowned. "Well, we'll be there if you finish your calls early."

"Thanks."

I put my phone back to my ear and replayed the first message.

Hey, Lain. It's me. Just letting you know I had a little mishap in the kitchen. Nothing to worry about, just a small fire. Bonus, I met a hot fireman today.

I rolled my eyes and skipped to the next message.

It's me again. So, our landlord isn't very happy about the whole smoke damage. Don't worry, because I have it covered, but you might want to stay out of the apartment for a while. It's…a little smoky. But hey, you like campfires, right?

Good lord, the girl burned water. I didn't even want to know what she was attempting to cook. For someone who planned every detail of their life, you'd think using a measuring cup would come as second nature. I dialed her number, and she picked up on the second ring.

"Did you get my messages?" she squeaked, and the background was a muffled murmur of numerous men talking.

"Yep, I got both."

"I'm so sorry. Things got a little out of hand with the brownies. I mean, a boxed mix shouldn't be this difficult."

"You made brownies?" Dear lord. What the hell possessed her to use the oven?

"Attempted. They're better off as doorstops at the moment." She sighed. "You know how *Top Chef* always gets me amped. I had the day off and wanted to give baking another try."

I put my head in my hand and stifled my groan for her benefit. No use making her feel worse than she did. "How extensive is the damage?"

"Just a little black around the stove, and part of the counter's melted, but other than that, nothing. I closed your room so your clothes wouldn't get smoky."

I leaned back in my chair and took a deep breath. It could have been so much worse. "Thanks."

"It should be okay by the time you get home tonight."

"Great thanks. And leave the baking to me next time,

okay?"

"Right."

We hung up, and I inhaled deeply, trying to use Zoey's yoga breathing to center myself. Screwed up tweets? Check. Apartment caught on fire? Check. With that out of the way, I could safely move on to my next task of the day—emptying my bank account into the healthcare system. *Good-bye, paycheck, it was nice knowing you for a whole forty minutes.*

The hospital had been nice enough to add me on the account so I could easily make online payments (how selfless of them). I powered up my laptop and logged into the site, clicking on the bill portion.

The amount loaded on the screen, and the yoga breaths screeched to a halt. I sat there and blinked.

No. This couldn't be right.

I refreshed the page five times just to make sure.

No, no, no.

I'd always heard bad things happened in threes. This must be a record.

I'd just checked the other week, and I was sure that there hadn't been that many zeroes. This would take me four years to pay off *if* I didn't have any other expenses. Surely this had to be a mistake. Yes, a clerical error, because even with crappy insurance, this fee seemed exorbitant.

My shaky fingers dialed the number of the billing company, and I sat through ten minutes of crappy, static-y hold music before I was queued in to a receptionist.

"Hello, St. Vincent Hospital billing center, this is Betty, how may I assist you?" she drawled in a thick southern accent.

Okay, Betty, get ready to make it rain, because I need a money tree right about now. "Hi, Betty. I'm calling about my mother's bill. I logged into the site, and it seems like there's been an error in the amount due."

I gave her my information and she *hmmed* and *huhhed*

and *yes, ma'amed* a few times before saying, "Yes, I see the account now."

"And do you see there is a big mistake in the amount owed?"

"I'm sorry, sugar, but it seems the new chemo treatment is more expensive than the previous one they were administering. Your insurance doesn't fully cover it."

My heart fell through a trap door in my chest and plummeted straight to the floor.

"Oh." My money tree, the one Betty was supposed to fix and replenish, was on fire, burning a hole in my dwindling bank account. My throat tightened, and I swallowed hard, trying to keep it together long enough to end the conversation.

"I'm sorry, sweetheart. Wish there was more I could do."

Me, too! I wanted to scream, but poor Betty with her sweet southern accent wasn't the one who decided my financial fate. As I learned earlier this morning, it sucked being on the receiving end of someone else's misplaced anger. So instead of screaming at a woman who didn't deserve it, I said, "Thanks," and hung up the phone.

I stared at the amount on the screen until my vision blurred and my head swam with words like "eternal debt" and "starvation." Suddenly, playing the lottery didn't seem like a bad idea.

I tamped down the hysteria that rolled in on the perimeters of my mind, waiting to blanket all my rational thoughts. No problem. I could live sparsely for the next few years. Discounted noodles were already my best friend, besides Zoey, so why not invite Spam and off-brand cereal to the party? It was all worth it if my mom didn't have to worry about this. She had bigger things on her plate, mainly staying alive, which was all that mattered to me at this point. The money situation would work itself out. Eventually. When I was gray.

Plus, there wasn't much I could do. Starr Media paid on salary, so no matter how many hours I worked, it didn't mean I earned more. Hopefully Brogan gave out Christmas bonuses because I sure needed a Scrooge McMoneybags right about now.

Chapter Twenty

Lainey Taylor Rule of Life #92
Sometimes a fling is just a fling.

At a quarter till seven I shut down my computer and grabbed my coat off the rack. December had brought a wet, bitter cold that seeped into my bones, chilling me to the core. I tied the belt tighter on my trench and started my ten block trek to Brogan's condo.

I hadn't spoken to him the rest of the day after the less-than-amicable exchange in his office. This was the first time that he'd been upset at me, and I wasn't quite sure what to expect when I got to his place. Were we supposed to ignore that I screwed up? Would he continue to be pissed? He hadn't sent an email or message telling me not to come over, so I took that as a good sign. Plus, I had to go over anyway to walk Bruce.

It was strange to think that I didn't go straight home after work anymore. Not that I was in any hurry to get back to my place. After the fire, it probably reeked of burned plastic (thanks, Zoey). And my roommate had to work overtime on her new project, anyway, so the company for dinner was appreciated. Nothing was sadder than eating ramen in an empty living room watching reruns of *The Bachelor*.

Luckily, tonight I didn't have to. Anything Brogan cooked was bound to be eons better than whatever I could conjure up in my currently non-existent kitchen.

Plus, after twelve hours of nothing but conversations involving tweets, Cloud pictures, and the number of someone's followers, I was ready for a much-needed reprieve.

On the surface, everything between us had been going great up until this morning. Getting to know him on a deeper level than joking about movies and funny requests from clients had proved more difficult. Any time I even hinted at asking more about his personal life and past, he'd shut down and mumble an *I don't know*. I knew from the beginning Brogan was a private person, but I figured he'd open up with time…I hoped. It would be nice to know more than that his grandmother was Italian and liked to cook. In fact, that was pretty much all I knew. Which, after a few weeks of our relationship, didn't bode well.

Bruce sat in the entryway wagging his tail when I walked through the door. Instead of jumping, he was now down to a scramble of paws that was a mix between tap and river dancing. I bent down and let him give me a kiss on the cheek. "Good to see you too, boy. Jitters is going to be very jealous."

"Hey there." Brogan stood in the doorway to the living room, and my heart leaped into my throat as his gaze lazily traced over me. "That skirt has been driving me insane all day." He strode over and skimmed his fingers along the curve of my hip.

Wait, wasn't he super pissed at me this morning? Okay, so I guessed he was done being mad at me. Interesting how he could flip it like a switch. Was that what I was supposed to do, too?

"I'm surprised you noticed, after what happened earlier," I said cautiously. How could he be so nonchalant after threatening my job if I screwed up again?

His lips pressed soft kisses along my neck. "Office stays at the office."

"Ah." That made sense, I guess. And yet, totally ignoring what happened this morning was impossible. "Right."

My misgivings must have been etched on my face because his eyes searched mine and his hands cupped my cheeks. "Are you okay with this? At work I run everything by my specifications. Nothing is personal. I have to treat you like I'd treat every other employee. We both agreed."

Now I just felt stupid. Of course he had to do that. I didn't expect preferential treatment, but I didn't know how to act outside the office after being chewed out. Guess it was something I just needed to get used to.

Because, even if it was in a limited capacity, Brogan was mine. His condo had turned into a safety net, a bright spot in long, strenuous days and worry-filled nights. A few hours with him was enough to recalibrate my system. "You're right. Everything's cool."

His lips pulled into a smile. "Good, because dinner's ready."

I dropped my bag on the counter, and he swept me into a hug. His lips found mine, and my body melted into his. A deep heaviness settled into my muscles as every part of me ached to connect with him. When his tongue swept past my lips, blissful numbness overtook me. Okay, yes, I could definitely let this morning go. "Good, because I'm starving. I'm going to be kitchenless for a couple weeks, so might as well pack it in now."

A crease formed between his brows. "What? Why?"

"My roommate caused a kitchen fire." I waved my hand

dismissively, like this was a common hiccup when living with roommates—which I guess it was when living with Zoey.

His hands cupped my shoulders and concern washed over his features. "Are you okay? Is it livable?"

"Yes, just a little…pungent. Really, it's nothing out of the norm. Zoey catches fire to anything she tries to cook."

"So you live with an arsonist?"

"She's harmless unless given a pot or pan. Then all bets are off."

"Remind me never to let her in my house." He mashed his lips together and cleared his throat. He shoved his hands in his pockets, and he shuffled nervously from foot to foot. "If you ever need a place to stay, there's always room here for you."

All of the anger and anxiety from today's earlier events evaporated. Goose bumps cascaded over my skin at the thought of staying with Brogan, sleeping in his bed, waking up with my head on his chest. I didn't know what that meant in terms of *us*, but I took his offer as a good sign. Opening up didn't seem to come easy to him, so this was a huge relief. "Thanks. I appreciate that."

Silence hung between us at the weight of the moment. This was a nice unexpected step forward in an otherwise crappy day.

A grin spread across his face, and he pressed his hand into the small of my back, leading me toward the dining room. "Right. We should eat before the food gets cold."

White china plates were placed in our usual spots at the table. A steaming bowl of macaroni and cheese (the homemade kind, not Kraft) sat in the middle of the table, along with a plate of fluffy dinner rolls and a mixed greens vegetable dish.

We sat down at the table, and Bruce curled up on his pillow in the living room, snoring.

"This looks amazing."

"I'm glad you think so. It's been a lot of fun cooking for someone else." He smiled at me, his dimples making an appearance. "Dinners together have been something I look forward to."

Would I ever get used to him? Or would he always steal my breath away with kind gestures and easy smiles?

I speared my fork into the tender macaroni, and the cheese stretched between the pieces as I brought it to my mouth. The sharp cheddar hit my tongue, followed by the creamy sauce and noodles. My eyes rolled back in my head, and for a split second I hated Brogan for ruining Kraft Mac and Cheese for me.

I took a sip of wine and said, "This reminds me of my mom's cooking."

"Your mom's Italian too?"

I shook my head. "She just likes to cook with a lot of cheese." I pointed my fork at him. "Although never trust her with pre-sliced packages. She had this bad habit of not peeling the slips of paper separating the cheese when she made my sandwiches. Nothing more disappointing than biting into plastic. She went through this vegan phase, and the vegan cheese almost tasted like plastic, so honestly I couldn't tell the difference at some point."

He grimaced, and his fork froze halfway from his plate to his mouth. "Gross."

"Oh, come on, didn't your mom used to make horrible lunches? Please tell me I'm not the only one."

Brogan shrugged and tore off a piece of bread. "Not really. I went to boarding school starting in seventh grade."

"Oh? Like one of those all-boys ones where people stand on their desks and yell *Yawp* and write poetry?"

He pointed at me. "I actually did see *Dead Poets Society*. And no, it wasn't nearly that exciting. But I did manage to singe off my eyebrows in chem lab. And we did sneak out to meet the all girls-school a few miles away." A wicked grin crossed his face as he remembered the memory.

"I bet you were quite popular with the ladies." I smirked and took another bite of pasta. I would bet my next paycheck that younger Brogan charmed the plaid skirts off many prep school girls.

A twinkle lit his eyes as he said, "I lacked any skill when it came to the opposite sex. Could barely form a coherent sentence around them." He chuckled.

The Hallelujah Chorus broke out, angels sang, and the Red Sea parted. Brogan was finally opening up, even if it was just a little. To think of him as an awkward, gawky teen was completely charming. It went to show that the nice guys in high school really did turn out okay. And Brogan was more than okay. Maybe that should be a PSA in high schools: *Awkward, gawky teenager? Don't worry, you'll end up being a billionaire CEO by the time you hit thirty. Keep doing your thing, nerds.*

I cocked my head. "I find that hard to believe."

"It's all true. Even when I started my company at twenty-two, I was painfully shy around women. Just ask Jackson."

"I'd need to see it to believe it." Brogan, Mr. Tall, Dark, and Tattooed, shy around women? I'd pay good money to see that. Even though he remained somewhat reserved in our interactions, he still managed to make me swoon without even trying.

"Cross my heart." He made the motion with his fingers. "I was a late bloomer, much to my father's dismay." He grumbled the last statement, and his expression darkened.

A boarding school boy with daddy issues? Oh, the plot thickens. "You don't get along with your dad?" I already knew the answer to this one after the shouty phone call during my first few weeks at the company. Even still, I couldn't help but want to know more, especially when he was finally opening up to me.

His frown deepened, and a crease formed on the bridge of his nose. "I don't really like to talk about him."

"I'll show you mine if you show me yours. I bet my daddy issues can trump whatever your dad did." I joked, keeping my voice light, when in reality, talking about my dad was the equivalent of dunking my eyeballs in bleach.

"I doubt that," he muttered.

"Did your dad live a secret life for fifteen years and have another family he visited every other week?"

His eyes widened at this, and he bristled. "That's horrible. I'm sorry."

"It's in the past. I haven't talked to him in a long time. It's better this way."

"Sometimes it is." He nodded solemnly. "Still, no one should have to go through that." He pushed a few noodles around on his plate, staring into space. Still not sharing anything about his family.

"I don't mean to pry." Let's be real here, I totally did. "I just want to hear more about you. I feel like I'm the only one that ever shares anything personal, and I don't want this to be one-sided." Future conversations would be pretty boring if it continued this way.

Awful flashbacks of family dinners washed over me with this déjà vu moment. Mom would ask Dad about his day, and he would shrug noncommittally. To think, he kept a whole other family hidden from us for years.

By no means did I believe I was the other girl in Brogan's life—because, come on, the guy barely had time for work and his dog—but I didn't want to fall into the same holding pattern that my mom had been in for twenty-seven years.

I pressed on. "Is that why you have so many rules? Because of him?" I couldn't help it. Brogan was like a damn bag of Doritos. Once opened I wanted to devour the whole thing. Even if it meant prying a little hard for information.

"Lainey." This time his voice was much harsher. "Stop pushing."

The pressure in my head continued to press against my skull. I'd tried hard to be patient, but it was clear I wasn't going to get through to him. His secrets, his desires, they all remained locked behind a door, and he wasn't ever going to give me the key. "Unbelievable. All I want is to know a little more about you. I'm not even asking for much. Shit, I ask about school lunches, and you treat me like I'm interrogating you."

He threw up his hands. "That's what it feels like."

Oh hell no. He would not pin this on me. Heat sizzled on the back of my neck, and I put my fork down. "I might be nosy, but like hell am I shining a police light on you." Everything from five years ago came pouring back. The call from my mom, listening to her cry over the phone while I sat helpless in my dorm room. Googling my half-siblings and spending the rest of the day in the bathroom, sick from the news.

I cut my gaze to Brogan, this man who wouldn't share a damn thing with me, who'd already made it clear he didn't have time for commitment. "This is what people in relationships do, Brogan. They get to know each other. You know what they don't do? Pretend everything's great on the surface while keeping their whole life a secret."

His fork clattered against his plate, and he looked up at me with unfamiliar eyes. Cold, unforgiving. Similar to when he'd chewed me out this morning. "You think I like keeping everything inside? Try having your life splattered over the front page of every tabloid." He shook his head, defeat flashing in his gaze. "People break trust, Lainey. If I've learned one thing, it's easier just keeping everyone else out. Living by my rules has gotten me this far, and I don't plan to change that anytime soon."

I sucked in my cheeks and swallowed past the tightness in my throat. Okay. This was not the way to go about getting to know Brogan better. If anything, he'd shut down even more. I should have let it go. I should have steered the conversation to something pleasant, something that didn't involve opening up whatsoever. But I couldn't. I deserved better than that. Hell, I liked Brogan. *Really* liked him. But what was the use of being with someone who would never let me in?

I frowned at him. "If we're getting into technicalities, you're doing a shitty job following your own rules when it comes to me."

His jaw ticked and he blinked hard. "You're right." He shoved a hand through his hair and let out a loud sigh. "I've lost my damn mind when it's come to you. This whole thing is insane."

"I mean, it's not *that* insane," I muttered. Unexpected, yes. But crazier matches have happened. Like Tom Cruise and Katie Holmes.

"No, it really is. I made these rules for a reason. Why would I break them? They've kept this company functioning."

He stared at his plate, then closed his eyes and took a deep breath. When he finally looked at me, a completely different person sat across the table. Someone who I could imagine fighting tooth and nail to get to where he was today. Someone cold. "My judgment is clouded. Obviously I haven't been thinking clearly for weeks." His voice took on an eerily calm quality. "If I hadn't been so unfocused, we might have prevented the hacking problem."

Low blow.

The jab at my work performance cut deeper than I expected, and my pulse jackhammered against my skull, an unease building in my chest. "I thought we weren't bringing up the office at home."

"You're right. But maybe I was too hasty in my decision to invite you here in the first place. It was simpler before I met you." The muscle in his jaw ticked, and he stared down at his plate.

Simpler? Why not just punch me in the face? There'd be less sting with a bloody nose.

I put my napkin on the table and crossed my arms over my chest, no longer hungry. "I don't know who hurt you in the past to make you this way, but I'm not some jerk looking for an edge on you. I'm interested in you as a person, Brogan, and I can't be in a relationship with you if you can't give a little."

His cold gaze sent a shiver through me. "I can't." Only two words. Two words that spoke volumes more than anything else he'd said tonight. They said "done," and, "you shall not pass."

My cheeks heated, and my eyes stung as I fought away unexpected tears. The tiny bit of hope that I'd clung on to deflated faster than a popped balloon. How did I go from an open invitation to stay at Brogan's house, and laughing about vegan cheese, to ruining the mood in two seconds flat? There must be some Guinness World Record for this. If not, I was phoning it in tomorrow.

Lainey Taylor: Fastest person to ruin a good time. 1.2 milliseconds.

"I need some time to clear my head. We need to have a little space." He pointed between us. "I think that it'd be best if you relinquish Bruce walking duties back to Jackson for a while."

I sucked in a shaky breath and cut my gaze to the dog, who was belly up, snoring on his pillow. "Okay." That news alone should have made my night. Bruce was nothing but a pesky, slobbery dog who ruined my clothes. And also had the cutest button nose, and did an awesome impression of a pig when he was happy. But what did this "space" and "time to clear his head" thing mean? I thought we were making a breakthrough, that I was really getting to know him, and yet I ended up pushing him away. My appetite suddenly vanished, the mac and cheese rolling around, threatening to make a repeat appearance.

There had to be a positive spin on this, right? Without dog walking duties, it freed up my evenings to…sit at home and watch TV and mope. Oh, man, I was worse off than I thought. My mom had been right. Work had taken over my life. I was wasting my early twenties in an office rather than indulging in bad choices. Yep, this totally sucked.

He blotted his face with his napkin and threw it down on the table. His chair groaned against the tile as he stood and adjusted his tie. "I need to get back to the office."

"Right." His schedule for the night was clear. I'd made sure of it before I left, because if tonight had gone well, I was planning on taking him up on his cookie-making offer.

Well, whatever *I* thought was obviously a moot point as of thirty seconds ago. "I should probably walk Bruce anyway. I'll have him back in a little bit and then head home."

He stared at me, his expression unreadable.

I always picked the most opportune times to babble. He'd made it clear the position we were in. Boss. Employee. Benefits currently terminated. Because even if he did want to start something, I couldn't do it, good cooking or not.

A few tears tracked down my cheek.

He lifted his hand, like he might wipe my cheek, but then he swallowed hard and dropped it to his side. He grabbed his coat from the rack and walked out the door.

Bruce got up from his spot in the living room and padded over to my chair. He nuzzled my hand, and I scratched him behind the ears, his favorite spot. He let out the snorting noise and I smiled.

"At least someone enjoys my company." My voice shook

and pitched up at the end. I quickly cleared my throat and swallowed past the thick knot. Nope. Not going there. If Brogan could barricade his feelings behind a Berlin-size wall, so could I.

He licked my hand in response.

Another onslaught of tears pricked at my eyes, but I pushed them back. I would not cry over something that was so silly to begin with. No one knew Brogan, and I was deluding myself to think I could get close to him. It was much better this way. I could focus on my work and my mom. Shudders wracked me as I sat hunched over, rubbing my arms in an attempt to fight the chills overtaking my body. I glanced around the empty condo. Barren, skin-deep, a shallow shell. This was what Brogan chose, what I had hoped he'd change once we spent more time together. Tears streamed down my face, and I pulled Bruce closer, nuzzling into his fur. At least we ended things before he could break my heart.

Jackson shook Bruce's leash, and the vein in his forehead throbbed double-time. "I can't believe I'm stuck walking that damn dog again. He destroys everything good in this world."

"He likes being scratched behind the ears when you first come in," I said, quietly. Tears pricked my eyes the instant I'd tossed his leash on Jackson's desk this morning.

"What?" he snapped.

"If you show him affection, he's less likely to eat your clothes," I offered. Although really, why would I want to stop Bruce from destroying the Italian loafers Jackson had been bragging about for the past three weeks?

"The only thing I'll show him is the door if he ruins my new loafers." Even I knew this was an empty threat, because Jackson would never do anything to purposely piss off

Brogan.

Both elbows were propped on my desk as I rested my chin in my hands, staring at my computer. I'd been reading the same email for twenty minutes.

To: LAINEY TAYLOR
FROM: BROGAN STARR
SUBJECT: LEASH

Please promptly return the leash and key to Jackson. He will take care of everything else. I expect files on the Anderson account on my desk first thing Monday morning.

Best,
Brogan Starr, *CEO Starr Media*

I'd pushed him too hard and lost him. But did I ever really have him to begin with?

I'd once had a membership to a purse website that rented out high-end bags for a great price. I'd gotten this cream Michael Kors bag that really was the mecca of all purses. When I'd mailed it back, I felt like a piece of myself had left with that bag. This was worse. So much worse, because purses didn't give me butterflies or make me smile even if I was having a horrible day. They also didn't look nearly as good in a towel.

Then again, how could I possibly be with someone I knew nothing about? The answer was simple: I couldn't. So, it was time to put on my big girl panties and devise a plan to get Brogan off my mind for good.

Chapter Twenty-One

Lainey Taylor Rule of Life #17
A jealous boy can be a good thing.

"I think we should go out," Zoey said, staring at me from across the living room.

I grunted, continuing to devour rocky road ice cream from the half-pint carton in my lap. The whole plan to get Brogan off my mind had tanked the second I'd stepped out of work. A person passed by with a dog that looked like Bruce, and I'd effectively lost all interest in doing anything but sulking on the couch. I'd been doing a fantastic job at this task for the past week.

She eyed me. "You're starting to scare me, cave girl. Use your words."

I glanced up at her, the spoon still in my mouth. "Me no want go out."

"Much better. We'll work on correct pronoun usage another day."

I shot her a look. I was completely fine binging on ice

cream and Netflix. Definitely not gummy worms, though, because that would make me think of Brogan and how he hated anything with ingredients that couldn't be pronounced.

"Seriously, whatever happened, you just need to shake it off. It's Friday. Scientifically speaking, we are never going to be as hot as we are now, and we need to use that to our advantage to get free drinks while we can."

"This is supposed to make me feel better?" I said.

"No, it's supposed to get you off the couch." She took the ice cream off my lap and placed it on the coffee table, and then grabbed my wrists and pulled me to my feet.

"Hey, I was just about to watch the swan episode on *Gilmore Girls*."

"Jess's black eye can wait. Let's go to Dean's. We don't even have to drink if you don't want to, but you have to stay out for at least forty minutes."

"Can I go in this?"

She smirked and gave my ratty OSU sweatshirt and stained sweatpants a once-over. "Only if you want to prevent us from getting hit on."

"Then I'm good to go." The last thing I wanted to think about tonight was impressing men.

She gave me a playful shove toward my bedroom. "Go get dressed. It'll be good to be hit on by men who are emotionally available and vulnerable in their drunken state."

I huffed out a laugh. "Because that doesn't sound predatory or anything."

"Put some real pants on," she shouted as I walked into my room.

A few minutes later, I walked out in skinny jeans, purple chucks, and my favorite AC/DC T-shirt. Zoey smiled and nodded. "Much better. Now we at least have a chance at not paying for drinks tonight."

"I thought you said I didn't have to drink."

She shrugged. "You don't have to, but I wouldn't mind one."

Before we locked up the apartment, I grabbed my coat and phone, my credit card and ID, opting to forgo a purse in case I got drunk enough to decide to dance.

A line wrapped along the side of Dean's as we strode up to the building. Rock music boomed out of the open door, blocked by a black velvet rope and a stacked bouncer talking to an equally muscular guy in a very nice fitting suit.

"Good thing I brought my coat." At the rate Mr. Muscles was letting people into the bar, I'd be a Popsicle by the time we were admitted into the place.

"You won't need it for long." She grabbed my arm and led me to the front of the line.

Closer up, the neon lights from the window shone on the man in the suit. He had extraordinarily high cheekbones and muscles stacked on his muscles. I'd have recognized him sooner if he'd had his shirt off, because it was none other than Shirtless Dude—er, Ryder.

His sullen look changed to a megawatt smile the second he spotted my best friend. "Zoey!" He beamed, and heck if I didn't hear her let out a soft sigh in response.

Apparently we had a lot of catching up to do, because this was the same look Bruce got when we passed the neighbor's poodle.

He nodded to the bouncer, and he opened one side of the velvet rope and motioned us in. "Have a good time tonight. If you need anything, I'll be around." He winked down at her, and it was my turn to sigh.

I bumped her with my elbow. "I see things are going well with Ryder?"

Her smile vanished the moment I mentioned his name. "It's purely professional. We work together, that's it."

"Please tell me by 'work' you mean 'in his pants.'"

Her shoulders tensed, and a line creased the skin between her eyes. "No. We're just friends. Barely."

I looked at her. "Oh, girl. You obviously don't see the way he's looking at you."

She rolled her eyes. "Just because he's flirty does not mean he's interested. He acts that way around everyone."

"And he winds up shirtless at ten in the morning at people's houses, too?"

She flushed.

Ha. I got your number, Zoey Reynolds.

Yeah, no. I wasn't convinced, but wasn't going to push it any further. She'd been nice enough not to get into my business—because I certainly didn't want to admit I was on the losing end of this whole fling deal. Nope, tonight was about hitting the reset button on life. We were here to hang out, just like we did in college, and that beer was sounding pretty good right about now. Who cared if Brogan's wine beat a Blue Moon, hands down? Certainly not me.

We managed to find two spots at the bar and plunked down our coats on the back of our stools. The bartender bustled over to us almost immediately and placed two napkins on the granite.

We ordered a beer and Tom Collins and swiveled to look out at the dance floor. People a few years younger than us were grinding, already drunk, hours before last call.

Dean's had been a regular spot for us the past couple months. It had a nice variety of country dancing, karaoke, pool, and an upstairs that was quieter for when you wanted a calmer atmosphere.

"That used to be us last year." I pointed to the drunk girls on the dance floor, gyrating their hips to the beat of the music.

She pursed her lips as if to say *ohh, girl.* "Please. We looked way better than that."

I smiled and sipped my beer. "True." Or at least the

alcohol made it seem that way. "Remember that one time you danced on the bar at Malone's like you were in *Coyote Ugly*?" I giggled and pressed my lips to the top of the beer bottle.

"No. I really did that?" Tequila was Zoey's kryptonite. Two shots and the girl went from southern belle to *Pretty Woman* in the span of an hour.

"It was the night you broke our toilet seat and then wore it around like a necklace."

She shuddered. "Yeah, I'm so glad we're over that phase." She lifted her Tom Collins as a salute to our younger, alcohol-hazed college years.

"Me, too. I was one hangover away from giving up drinking until I turned forty."

"Thank God it didn't come to that." We clinked glasses, and I settled into the bar stool.

I grabbed Zoey's arm and bit my lip. "Thanks, Zoey." If she wasn't around, I'd be home, sulking. Which sounded really pathetic, seeing as I didn't have anything to really sulk about. I refused to pity myself. If my mom was strong enough to make it through chemo, I should be able to make it through the night without thinking about my boss. And his dimples. And his cooking skills. And his complete inability to play vintage video games. And his way of making me smile even if I was having a crappy day.

Yeah, I was doing a fine job putting all that behind me.

My completely unwanted fantasy about my boss was ruined when a guy in need of a good shower and deodorant sauntered over to us at the bar.

"How's it going, ladies?" As he put both hands on our bar stools and stood between us, the odor of his pits was enough to turn my wavy hair into corkscrew curls.

"Good." Even if I did want Pepé Le Pew to take a hike, preferably to the nearest shower, I didn't have it in me to tell him off.

"What are you drinking?"

I held up my beer and breathed through my mouth.

He leered at both of us, and I had a sudden urge to expel the contents of my stomach onto his shoes. "Need a refill?" he asked.

"We just sat down. Listen. This was very nice of you, but we're just trying to enjoy a girl's night." I gave a weak smile and turned back to Zoey, trying to politely give him the hint to screw off.

"Oh." The tiny little hamster wheel in his head spun for a moment, and his eyes brightened. "I get it. I'm all for the lesbian movement." He lifted his fist and said, "Right on."

Zoey spit out the contents of her Tom Collins in a spray across the bar top. "What?"

"If you ever want to expand your horizons, I'll show you what a real man feels like." He wriggled his eyebrows and cupped his crotch. That, paired with the BO, was enough to get my gag reflex going.

A hand gripped the guy's shoulder, and he was pulled away from us. "Take a hike, buddy, I think if she wants a real man, she knows where to go."

My beer bottle froze midway to my mouth as I took in my boss in a grungy bar, with his hands on Pepé. Brogan postured, his chest puffed out, a very primal display of *fuck off.*

"I didn't mean nothing by it, man," the guy stuttered. He was at least six inches shorter than Brogan, and even without the height difference, my boss had the intimidation factor in spades.

"Go home. Shower. Sober up." Brogan commanded in his boardroom voice, and the guy stared at him in awe. "Go," he said once more, and Pepé sped toward the door.

"What the hell are you doing here?" I asked, not quite fully comprehending that he was here. In the same bar as me. Hell, was he here for me?

"Friend's birthday party." He nodded over to the group of guys by center stage, stumbling with mics and arguing over the black binder of karaoke songs.

"Thanks for being our savior," Zoey said.

All I could do was stare at Brogan in his bicep-hugging black T-shirt, wishing that he'd pull me into a much-needed embrace. His tattoos were very visible tonight, and as I glanced around the bar, many of the girls were sending appreciative stares his way. I felt a full-body burn, starting at my toes and ending at my scalp, both from Brogan being this close to me and the fact that I'd ruined my chances with him. Any girl in here could wind up going home with him tonight, and a spear of jealousy sliced through me. See, this was why flings were a bad thing. Obviously, I was way in over my head and turning into a crazy person.

A jovial smile played at his lips, but his brows were pulled together into dramatic slashes. He seemed just as uptight, maybe even more, than last night.

Zoey cleared her throat, breaking the long moment that I'm sure we were standing there silently staring at each other.

I regained my composure and remembered that these two hadn't officially met, unless behind-a-tree-stalking counted. "Brogan, this is my best friend and roommate, Zoey. Zoey this is my boss, Mr. Brogan Starr."

"Please, call me Brogan." He extended his hand, he and Zoey shook, and the dip in her shoulders told me she was already under his spell.

He looked her over, his brows creasing. "Have we met before?"

"Maybe we ran into each other?" She shrugged.

I elbowed Zoey, not appreciating her reference to the whole hiding in the bushes incident.

His gaze flicked down to my shirt. "AC/DC is a good look for you." He smiled, but not enough to elicit the dimple effect.

"I wasn't expecting to run into anyone tonight." Gah, why didn't I take Zoey's advice to dress up more?

I stopped that thought process. Like hell I needed to dress up for the guy who told me our fling, or whatever it was, had been a mistake. No, I wouldn't care one bit what he thought of my wardrobe choice.

He held my gaze for a few seconds before saying anything. "Well, I just wanted to come over and make sure you were okay." His swallowed hard and cleared his throat. "I can see that you are, so I'll leave you to your girl time." He wasn't able to meet my eyes, instead opting to look at his group of friends.

Was Brogan...jealous? The sting of his rejection gave me pause in thinking this was anything more than him being friendly. Because that's what Brogan did. He was nice to everyone. Everyone loved him. And everyone was content to not dig any deeper, only taking him at face value. Not me, unfortunately. Seems like I was the only one in the Emerald City who was glutton for punishment enough to want to know more about the one person who guarded his secrets tighter than a Las Vegas magician.

I wanted to know what each of those tattoos meant. I wanted to know why he stayed at the office long past when he needed to, and why he'd never watched the movies that were part of our pop culture growing up. It hit me like a stiletto to the stomach how badly I needed to know all of this.

A clean-cut guy with a fauxhawk strutted over to our little group and clapped a hand on Brogan's back. "You singing Journey with us, bro?"

Brogan motioned to the guy, who seemed to have a few too many beers in him, and said, "Lainey, Zoey, this is Jace. He went to MIT with me, but the bastard moved to New York."

Jace slugged him in the shoulder. "Wall Street isn't as bad as you imagine, Starr. Not everyone's a prick like your dad."

I'd already gotten the sense that his dad wasn't the

nicest—I mean who sent their kid off to boarding school and deprived them of video games? But I could tell there was more to the story from the way Brogan leveled a glare at his friend.

Jace shook our hands. "Is this the Lainey that you were moping around about?" He jutted his chin to me, and if it hadn't been so dark, I could have sworn Brogan's cheeks turned ten shades of red in the span of a few seconds.

My heart jackhammered in my chest. Brogan was sulking about me? And he actually *told* someone about it?

He pointedly ignored Jace's question and asked, "What are you ladies drinking?"

I swallowed hard and tried to read Brogan's expression, but he kept his perma-smile affixed to his face. But those dimples were no longer kryptonite for me (okay, they totally were, but I was getting used to them).

"Blue Moon and a Tom Collins," Zoey said. She never was one to turn down a possible free drink. Except from Pepé.

He turned to Zoey. "Nice choice in drink."

She lifted her glass in a salute. "They're highly underrated."

"I whole-heartedly agree. Need a refill?"

Just as I said no, Zoey blurted out a yes. She elbowed me, and I remembered her "all bar expenses paid by other people" goal for tonight.

I rolled my eyes and nodded. "That would be really nice, thanks."

The bartender brought us another round of drinks, and the guys stood in front of our bar stools, sipping beers. As Brogan looked out at the dance floor, I took the opportunity to take a greedy gaze at the tattoos running along his forearm. Especially the ellipses that covered most of the inside of his wrist. Above that was something scrawled in script, which I couldn't read unless I was sitting a few inches closer. Just a few inches and my legs would brush his. Just a few inches and those deft hands could roam freely over my skin. Okay, my mind and body were totally not on the same page.

This had to stop. He didn't want me. He'd made that clear. And I wasn't some love-sick girl pining for Mr. Whatever. We were done.

He cleared his throat and said, "It's Latin for 'keep your friends close and your enemies closer.'"

I shifted in my seat, realizing my gaze was still awkwardly pinned on his arms.

Crap. Caught. "They're interesting."

He leaned in closer and murmured, "I like when you look at me." His stubbled cheek brushed against mine, and his warm breath caressed my skin. A shudder rippled through me.

Boom. RIP ovaries, it was nice knowing you.

I choked on my beer. I didn't know if this was my head playing games with me, my inner romantic filling in words that I wished he'd say, or if he'd actually just said he liked when I checked him out.

The guy was giving me whiplash. What kind of asshole leaves a girl crying in his apartment and then ignores her for a week? If he thought he could swoop in and expect me to just forgive him without batting an eye, he had another thing coming.

"We have a couple songs before our group sings karaoke. Want to dance?" Jace asked Zoey, holding a hand out to her.

She shot a nervous glance toward the front of the building, where Ryder stood talking with another guy, and took Jace's hand.

As soon as we were alone, Brogan brushed his hand down my arm—sweetly, slowly—and said, "I'm sorry for how I acted the other night. It was immature and stupid." He frowned and looked down, embarrassed.

I shrugged away from his touch, even though it took

every bit of restraint not to lean into his fingers. "Doesn't matter. You were right. It's probably best, like you said." I'd be absolutely nuts to be with a guy whose emotional stance on a relationship ping-ponged in a handful of days.

"And I told you what I said was stupid. I'm really sorry, Lainey. Truly. The thought of putting my trust in someone, opening up, scares the shit out of me."

Damn him for sounding so earnest. How was I supposed to resist him when he looked at me like that, when his touch sent a million pinpoints of heat through my body?

Must. Stay. Strong. I wasn't a damn doormat.

"I'm not looking for you to share your social security number. All I want is to know more about the person I'm"—I motioned with my hands—"spending time with. Or *was* spending time with." So maybe that seemed a little casual compared to what I'd built it up to be in my mind, but my pride was still a little wounded from last week, and I sure as heck wasn't going to give in that easily with one meager apology. "You say you're scared, but everyone's scared. Relationships involve taking risks, but finding the right person can also have its rewards. You'll never know unless you try. But when you shut down, it makes that impossible."

His lips tipped into a frown, and it took everything in me not to run my thumb along the seam of his mouth. "I know. I handled it like an asshole, and I'm sorry for that," he said.

"It's hard to know where I stand with you. If I'm just another employee to you, then maybe it is for the best I don't come over to your house anymore."

His eyes sparkled in the lights, and he shook his head. "You're more than that to me. So much more."

"Am I?" I crossed my arms, but inside my inner fangirl was flailing. This was the first time I actually felt like we were getting through to each other, finally on the same page. "Because at times it doesn't feel that way."

"Yes." He chanced running a finger over my cheek. This time I let him. "You deserve better." He frowned.

I nodded. "I do." Because hell if I'd cheapen myself for any guy.

"This past week has been miserable without you. It just hasn't been the same." He frowned. "The other night, I opened up Netflix and watched *Mean Girls*."

I choked on a sip of beer. "I am slightly jealous I didn't get to witness this."

"It was horrible, by the way. And you have the worst taste in movies, but you know what I was thinking the whole time?"

"What?"

"How I wished you were there, because I like hearing your commentary. I wanted to know what parts you found funny. I wanted to share that with you." He tucked a stray curl behind my ear and said, "And that scared me, because I haven't wanted to share anything with anyone in a long time. I'm not used to trusting people, but I want to try with you."

My breath hitched at the sincerity of his comment. Who knew what changed his mind from last week. "I'm not big on the trust thing, either, and after last week…you made it seem like you could turn it off just like that." I snapped my fingers. "I get that we aren't supposed to be serious, but you were so cold. I just wanted to know what things were like when you were a kid. You didn't just shut me out, you ended it. That's not how it works—this is a two-way street."

His gaze searched mine and we were standing close enough that I could see the tiny flecks of gold in his eyes. "I'm pretty sure I've used the word stupid a couple of time. I–I'm not sure how to make it up to you."

I shrugged. "I don't know either."

I thought he might walk away. Then he smiled, and it was like a riptide pulling me under. "How about, will you dance with me?"

I stared at him, wondering why it had taken him a full week to say this. But his sincerity spoke volumes. What could one dance hurt? "What about the no dancing rule? I thought your mother scarred you for life."

"Lainey, when it comes to you, I'm breaking all my own rules." He held out his hand. "Please."

I pushed my empty beer across the bar and grabbed his hand. "Fine, Starr. I'll give you one dance."

He smiled. "That's all I need." He led me to the dance floor. A fast country song boomed in the room, the beat vibrating through my bones. Brogan grabbed both my hands and took the lead. Within the chorus of the song, I'd been spun, dipped, and sufficiently wooed.

His warm hands on my hips, the heartfelt look in his eyes—it was more than I could handle. Call me stupid, but if he was really serious about giving this another shot, I was willing to give it one more try.

I laughed as he pulled me up from the final dip. "Can I write a letter to your mom thanking her for putting you in dance classes?"

He shook his head and smiled. "You could, but I wouldn't know the address."

He said it so matter-of-factly that it made my heart ache, because I couldn't imagine a life without my mother.

At the end of the song I was out of breath, and I didn't know if it was from being this close to him or the fact that no matter how many miles I ran, dancing always seemed harder on my body.

His heated gaze pierced through me, and he ran his tongue over his top lip. "Do you want to get out of here?"

I searched his eyes, still slightly apprehensive. I needed to be totally sure before I'd put myself out there again. "Depends."

He cocked his head. "On?"

"Are you really ready to let me in?"

"I just said I am."

I frowned. "Words are cheap, Starr. Someone with your business sense knows this."

He leaned closer to me and said, "I can't really *show* you in a bar, when a bed is far more suitable." His breath ghosted over my skin, and a shudder rippled through me.

Well, crap. He got me. An offer I couldn't refuse. Not with the promise of soft sheets and our bodies pressed together.

"That sounds slightly more convincing," I mused.

"I think my mouth could do some additional persuading if given the chance."

Hello, neglected downstairs. Did you hear that? Without wanting to look too eager, I managed a nod. "I need to check in with Zoey first."

I scanned the floor and spotted her with Jace. She was grinding into him, and her lips pulled into a smile when she saw me.

"You having a good time?" I nodded toward Jace's hands firmly planted on her hips.

"Very good." She looked between Brogan and me. "Can I say the same for you?"

A flush filled my cheeks. "Yes."

"If you need to…you know…get out of here, I'm perfectly fine," she said.

"I don't know." I hated leaving her at the bar by herself, even if she was with Brogan's friends.

"My driver can take you home," Brogan offered to Zoey.

Her eyes lit up. "You have a driver?"

Brogan smirked. "Yes. Jace will make sure that no one bothers you, and you'll get home safe. Right Jace?" He leveled a serious look at Jace, who nodded.

I turned to him. "Thank you." The fact that he was willing to make sure my friend got home okay made my heart beat sideways in my chest. "Are you okay with that, Zoey?"

"I'm just going to have a couple more drinks with them, and then I'll have the driver take me home."

"Okay. But call me if you want me to come pick you up. I'll only be a few blocks away," I said.

She looked between me and Brogan again, and then gave me a wink. "I expect a detailed report on my desk tomorrow," she said.

Chapter Twenty-Two

Lainey Taylor Rule of Life #46
A girl should be properly kissed in the snow at least once in her life.

The air was thick with the promise of snowfall as we stepped out into the dimly lit side street. Frost glistened on iced-over car windows, and the only sound was the occasional truck passing by and the soft clomps of high heels on the pavement.

Brogan walked close beside me, his arm brushing mine a few times. Each time it happened, a fresh set of goose bumps cascaded over my skin, and the deeper I fell into the trap of getting my hopes up. Which was completely silly. But no matter how many times I told myself that he was my boss, that didn't hit a magic off switch to my wanting him.

His voice finally cut through the silence as we neared his building. "Your friend seems like she'll give Jace a run for his money."

I smiled and pulled my coat tighter around me. Zoey always spoke her mind, never was able to lie to save her life—

something that got me into a lot of trouble whenever I asked her to cover for me when we were younger. "You could say that."

We walked in silence for a few minutes more, then Brogan spoke. "I started getting tattoos when I was seventeen. My friend's brother owned a tattoo parlor a few blocks down from my boarding school, and I'd sneak out after curfew and get inked. It was a way to get back at my parents."

I kept my gaze focused straight ahead, not wanting to break the spell of the moment. He was sharing something with me, and I wasn't willing to let this slip through my fingers like grains of sand.

"Which one is your favorite?"

He pointed to the one on his wrist, the one I'd been drawn to since the first day I met him. "The ellipses. To me it means that my story isn't over. And no matter what obstacles come my way, I can always change it."

"That's beautiful." The hot flush of embarrassment crept up in my cheeks. I was sure he didn't want his tattoos to be called beautiful, but they were.

"I've never told anyone that before."

Brogan stopped abruptly and an intensity washed over his face, hardening his features, and I was sure that he was going to shut down, stop the whole sharing is caring thing we had going on.

"You make me want to do all these things I've told myself I can't have. It's fucking scary."

"Like what?"

He smoothed his thumb over my cheek. "Like have a relationship that is based off of feelings, not convenience." He leaned in, and his lips swept over my skin, feather light.

I let out a shaky sigh and closed my eyes. My mind went in a tailspin, trying to make sense of what was happening. This was a complete one-eighty from last week's events. I liked this version much better.

His hands worked up my sides, down my back, cupping my ass and pulling me closer to him. "I want to claim every inch of your skin."

My breaths came in tiny pants as he caressed my body.

"I knew last week was a mistake the second those words came out of my mouth. I want to trust you, but it's hard. I've been burned in the past."

I nodded. "What else do you want?"

"What?"

"You said you want *all these things.* That's plural. You've only listed one."

"Always the rapt listener."

Flecks of cold bit at my cheeks, and I looked up to see snow falling. It was the wet kind, big flakes that would surely melt as soon as they hit the ground. We didn't move, still staring at each other, one block from his apartment. "I want to wake up to you in the morning. I want to share my day with you. I want to know you in every way possible."

I didn't even know how to respond besides dissolving into a puddle of goop on the sidewalk. My chest felt heavy due to the fact that my heart had grown ten sizes. "I…wow." How could I even respond to that?

The fabric of my thin jacket clung to my skin as snow began pelting down harder. Brogan held my cheeks with both of his hands, and his eyes searched mine. "I crave you," he said. "Everything about you."

I nodded, still stunned into silence. My need for him pulsed strong, low in my belly.

His body pressed against me, his hands snaking through my hair as his lips hovered inches from mine. As soon as our lips connected, my body melted into his, now completely under his spell. Everything else fell away, not even nearly as important as the need to taste his lips, to sweep my tongue over his, to get a reaction from him.

He reluctantly pulled away and groaned. "We should get inside. You're soaked."

We sprinted toward his building as the sky opened up to a downpour of flurries in epic proportions. By the time we made it to his condo, my shoes squeaked, and if I wrung out my shirt, a good four inches could collect on the floor. Bruce met us in the entryway in a blur of skittering paws. After Brogan snagged a few treats from the pantry to placate him, Bruce padded over to his doggy bed and lay down.

Brogan smiled and focused his attention to me, grabbing the back of my neck and placing kisses along the bridge of my nose, my cheeks, the line of my jaw. "I love your freckles."

He continued down the curve of my neck. "And the way you look at me when you think no one is watching." His fingertips scorched a path along my spine. "Wanting you isn't even a strong enough word. I *need* you." Soft fingers edged their way along the strap of my bra. "I've needed you so much this past week, it's driven me insane."

I blew out a shaky breath. All I could do was close my eyes and lose myself in the moment, in this gorgeous man.

"Every freckle. Every curl. Every inch of skin."

My hands were everywhere—in his hair, skimming across warm skin under his shirt, raking down his biceps. "I could get behind that. I like when you break your rules," I said, breathless.

His gaze softened, and the tenderness in his eyes made my heart pound heavily against my ribcage. "I'd break every last one for you," he said. "I never knew what I was missing until the day we met."

I cocked my head. "You mean when I called you the devil."

Dimples indented his cheeks when he said, "I believe you used the term 'Antichrist.'"

I smiled. "Technicalities."

His hand swept across my jaw, his eyes conveying nothing but adoration. "The way you move. The way you smile." His teeth nipped at my bottom lip, and heat unfurled deep in my belly. "Hell, the way you challenge me. Everything about you speaks to my goddamn soul, Lainey."

"I told you my determination would grow on you," I managed to say as his thumbs swiped over my nipples. A shudder wracked my body in response, and I fell against him.

His arm wrapped securely around my waist as he inched me against the hallway wall, my legs between his, my body in desperate need of him. My back hit with a soft *thud,* and his lips were on me, everywhere, unrelenting, driving me mad.

The way he was baring himself, leaving himself open, vulnerable—it sent me reeling. He *was* ready for us. And lord knew I was ready, too. The fact that this was happening, something I'd waited for, that I'd wanted for months, and to know he felt the same way, too…it made me dizzy.

My heart crashed against my chest in a rhythmic chant of his name. *Brogan. Brogan. Brogan.* I arched my back, pressing into him, my chest brushing against his. I couldn't get close enough. Needed to get closer.

I made deft work of the buttons on his shirt, and in a matter of moments it lay pooled on the floor. I took my time, studying him. The massive shoulders that filled out his suits so nicely. The dip and swell of muscles taught under lean flesh. The dark ink against tanned skin. Brogan was better than a fantasy.

My fingers raked across his inked chest, down his abs, along the *V* of his waist. He shuddered under my touch and closed his eyes. *I* did this to him. The rule-maker broke all his rules for me. And that meant everything.

His brown eyes darkened, and his tongue ran across his lips as he edged his hands along the hem of my shirt. He cocked his head, asking silent permission.

Yes. So. Much. Yes.

I lifted my hands up in response, and he tore my shirt off, throwing it on top of his own.

He let out a low groan as his eyes made an appreciative perusal. "You know what I'm thinking about in all those meetings and phone conferences? What I think about in the shower and my bed—every goddamn second of the day?" he growled. His voice vibrated through my chest, stirring up everything inside me, all the pieces aflutter like the flecks of a shaken snow globe.

"What?" My voice was barely a whisper.

"You, Lainey. All I can think about is you." He pushed me harder against the wall. "I can't get you off my mind." His hands cupped the backs of my thighs, and he pulled me up, my legs wrapping around his waist. God, at this moment I'd give this man anything he wanted. Anything. He asked, it was his. I wanted to lose myself in him, for him to show me exactly what he meant by his words.

"Looks like we have the same problem." My hands scraped along the tight muscles of his back.

He pulled away and looked at me. I mean *really* looked at me, hitting a point so deep, I'd never come out of this unscathed. "You are not a problem to be solved, Lainey." His eyes held so much intensity they robbed the breath out of my chest. "You are the answer to my fucking prayers."

His mouth crashed against mine, unrelenting, as he carried me to his bedroom.

• • •

A slash of sunlight cut through the curtains at approximately a quarter till way too early. I groaned and turned to my other side, and came face to face with Brogan. His eyes opened lazily, flecks of gold glistening in his brown irises. He smiled and wrapped an arm around me, pulling me closer. "Morning, beautiful."

Being cocooned in his arms, in the warmth of his body, the scent of his intoxicating mint body wash...everything made me melt into him and never want to come up for air. What we shared last night, felt like we traded a piece of our souls, a connection I'd never experienced with any other guy before. "Morning," I said softly, still letting the moment wrap around me like a warm blanket.

"What do you want to do today?" I asked.

He took a deep breath, and his heated gaze raked over me while his hand disappeared under the covers. "You."

Well, then. A round four? Praise all that was holy, because Brogan was a god in and out of the boardroom. His fingers found their way to the space between my thighs, and I knocked my head back against the pillow, savoring his touch. I could definitely get behind spending an entire day in bed with Brogan.

Unfortunately, Bruce had other plans. He let out a loud fart and began to whine from the end of the bed.

I buried myself under the covers as the smell began to waft my way.

"Bruce, you really know how to ruin a moment, buddy," Brogan said. He joined me underneath the covers, and his smile softened. He ran his hand along the curve of my hip and said, "Now where was I?"

I pressed my forehead to his, and my fingers traced the stubble on his chin. "I believe you were about to kiss me again."

"Ah. I think you're right."

His lips brushed mine, and I melted into him. His hands gripped my hips and he rolled me over so that I was straddling him. It was apparent through the thin material of his boxer briefs that he was up for round four. I ground against him, and he let out a low growl, roughly cupping my ass.

"I wish I could wake up every morning like this," he murmured into my ear.

I deepened our kiss, my tongue sweeping past his lips, putting every bit of myself into this. The sensation of falling without knowing if there was anything below to catch me crashed over me like a wave. It stole my breath, every sensible thought, until the only words coursing through my mind were *need, want, must have*. Brogan wasn't something that I could consider a luxury anymore, he was a necessity.

Part of me understood that should scare the hell out of me, but I was too busy losing myself in him.

Brogan reached over to his nightstand and pulled out another condom. Just as he pulled the foil apart, Bruce whined again and pawed at the door.

I sighed and rested my forehead against his. "Do you want me to take him for a walk?"

He pulled the covers off and sat up, bringing me with him. His bare chest against mine was enough to make me want to ignore the dog altogether and continue where we'd left off. "No. He's my dog. I'll walk him. But I'd like for you to come with me. And…we'll continue this later." The determination in his eyes sent a wave of goose bumps cascading over my arms. It was a promise. One I'd make sure he kept.

Tufts of gray clouds rolled across the hazy Seattle horizon. A thin dusting of snow covered the cars parked along the streets as we made our way down the block an hour past what Bruce deemed as an acceptable time to be walked.

There was one question that was still bugging me from last night. Brogan's friend Jace had mentioned that his father was the asshole Wall Street type. It made me wonder why Brogan decided to build his own company. This business was hard enough as is. I steeled myself and gripped Bruce's leash a little harder. "Does your dad live in New York?"

In my other hand, Brogan's tensed a fraction, but relaxed a moment later. "Part-time. He also owns a home in Bellevue. That's where he conducts business when he gets tired of the city. He's been doing that for years."

"Must have been tough on your family."

He shrugged. "My parents divorced when I was fifteen," he said. His voice held a hint of sadness that came as a punch to my stomach.

I nodded. With the number of trust issues he had, it didn't surprise me. "I'm sorry to hear that."

"Don't be. My mom cheated on my dad."

Oh. I hadn't seen that coming.

"Now he has a new girlfriend every month. It's like a revolving door in that house." He pulled up a picture on his phone of his dad in a power suit, and handed it to me. "Meet Brandon Starr. He wants me to take over his firm. Cut me out of his will until I agree."

I raised a brow. "It's not like you're lacking for money." Brogan had more money than I would ever know what to do with.

"No, but he thinks it's the ultimate betrayal that I started my own business. He's tried to buy out my firm a couple of times since the startup. He's ruthless."

"That's horrible." I stared at the photo. He looked like an older version of Brogan, with his strong chin and lean build. But his eyes held a darkness that Brogan's didn't possess.

He turned to me and his gaze flashed with a sudden remembrance. "I forgot to tell you the good news about the hacker on the Willington account. I was a little distracted last night." He managed a sheepish grin.

"You found out who was behind it?" I'd almost forgotten the whole thing, it'd been so long.

"Turns out it was Craig's younger brother. Got ahold of his iPhone and thought it'd be funny to start shit with another country star." He smiled. "No hacker involved."

I scoffed, but relief ebbed through me. Thank goodness this was just a joke, even if it was in poor taste. "What a twerp."

"Craig's handling it. I taught him how to put a password on his phone."

"Good idea."

We walked around the park a couple times and then made our way back to Brogan's condo. As we rounded the corner to his block, a guy with a professional grade camera stood by a car on the other side of the street and snapped a few photos of us.

"Does that usually happen?" I jutted my chin toward the guy wearing a baseball cap, blue jeans, and a T-shirt.

He frowned. "Goes along with the territory of owning a company. I'm usually not interesting enough to make the tabloids, though."

I moved a few steps further away from Brogan, not wanting to cause any type of scandal in the media. No one would know who I was, but it was best to be careful.

My mom probably wouldn't be too pleased if she saw my face on the front cover of the *National Inquirer*. The thought of her triggered the memory of dancing with Brogan last night, how he'd said he hadn't seen his own parent in years.

"Do you ever talk to your mom? You said back at the bar you didn't know her address."

"I haven't talked to her since she divorced my dad. She left with her assistant and never looked back." The matter-of-factness of his statement gutted me. How could anyone do that to their family? Just up and leave.

We made our way back inside the building and waited for

the elevator. The expression on my face must have changed, because he stopped and squeezed my hand. "Don't feel bad for me. It happened, it's over, it's a part of my past."

"Is that why you have so many rules? I find it hard to believe the rules are in place just because you're young and worried about things that might affect your company." It made sense. His family history was enough to make even the sanest person go crazy.

He paused and seemed to contemplate it. "Maybe. But I think that rules help me keep boundaries. It's the stuff I can't define that scares the shit out of me."

I smoothed my hand down his arm and looked up at him. "The indefinable is what makes life worth living. People aren't meant to live by a book."

"That may work for you, Lainey, but I can't afford for my business life to get muddled with my personal. The only exception is you. I'm willing to try this, because you're worth it."

"Thank you for letting me in."

He nodded. "I'm not perfect. This is really hard for me, but I'm trying."

The elevator opened, and we stepped inside. Brogan hit the button for his floor. "Since you're so determined to try, how about a round four?" I smiled up at him.

The doors closed and Brogan pushed me against the wall. "Now, that I can manage."

Chapter Twenty-Three

<u>Lainey Taylor Rule of Life #72</u>
Never assume parents always have their kid's best interests in mind.

The week after Christmas, I returned to work. Brogan and I had been inseparable except for the few days I was at my mom's house, which I'd spent on her couch watching movies. The doctors said the new chemo meds were effective, and she'd be given her last dose in a couple weeks. She was a fighter and was kicking cancer's ass.

The past few weeks with Brogan had been a whirlwind of stolen kisses, staying up *way* too late, and the giddy, sleep-deprived new relationship feeling that washed over me every time I thought of him.

Yellow sunflowers sat on my desk when I entered the building. I smiled, and my heart swelled past capacity. We weren't in an open relationship in the office, but this was close enough.

A string wound around the base of the flowers, holding a

tiny envelope. I slipped it out and opened it.

Meet me at Hillside Park at 8 p.m.
B.S.

Okay, were we going running? Talking about this during work was completely off-limits, but this seemed like a weird request. I shook it off and continued my usual morning ritual of checking my clients' social media accounts, checking the Cloud, and preparing posts.

I spent the rest of the day buried in paperwork, and by the time I got home to the apartment, I only had forty minutes to shower and change before I had to leave for the park. Such an odd place to meet, but I guessed since he walked Bruce there everyday, it wasn't too out of the norm.

After washing my face and reapplying my makeup, I pulled my jacket off my chair and breezed out of the apartment. The early-January night still had a bite of winter, and my wet hair started to crisp at the ends.

I sat on the bench that was a central viewing point of the small park.

"You're very punctual," came an unfamiliar voice.

My gaze shot up to an older man who I recognized from a photo Brogan had shown me. Brogan's father.

I wrapped my coat around me tighter. "You sent the flowers?"

"You sound surprised."

Uh, ya think? "How do you even know me?" But it clicked before he could answer. The guy with the camera a couple weeks ago. He wasn't from a tabloid. But would Brogan's father really stoop so low as to have him followed? And why?

"I've been following you for a few weeks now." He tossed a manila folder onto the bench beside me. I opened it up and found zoomed in pictures of Brogan's condo. Us sitting at the kitchen table. Us kissing at the stove, Brogan's hands climbing up my back. Us in the bedroom. "Seems you guys have gotten to know each other very well lately."

My heart sank. If these got out, what would it do to Brogan's company? And the bigger question—what kind of monster would take photos of his son without his permission?

"What do you want?" I spat the words, closing the folder on our most private moments. My stomach rolled, and I thought I might be sick. My privacy. My body on full display. Someone other than Brogan had seen this, and that invasion sent a ripple of anger and disgust blasting through my veins.

"I have a business proposition."

"Oh?" What was this, the friggin' mafia?

"I want you to leak a few of these pictures onto your clients' accounts tomorrow." He passed over his phone, and I swiped through images of clients of Starr media in very compromising positions. Positions I'd need at least ten years of yoga and a bottle of wine to even attempt.

My cheeks heated, and a wave of nausea washed over me. "This would be social suicide for these people."

He grinned. "Yes."

My lips curled in disgust. A father trying to ruin his only son's career? *Sick.* "That would go against everything Brogan stands for. This company means everything to him. What makes you think I'd do that to him?"

He sneered. "Because I have something you want."

I half expected him to pull out a horrible Italian accent and tell me "I have an offer you can't refuse."

"And what would that be?" What could possibly be worth ruining someone's career, including my own? Nothing.

"I heard your mom is sick."

I sat there, unable to move. This man had serious connections if he'd found out my mom's medical history and who I was just by having someone follow me.

"I will pay for all of her medical bills."

I glared up at him, working to keep my mouth firmly shut. The one thing I desperately needed, and he was dishing it up on a silver platter. Mom wouldn't even have to worry about paying off the bills. What would it be like to actually be able to buy things I wanted? Splurges on a new wardrobe, accessories, eating out. Things I ached to do. All for the small price of killing Brogan's dream.

I folded my hands in my lap and stared at a tree in the distance, unable to look this man in the eyes. "Hell no."

"I'll let you reconsider that." He pulled an envelope from inside his suit jacket and handed it to me, true mafia style. "A position with your name on it is ready at my firm, if you so choose."

I tentatively opened the envelope, and my eyes about popped out of their sockets when I caught a glimpse of the amount on the check. There were more zeroes than I ever could expect to have in my bank account before I reached retirement age.

I bit back a growl and pushed the envelope aside, sick I'd even contemplated this for a second. Even if the money would mean everything to me and Mom, I could never do this to Brogan. I—cared for him. No, I more than cared for him.

Caring for him didn't explain the spine-tingling sensation that came with his every touch. It didn't explain the trust I put into him with every kiss. And it sure as heck didn't even begin to describe how I fell harder with every soft look from those gorgeous brown eyes.

I loved him. Completely.

Jesus. I just had an epiphany that I loved the guy after I'd just been offered millions of dollars to destroy him.

Before I could make myself sick over this, my fingers found the center of the check and swiftly ripped it in half. "As I said before—hell no." I stood and walked away before my words came back to me and I really dug into this guy. Not worth it—he was slime, just as Brogan had said.

Just as I neared the edge of the park, I thought I saw Bruce being walked by someone, but they turned a corner before I got a good glimpse. Really, I was feeling paranoid from the whole situation. I half expected someone to come out wielding a machine gun and threatening to send me to sleep with the fishes. Maybe Brogan was right—Netflix was rotting my brain.

At home, I sunk into the couch and turned on the TV. Zoey had left a note on the counter saying she was out with a coworker and she'd be home late.

I frowned, thinking of all that money I just gave up. But what good would it do if I felt guilty for the rest of my life? It wouldn't be worth it. Nothing was worth hurting Brogan.

Chapter Twenty-Four

<u>Lainey Taylor Rule of Life #57</u>
Have Clorox wipes handy for when the shit hits the fan.

I should have known the second I stepped into the building that something was wrong. Jackson was at his desk, actual beads of sweat dripping down his face.

Coworkers caught my eye on their way to their cubicles and grimaced. Each one shook their head, their expressions pained.

I'd had this reoccurring dream when I was younger that I'd come to school and the entire student body would suddenly hate me, whispering to friends right in front of me, calling me names, keying my car. Reality was so much worse.

"What the hell did you do, Lainey?" Jackson shrieked.

"What?"

Before he could elaborate, Brogan's voice boomed over the intercom on my desk. "Lainey, get in here now."

My heart lodged in my throat.

Jackson shook his head in disgust. "Might as well start

packing up your shit."

"What?" Seriously, this had to be a nightmare, and I was going to wake up in a cold sweat any minute.

"Really? You're going to play dumb? Even I didn't think you were that stupid."

What the hell was he talking about? And what had I done since I left the office last night that could possibly elicit such a reaction from all my coworkers?

Everything was happening at whirlwind pace. Without realizing it, my legs had propelled me into Brogan's office, and I stopped in my tracks as soon as he turned around.

He looked at me as if I were—nothing. Like I was less than nothing. The corners of his lips curled into a sneer— what I'd assumed I looked liked when I met with his father last night.

He turned his computer monitor around to face me, and I gasped as one of the pictures his father had shown me yesterday was plastered across the screen. To make matters worse, they were posted from the client's account—*my* client's account. "Did you do this?" His soft tone had an edge that could pierce through steel.

"No," I matched his whisper, a full body shiver striking through my body. I couldn't do it, no matter how much I could gain. "I'd never do this to you."

He let out a heavy sigh, and momentarily I thought he would accept my word and we could discuss a game plan for damage control. "I stared at this all morning, wondering how someone I care about more than anything could do this to a company that means everything to me."

"I wouldn't." My lip quivered, and my knees felt like they would give out at any second. I braced myself against the back of the chair and tried to meet his gaze, but he refused to even look in my direction. To see him so disappointed, so hurt…it was a million tiny paper cuts to my heart.

"I want to believe you. I really do." His expression was a swirl of emotion, and I could tell he was at war with himself over this.

"But…" There was always a but. I'd seen it in every show where someone gets screwed over.

"It's from your account. I don't know what to trust anymore." He scrubbed his hands through his hair and leveled a distant gaze at me. "I have to follow my code of conduct that I wrote, Lainey." His lips mashed together, and he looked absolutely pained when he said, "It's the rules. I have to fire you. Ever since I started breaking them, it's been a distraction. Now this happened and…" He trailed off.

He didn't believe me. He thought I could do something this monstrous, cause him this much pain.

A cold, dark mixture of emotion swirled inside me—a blend of fish hooks ripping open my organs, a pair of Italian loafers smashing the remains, and a dash of salt to really amplify the pain.

I didn't know whether I wanted to add a few dents to his desk with my foot or ugly cry in my car with *Bad Day* blaring.

This man who I'd given my heart to was taking away the one thing that meant the most to me. His trust.

The spear of betrayal morphed into hot anger at how screwed up this whole situation was. He *had* to fire me? What the hell was that bull crap response?

Hell. No.

Screw him and the holier than thou shit he spouted. Screw the progress we'd made in the past few weeks, learning to open up to each other. Obviously it was all complete crap just to get in my pants. If he really trusted me, my ass wouldn't be on the chopping block. We'd be working to combat this as a team.

That was it. I'd never be able to compete with his company. His stupid rules would always win over feelings and relationships. I should have known. He'd been clear about it from the beginning, but did I listen? Of course not.

"Fuck your rules." I threw my hands in the air. "How about you find the person who did this? The person who posted it on my account."

Brogan's brows furrowed at my outburst. "I don't know *who* it is, but I can't keep you employed here. This is my entire world. My company might not make it through this as is. You've been a liability from the start." He didn't even have the decency to look me in the eye. He'd completely shut down. Game over. Brogan was back to the closed off CEO I'd met months ago. The Brogan I loved wouldn't do this.

"A liability," I repeated. "Really? So forget the fact that the crap clients I was given when I started here now have more than a hundred thousand followers. Or that four of the ideas I came up with to increase productivity have shot your numbers and your client list through the roof. No. You're right. I'm just a big fat distraction. I'm glad we have everything cleared up. I'll make sure to get out before I jeopardize your company any further, Mr. Starr."

"It'd be best if you were out by lunch," he said, staring at the door.

The coldness of his words crushed my insides in a slow painful twist.

I bit the inside of my cheeks and *really* looked at him—and it finally dawned on me. He would never change, and I was deluding myself thinking I could ever have a fighting chance with him. Work would always come first, and his trust issues ran too deep.

"You know what, Brogan? This is good to know. I'm glad I found out early on just how fucked up you are. I hope you and your rules have a happy life together." The loss of everything in that moment wrung my heart in my chest, and my lungs squeezed tightly, barely letting in any air.

I bent down to Bruce, who was laying on his doggy bed next to Brogan's desk, and scratched behind his ears. "He doesn't deserve you."

Bruce whined and dragged his chubby little doggy paw across my arm, and I almost lost it. I straightened and wiped a stray tear from my cheek.

A box was already waiting on top of my desk when I walked out of Brogan's office. Jackson's face still held that look of disgust. "Figured you'd need it. Don't let Betsey bite you on your way out."

He walked into Brogan's office and the frosted glass door whooshed shut with finality.

A moment later, Zelda came rushing through the hallway and threw her arms around my shoulders. "I heard you were fired."

I nodded, numb. The mountain of pending debt came tumbling down on me faster than a lost game of Jenga.

Jobless. Rent-money-less. Brogan-less. This was all too much to process.

How was this even happening? Why was I losing my job for something I hadn't done, and yet getting none of the benefits from the act that I'd supposedly executed.

"I'm so sorry. If there's anything I can do, I'm here for you." She squeezed my shoulder. I couldn't even look her in the eye—first, because my eyes were clogged with tears, and second, because I didn't want to see any other people disappointed with me.

Again I nodded, and continued piling my pictures and stash of food, toothbrush, and other toiletries into the box.

"I'll miss you," she said.

"Me, too." My pulse hammered in my temples at the thought of this being the last time in Starr Media. I'd miss everything about this job—the people, the feeling I got every time I posted something that was well-received, the way

Brogan made me feel both in and out of the office. I can't believe I trusted him.

Sorrow quickly bubbled to anger as I debated how this happened to me. How did Brogan's dad have the power to post from my account? How did he get past our security? If he *did* have that power to do these things, why bribe me? It just didn't make sense. Too many questions with zero answers.

With my box stuffed past capacity, I was almost ready to leave the building. All I needed was to clean off my runny mascara, straighten my pencil skirt, and walk out with at least part of my dignity.

I sat in the bathroom stall to collect myself, my hands still shaking and my lip in a constant state of quivering. My teeth raked over my lips and I pressed my palms to my eyes while sitting on the toilet. Just as I was about to flush, the door to the restroom opened and Zelda's familiar voice flooded in.

"—according to plan."

I decided to stay perched in my spot, lifting my feet so she wouldn't know I was in the stall.

"Hold on," she told the person on the phone, and she was silent for a moment, most likely making sure the bathroom was empty.

"I can't talk long. I need to get back to work, but he totally bought that it was Lainey."

What the hell? Who was she talking to? Was it Brogan's dad? Had he decided to go to her when I wouldn't say yes?

My anger quickly turned to rage at the fact that the *one* person who I hung out with at the company was the one to screw me over. She was my *friend*. Well, obviously not. I continued listening, stewing in the stall, wondering if I should barge out there and scream at her, or keep listening to get the whole story. Inner Nancy Drew won out, and I stayed perched on the seat.

"When do I get the cash? It was difficult to make it look like I did it under her account, that should mean I get a bonus."

I couldn't hear who was on the other end of the call, but I was ninety percent certain it was Brandon. How could someone want to hurt his son so much that he'd resort to destroying his business and credibility? My dad may have earned a spot on the Worst Dad List, but he'd never do anything like this to me, no matter how badly he wanted me to go the lawyer route.

"I'm not greedy. It's not every day I commit company espionage."

She argued a little more and then gave a clipped, "Good-bye."

As soon as she got off the phone, I opened the stall and our eyes met in the mirror's reflection. Her eyes widened a fraction, but she kept the rest of her expression motionless.

If anyone in the company had the capability to hack into my account, it would be the tech guru. Why hadn't she been the first person I thought of when this happened? Oh, yeah, because friends didn't set each other up to take the fall for espionage—obviously rule number five in the friendship manual. "How could you?"

She gave a pitying look. "Money's money, Lainey. I couldn't pass that up."

All I could do was stare. How could she be so cold to a boss that gave her a job, a damn good one at that. "You could. I did."

"Then you're stupid. Didn't you say your mom was sick? Why not use that for her?"

I scoffed, disgusted. "Because I'm a decent human being. I'm not willing to screw people over because of money." I shot her a look through the mirror. "And next time, you should really check to see who is in the bathroom before you talk about corporate espionage. Pretty sure there's something in the rule book about that." I gnashed my teeth together, keeping anything else I had to say safely pressed behind my lips. She didn't deserve to be chewed out. She deserved handcuffs and a jail cell. Never in my life had I wanted to punch someone, but I *so* did.

I shook my head. Someone who'd be willing to throw someone under the bus obviously wouldn't understand anything else I had to say. I walked past her in silence and left her in the bathroom alone.

This whole company was backward today. My boyfriend/boss/whatever thought I was a liar and a life-ruiner, and my only friend here screwed me over. The real world blew.

I strode over to my desk and took one last look around me. Good-bye to the stupid set of rules that I failed to follow. Good-bye to the first assistant who thought I was lazy and incompetent. Good-bye to the one person who shredded my heart into confetti-cut pieces.

I grabbed my box and headed for the elevator.

Just as the doors opened, Brogan came rushing out of his office.

"Lainey, wait," he said, out of breath as he sprinted toward me.

"Whatever you have to say, I don't want to hear it. I'm done with you. Oh, and you might want to check Zelda's computer and call log. I think you might find you've got it way wrong."

I clutched the box's cutout handles and lifted my head proudly as Betsey's doors zoomed open. I walked into the elevator and pressed the first floor button for the very last time, then turned to face Brogan. I blinked away tears and managed to fix my features into something that remotely conveyed the proper amount of *screw you*. His face fell, and it took everything in me to stay put and not run to comfort him. Our eyes locked, and I took solace in knowing that nothing could quite possibly hurt worse than this.

"Good-bye, Mr. Starr."

Chapter Twenty-Five

No one's there for you like your mom.

By the time I got back to the apartment, Zoey was already there with a carton of rocky road ice cream and store-bought brownies sitting ready on the counter.

She ran to me and wrapped me in a hug. "What the hell happened?"

"I was framed." I burrowed my head into her shoulder, wishing I could escape from this whole day. Seriously, I thought only people in lockup said this crap. I grabbed the bowl of ice cream and flopped down on the couch. "By Zelda."

"What? Why would she do that?"

"Money." I stabbed my spoon into a chunk of chocolate. "Brogan's dad got to her, and she set me up to take the fall. She even used my login. My clients. The evidence was stacked against me."

"He really didn't believe you?"

I shook my head and swallowed past the thickness in my

throat. "No. Not initially." That was what hurt the most. Not being fired and having zero income now. It was that Brogan and I had finally gotten to a place where we trusted each other. I could see myself with him. A future. My bright future now felt like sand sifting through my fingers—gone, and impossible to pick up the pieces.

"Then he didn't deserve you in the first place. What an asshat."

But that was the thing—he wasn't. Brogan was a lot of things, but that word was only saved for the Do Not Use pages of his employee manual. Deep down, I knew that I should be angrier, but I understood where he was coming from. This was his company, his life. He'd do anything to keep it afloat, even if it meant firing me. How could I ask him to choose between me and his life dream? I couldn't.

• • •

The next day, I pulled the masking tape over the last of my boxes and kicked it toward the front door. A lot could be accumulated over the course of five months, and I barely had enough room in my Corolla to get everything down to Portland.

Zoey wrapped her arms around my neck and sniffled into my shoulder. "What am I going to do without you?"

"The same as you always do. Work. Binge on *Gilmore Girls*. Just do me one favor and don't get your next roommate off Craigslist. I hear there are a ton of crazies on there."

"I have a few months until I need to think about that. The room will stay open for you."

I frowned. "You know that's not necessary."

She nodded, serious. "Yes. It is."

I pressed my lips together and tried to keep my composure long enough to take this last box down to my car. She'd tried to convince me to stay in Seattle and find a new job, but what was the point when I could be with my mom as she went through her last round of chemo? This was for the best. I'd find a job in the city and spend some much-needed time at home. Really, Brogan's dad had done me a favor. He taught me who was really going to be there for me during the hard times, and unfortunately my heart had been caught in the crossfire in this little experiment.

Zoey walked me down to the car, and I managed to not cry until I hit the interstate. Which was particularly dangerous because everyone should be able to see while going seventy miles per hour.

A little after noon, I unlocked the familiar red door and was met with Mom's outspread arms. I collapsed into her and released all of the pent-up tears and frustration of the past couple of days.

"I'm so sorry, love bug. I'm here for you."

"I'm sorry, Mom. I failed you." This was the first time in my life that I hadn't followed through with a promise, and it was every bit as painful as disappointing Brogan.

She pulled me away from her and looked me in the eye, her expression turning serious. "You did not fail me, or anyone else, for that matter. You are the strongest, most dependable person I know, and if this idiot can't see that and believe your word, then he didn't deserve to have you as an employee in the first place."

I hadn't told mom the whole story. I left out the part about Brogan's father and the exorbitant amount of money, because it didn't seem fair to dangle that in front of her to add insult to injury. Plus, she was already upset enough that I was putting any of my money toward her treatments.

She smoothed a hand down my arm and squeezed my hand. "Can I get you anything? I know it's been a long drive."

"No, I think I just want to lay down for a bit." The weight

of the past day settled deep in my bones and drained the energy from my body.

She nodded and rubbed her hand over my back in small, soothing circles. As much as I needed her right now, I immediately began to miss the life I had created in Seattle. This felt like I was taking a step backward.

I tried to close my eyes as soon as my head hit the pillow of my old bed, but the dread of job hunting scrambled all my thoughts. How was I supposed to get a job when I'd been fired? I'd be blacklisted from media and advertising for the rest of my career thanks to this. Even though it hadn't been me.

I could see how the conversation would go:

"Can we use your previous employer as a reference?"

"Uh, no. You see we slept together, and then he believed I sabotaged his career. Probably best not to ask about that."

Yeah, the interviews were going to go great.

If I didn't list him as a reference, I then had zero experience to put on my resume. All because I'd said no to protect the person I loved. Was it love when that person didn't feel the same way?

Yes…just unrequited.

Chapter Twenty-Six

I spent the next day locked in my room, researching jobs online. I'd only left my bed to grab sustenance and the occasional bathroom break. A film covered my face and teeth, and in the span of forty-eight hours of unemployment, I'd turned into the kid who moves home and lives in Mom's basement, minus the basement. Apparently no one was hiring in advertising in the Portland area at this time, probably waiting to open positions when school let out this summer. Until then, I'd hunker down and grit my teeth and work at a job I was overqualified for.

I figured if I could hold two jobs, we'd be okay. The salary wouldn't be comparable to what I made at Starr Media, but it'd make a dent. We'd pay the minimum balance of the bills until I was able to land a job that paid a little more. Mom would have time to recuperate, and I'd be too busy to miss my old life at the firm.

Mom walked into my room, and she wrinkled her nose. "Have you showered?"

I folded my arms over my chest just in case I forgot to put deodorant on. "No."

She took a shallow breath and moved a little farther away. "You smell like bean dip and bad decisions."

"Better get used to it, I guess," I muttered, still looking at my computer screen. There had to be *one* job out there that paid over minimum wage.

She grabbed my laptop and placed it on the bed beside me, and then sat down. "I want to talk to you about something."

"Yeah?" I could barely lift my head off my pillow. Unemployment was exhausting. Or at least I was blaming my fatigue and general stabby feeling toward life on that. It was safer than contemplating the real reason.

"I'm going back to work," she said, her tone final.

I shifted in bed and propped myself up on my elbows. "But you can't. Your immune system is too weak."

"I talked to my old admin today. I'm going to teach for an online school. It pays almost as well as my classroom position." She put her hand on my calf and squeezed. "I want you to take your time finding a job."

"There's nobody hiring here. It's no problem—I'll take on a couple minimum wage ones and—"

She grabbed my hand, silencing me. I looked up at her, feeling the most helpless I'd felt in years. This woman who raised me, was my everything, I'd failed her by getting fired. She needed me and, dammit, I was going to do anything in my power to help her.

"Sweetie. You need to stop. You've done more than your fair share. More than I ever should have let you contribute."

I wanted to scream *but I could have had it all paid off by now if I'd just done the horrible thing I'd been accused of.* But instead I shut my mouth and frowned.

"I want to help you." My voice sounded so small, so foreign. I hated the way this situation made me second-guess everything I'd done in the past six months. Why did doing the right thing have to suck so damn much?

"I know. And I love that I've raised someone with such a kind heart, but you need to live your life."

I shook my head at her, not understanding. "I can do that from home."

She took a deep breath and a mixture of peppermint and chocolate wafted under my nose. "No, you can't."

I frowned. "What do you mean?" Was I being kicked out? Man, I wasn't even cool enough to be a basement kid.

Her gaze raked over my face, a resolute expression in her eyes. "You're meant to be in Seattle. Zoey is there. You're building a life, on your own." She nodded as if assuring herself.

"But what about..." I trailed off. By asking what about *her* I made her sound weak, which wasn't the case. But if I moved back to Seattle, she'd be here by herself.

She blinked hard. "Me?"

I picked at a snag on my comforter, too embarrassed to look her in the eye.

She cleared her throat and waited to speak until I met her gaze. "How do you think you learned to be so independent?"

Good point. Even if we were both independent, wasn't it okay to lean on someone in a time of need? But it hit me. Maybe she didn't need my support as much as I thought she did. Maybe I hadn't given her enough credit. Hell, she was kicking cancer's butt—of course she didn't need me hovering over her.

I smirked. "I thought I learned my co-dependence skills from you."

"Is it still socially acceptable to smack children?" She playfully swatted my thigh. "I need my space, too," she continued. "What if I wanted to bring some guy home and you were here. That would be a total buzz kill."

Even if she was my best friend, I *really* didn't want to know about that side of my mom's life. "You're worried about me cock blocking your hookups? Are you even dating?"

"No, but when I feel better, I'd like to start." She smiled.

I was still processing the fact that my mom said she was bringing home men to our house to hook up. "I don't even know how to respond to that."

She laughed and patted my leg. "I'm divorced, not a nun."

Okay, I so wanted to be my mom when I grew up. "Noted."

She grabbed my phone from the nightstand and switched it from hand to hand before placing it next to me. "Why don't you consider moving back up with Zoey. You know she misses you," she said, hesitantly.

I sighed and flopped back on my pillow. Right, because a more expensive city with zero income was clearly a good choice. "There's no point. I don't have a job. So even if I wanted to move back, I can't. It's just not fair, Mom." Oh God, I had reached an ultimate low if I was whining like a three-year-old about fairness. But the feeling of complete helplessness, and the utter desperation for this to all be a horrible dream pummeled me into the ground.

She frowned and looked at me for a long time, with eyes that penetrated straight through my soul. After a moment, she said, "It's not fair that you were fired, but it happened. Life happens, sweetie, and you just have to roll with the waves and eventually your feet will hit shore again." She ruffled my hair. "In the meantime, there's ice cream and a healthy dose of sulking."

"What if I never get another marketing job?"

She scoffed, like I'd just said something so incredibly insane it wasn't even worth acknowledging. "You're a Taylor. You'll make it happen. You're one of the hardest working people I know." She grabbed a picture of my senior year prom, with me and Zoey posing on the staircase. "But you'll have a better shot if you go to a bigger city. Life's a bitch sometimes, but you'll get back up on that horse, sweetie."

That immediately made me think of the employee manual at Starr Media. Was it possible to have homesickness for a company? I missed everything about it—well, maybe not Jackson or that traitor Zelda—but everything else.

And Bruce. I missed his cute pudgy nose.

Mom was completely right. I wouldn't be happy living at home. I'd outgrown my old life, and I needed more. Unfortunately, *more* was two hundred miles away and thought I'd actually try to sabotage his company.

I nodded, resigned to the fact that I had to stay true to myself and give myself the best chance to get ahead in my career after such a disastrous setback. She was right. I was a Taylor, and I was going to land on both feet like a frickin' Olympic gymnast and find another job. "Thanks, Mom."

She kissed my forehead and shifted off my bed. "Any time."

I needed to make a plan to get my life back.

Chapter Twenty-Seven

Lainey Taylor Rule of Life #99
Gossip shows can be very educational.

"Do you want something to drink?" I asked. Anything to keep busy while Mom was strapped to the machine.

"Kid, if you keep loading me up on drinks, I'm going to have coffee coming out of my eyeballs."

"Sorry."

She skimmed her hand over my cheek, and a calm smile creased the corner of her lips. "Hey, I know this is all new to you, but I've been around the block a few times with this. I appreciate it, though."

I nodded, frowning. She'd done this alone for months and every ounce of my coffee-flooded neurons felt like crap about it. "I wish I could have been with you for all of them. I'm sorry, Mom."

"Honey, I didn't raise you to be sorry for everything. The only time you have to apologize is if you're the first one up in the morning and you don't make any coffee."

She pulled me into a hug, and I wrapped my arm around her, avoiding the IV hooked to her arm. Her very last treatment. This nightmare was finally going to be over, and she could finally start to heal. Even if I didn't have my dream job anymore, I had what counted most—my family.

Which reminded me—since I didn't have a high-paying job anymore, I needed to reduce the payments to the hospital. It'd be much easier to do in person than over the phone.

"I'll be right back." I untangled myself from my mom's embrace and stood.

Mom lifted up the arm hooked to her chemo meds. "I'm not going anywhere."

I walked down the corridor until I found the accounts office. A woman wearing a black pashmina sat behind the desk, taking a sip from a mug that said, "My book boyfriend's better than yours." Unless that book boyfriend was Mr. Darcy, she was probably wrong, but now wasn't really the time to tell her this.

"Can I help you?" She put the mug down and typed something into her computer.

"I'd like to change the payment options for my mother's account."

She looked up, bored. "Name."

I gave her my mother's name, and she typed a few more things on her keyboard. Her brows furrowed as she scrolled her finger over the toggle button on her computer mouse. "The account looks like it was paid in full."

I froze. Could a miracle have happened? A mistake? A computer glitch? "Excuse me?"

"The account is closed," she repeated, fidgeting with her scarf.

I leaned my elbows on the counter and held my head between my hands, staring down at her. How could this be? "As of when?"

She squinted at the screen and hummed under her breath as she scrolled through the account. As soon as she found the information, she stopped the tune and looked up at me. "Yesterday."

"That's impossible. We owed…" A shit ton of money. "A lot."

"It was paid in one large sum yesterday."

"Can you tell me who paid it?" Who the hell would pay Mom's medical bills. The only explanation I could think of, with a glimmer of hope, was that my father had grown a conscience and stepped up to cover the costs. But that was about as likely as the damn bill being paid in the first place.

"It doesn't say on the account, sorry."

I looked around her desk, leaning over to check for camera crews or a television host that said this was all a big joke. "You're sure I'm not being punked?"

She shot me a look, and I could tell this conversation was getting a little old on her end, but I just couldn't let it go. Who could have paid off that sum of money? And why?

It was over. No more Tastytarts. No more ban from online shopping—well, maybe until I got a job. No more…bills. The suffocating weight of debt lifted for the first time in a year, and tears streamed down my face. We were free to live our lives how we wanted, not having to worry about enormous payments. My life could go back to normal. I could get a shit job up in Seattle and worry about which purse I should waste my paycheck on. We were going to make it through this.

I walked back into the room where Mom was watching CGC—a show that discussed all the latest celebrity scandals. Her eyes fluttered shut as the chemo treatment was being administered. I leaned against the doorframe and watched her, hope bubbling up over the rest of my jumbled feelings.

"We don't have to worry about hospital bills anymore." My voice was thick. Whoever did this, I wish I knew who it was so I could thank them. This wasn't a simple act of charity like dropping lightly used clothes off at the Goodwill. This was something I'd never be able to repay, not in this decade, at least.

Her eyes flew open. "What do you mean?"

I cleared my throat and fidgeted. "Someone's paid the medical bills?" Even I didn't quite believe it yet.

She shook her head and her expression matched what I felt—shock. "How is that possible?"

"I don't know, but right now I don't care. As soon as you're feeling hungry again, we're having a junk food movie marathon."

"Deal." Tears welled in her eyes, but she blinked them back and smiled. Even during these horrid treatments, she was a warrior. If I turned out with even a tenth of my mom's strength, I'd hit the jackpot.

Something on the TV broke through our moment. A lady in a peplum power suit said the one single word that could ever hold my complete attention—*Starr*.

I focused on the show. "Allegations against Starr Media have been addressed personally by Brogan Starr, CEO of Starr Media. He spoke in a press conference earlier today," said the woman.

It panned to a clip of Brogan speaking into about twelve microphones at a podium. Cameras flashed as he gripped the sides of the stand, his knuckles turning white as the skin strained against his bones. Worry lines creased his forehead, but a smile remained plastered on his face. I knew him well enough that this wasn't a genuine grin. No dimples, no little lines in the corners of his eyes. But even so, he still took my breath away. The man was gorgeous, and my heart ached for him and his company.

"Starr Media is cooperating with authorities in the investigation of the leak of unapproved photos on five different accounts. We have found the perpetrators, and they have been taken into custody. Causality and motives are still under investigation." He paused and looked into the camera, his gaze heavy with hurt. "I want to personally apologize to all of the clients affected by this tragedy. I also want to say that I deeply regret that an employee of Starr Media was wrongfully accused and punished because of this."

Was he apologizing to me? To my knowledge, no one else had been let go. And I was the only one who'd been personally screwed over.

I stared raptly at the TV as he continued. "If it weren't for those employees, I wouldn't be where I am today. I've hurt someone I deeply care about and I can't even begin to ask for forgiveness. I don't think I can even forgive myself for my hasty actions."

He paused and looked down thoughtfully at his hands clasped atop the podium. "As the wise Abraham Lincoln once said, 'The people when rightly and fully trusted will return the trust.' This person gave me their trust to be a leader… and more, and I was not there in the moment of need. And because of that, I lost a truly valuable asset. A person who taught me trust is a strength, not a weakness. I should have been more vigilant before jumping to conclusions, and I assure you, that this will never happen again." He looked directly into the camera, and his eyes held more sadness than I ever thought possible. "Thank you," he said, more emotions running through those two words than I could name. He collected his notecards and turned to exit the stage.

All I could do was stare as camera lights flashed on his retreating figure. He'd just apologized to me on national television. Not naming me personally, but I knew it was for me. I pressed my lips together to keep them from quivering. That was one of the nicest things he could have done. He could have easily left that out of his speech, but he didn't.

"Wasn't that your dickhole boss?" my mom cut in.

"Mom!" I put my hands on my hips. That was the last word that would have come to mind if I'd been asked to describe him right now. I didn't know if I'd ever get a chance to talk to him again, but at least I had closure in the fact that he knew it wasn't me, and he felt bad enough about it to publicly announce it.

"Isn't he one, though? He fired you without even blinking an eye."

"It isn't like that. He has a company to run. He had to save his life's dream," I argued.

"He should have had all his facts straight before acting so rashly." She frowned, shutting off the TV. "That's what a real leader does."

"She's right, you know." A familiar voice came from the doorway.

I turned and spotted Brogan leaning against the doorframe in a pair of jeans and a fleece zip-up. My whole body froze. What was he doing here, in a hospital hundreds of miles away from his home? I had to blink a few times just to make sure I wasn't imagining the whole thing. By the third blink, I was sure that yes, he was in fact here, and that he probably thought I had an eye twitch problem.

"Dickhole is a great word to describe my actions." He strode over to my mom and extended a hand. "Hi, Mrs. Taylor. I'm Brogan Dickhole Starr."

She shifted her gaze from me to Brogan, skepticism in her eyes. "To what do I owe the pleasure?"

"I wanted to personally apologize for my dickholery, and to meet the person who raised such a smart, business-savvy woman."

She turned to me and murmured, "This one'll charm the pants right off of you." Then she shifted her attention back to him. "I assume you also came to compensate Lainey for time lost being out of work the past couple days, and to assure her she'll have a position ready for her return on Monday?"

"Mom!" Who said I wanted to go back to Starr Media? Even if I *really* did, it wouldn't be the same. People would look at me differently, and even if my name had been cleared, the damage to my reputation had been done. There was no coming back from that.

A bemused expression flitted across his lips. "Are you bartering for a job on behalf of your daughter?"

Even with IVs in her arm, Mom was still able to pull off a *boy, you're messing with the wrong woman* look, complete with silent finger snaps. God, I loved this woman. "Where do you think she got her business sense from?"

"Undoubtedly from you." He smiled. "I'd also like to congratulate you on your final chemo treatment. Lainey's kept me posted on your progress throughout, and I'm so glad the treatment was effective."

"She's a sweetheart." She patted my hand and gave a soft smile.

"Yes. She is." The heat in his expression sent a shiver through me.

Mom cleared her throat and produced a very artificial yawn. "I'm very tired. If you guys don't mind, I'd like to be alone for a little bit." She gave a quick wink in my direction and then closed her eyes.

I looked to Brogan. Did I want to talk to him alone after what had happened the other day? I did deserve an in-person apology. We walked into the hallway in silence.

"Lainey." The whisper in his familiar voice caressed my ear, and if I hadn't been paying attention, I'd have passed it off as my imagination.

Slowly, I turned to face Brogan. His hands were shoved in the pockets of his jeans, a sheepish expression set across the lips that played front and center in my dreams the last two nights.

"What are you really doing here?"

"I made a mistake."

I pursed my lips and leveled a glare at him. I may have forgiven him once, but the second time wasn't going to be as easy. He deserved to squirm. "Just one? I'm pretty sure there were several. Which one are you referring to?"

His frown deepened. "Yes. I screwed up a lot. I should have believed you when you said it wasn't you." He paused and added, "I really didn't think it was, but I couldn't get over the fact that I needed to abide by my own rules. And it hurt you." He looked away, ashamed.

"Trust isn't exactly your strong suit." And because of what he'd done, I wasn't doing so great with it myself.

"I'm working on that. I was wrong to jump to conclusions. It was a dick move, and you deserve better." He looked around the hallway and then back at me. "I did some investigating, and you were right, it was Zelda."

I tilted my head at him. "Glad to hear that MIT education did you some good."

His tongue ran nervously over his top lip, and he shifted his weight side to side as he looked at me. "I talked to my dad and realized what he had offered you. I can't believe you turned him down."

"Really? Then you don't know me at all," I spat. "How could I hurt you?"

"You mean the way I hurt you?"

"Yeah." Exactly. Because just when I'd thought we took the next step in our relationship, we took five hundred steps back.

"It was a mistake that we worked together. I should have fired you from the start."

I gaped at him, words momentarily escaping the confines of my brain. *What?* "That…is not what I was expecting to hear. Did you really just come all the way down to Portland just to tell me this? If so, you can go now." I turned away. What a jerk.

"Just hear me out," he said.

I faced him reluctantly, but didn't say anything.

"I'm glad I didn't, because you have taught me so much, but it's too distracting. I missed the compromising position Zelda put us in, where I would have caught it otherwise. I'm usually on top of the security. The first time there was a glitch with one of your accounts, I should have been more vigilant. But I wasn't, and I don't mean this is your fault in any way, but I was distracted by you."

I shook my head, not understanding what he was getting at. Was he still blaming me but in a different way? "Are you expecting an apology? Because it's not happening."

"Absolutely not. You've made me feel things I never have before." He grabbed my hand and ran his thumb over my knuckles. I'd give anything to melt into his touch, but I pulled my hand away. He'd hurt me. And I would not be a doormat he could step on whenever it suited him.

"Everything about you is good for me. You make me a better man. I miss you hogging the couch. And stealing the covers at night. And the way you pretend to be annoyed by Bruce but actually love him. I love everything about you, Lainey, and can't imagine spending another moment without you."

These words were too little too late.

"That's a sweet sentiment, Brogan, but actions speak louder than words. You don't trust me. This is what broke up my parents and broke up yours. How can we build a relationship on something so broken? You'd rather stick to a set of rules than follow your heart. Every time something goes wrong you bail. It isn't right. You've done it to me twice, now. I refuse to live that way, always worried that if I make the wrong move, you're out."

"No more bailing, I promise you. Screw the rules," his shout echoed through the hallway and the intensity in his gaze was startling. "The difference between me and you versus our parents is that I want to work on us. I want to try to be better. And that was the worst mistake of my life. Letting you go. Please, trust me. Give me a chance."

I shook my head. My heart tugged in my chest, but he'd been this earnest before, and the same thing had happened again. I wanted to believe him, so badly. And after meeting his father, hell, no wonder he was so screwed up. I could forgive him. With what my mom put up with, she was living proof that people can forgive. But I wasn't sure I could trust him again.

"So what is it you want exactly?"

"You," he said. "With me."

"What do you mean? I can't just move back up to Seattle without any job prospects. Obviously I'm not going back to work with you."

"No. You're not," he agreed.

Okay, I wasn't quite expecting that. A little voice in the back of my mind hoped that he would ask me back, just so I could have the chance to say no. "Right. Well, I'm going to go back and spend time with my mom." I hitched my finger toward her room down the hall.

He touched my arm before I could walk away. "Lainey, I'm just so sorry."

"I forgive you, Brogan, but I don't know if we can come back from this. Not after what happened." At least Brogan's dad would be prosecuted for his actions, along with Zelda. Maybe he was the one that had paid the medical bills. It made sense. He'd screwed me over and wanted to make things right. "Although you can tell your dad that it was nice he finally grew a conscience."

Brogan shook his head, his brows pinched together.

"What are you talking about?"

"Paying my mom's medical bills." Who knew someone so corrupt could actually grow a pair?

He cleared his throat and scuffed his foot along the linoleum floor. "He didn't pay your bills."

"But…" How could I not see it before? Of course. It all made sense now. The reason he showed up to the hospital, the apology. It was Brogan.

He nodded. "Yeah."

"Why?"

"I love you, Lainey. I saw what you gave up. You did that for me, and I will be forever grateful. I don't want to live my life by a damn rule book anymore. I want you and only you."

I didn't know how to respond to his words. They filled my heart and tore it to shreds at the same time. "I can't let you pay for that. It's too much. Once I get the money, I will pay you back."

"Not happening," he said.

Hot tears burned at the back of my throat. He'd just given me the biggest gift I could never accept. Financial freedom meant everything, but I couldn't let him take the burden. "It might take a while, but I promise to return every penny."

"Consider it a bonus for helping find a corporate spy. Who knows how much worse it would have gotten if you hadn't told me."

"I can't. It feels weird. Like you gave me money for hurting me." I looked him in the eye. I wanted him to see what he'd done.

"No. That isn't it at all, Lainey. Really. I mean, I do feel guilty for what I did. But I paid your mom's hospital bills because my family wronged you. What my dad did—there aren't words." He shoved a hand through his hair. "You and your mom are good people. You're what's right with the world. Me paying the bill was saying thank-you for showing me that. If you pay me back—I don't want your money."

"I don't know," I said. This was all too much to process.

He huffed out a sigh, and I could tell he was starting to lose his patience. "How about this. I have another proposition." His eyes searched mine. "I'm taking over a new social media company in Seattle, helping them rebuild their infrastructure. I can't oversee them all the time, since I will still be dealing with the mess at Starr Media. I need someone I can trust. I'd like to extend the invitation of employment. We could say that the medical bills were an early signing bonus."

A job. Where I wouldn't have to walk dogs or fetch coffee. One without grinchy Jackson and a carnivorous elevator. A *real* marketing job. I looked at him, still skeptical. "Why not put Jackson on the job?"

"He's going to stay with me at Starr."

I nodded. This would be huge. I wouldn't get an opportunity like this for years to come with other companies, not with the current state of the market. "What would the position be?"

"Marketing manager. You could put those MBA skills to good use at the company."

Inner Lainey was dropping it like it was hot. Lainey that Brogan could see remained cold and aloof. "I'd need some time to think about it."

His frown told me he'd expected a different answer.

He put his hands on my shoulders, and those chocolate brown eyes pierced straight through my soul. "Please, Lainey," he pleaded. "I miss you so much. I made a mistake, but hell, I'm human. Is there any way you'll forgive me? Please just consider taking the job."

I frowned. "I'll think about it," I said again. As I turned to walk away, my chest ached. It hurt to breathe.

"Your mom is right, you know." His voice was quiet, but it carried in the empty hallway.

I swallowed past the lump in my throat and turned to face him. "How so?"

"I couldn't even dream of finding someone like you in this lifetime or the next. You're smart, and kind, and everything I could ever ask for in a partner—both in and out of the boardroom. You showed me what love is, and no matter what you decide, I will be forever grateful for that Lainey. It hurts like hell that I broke your trust, because you are my heart. I can't live without you."

My wall crumbled into dust. He was everything I could ever want in a man. He didn't complete me, because hell, I was complete to begin with, but he was the perfect complement, one that I'd be hard pressed to find in someone else.

I let out an exaggerated sigh and put my hands on my hips. "What are the starting wages?"

His expression turned hopeful. "What?"

"For the marketing position." I tried to act bored, like I'd seen on the law shows when people bargained for more money, even if a grin twitched at my lips.

His dimples made an appearance. "I'm sure it can be negotiated."

"I want at least ten thousand higher," I said, completely serious. "Make it twenty."

"But you don't even know the wage yet."

"I know. But I've been on a shoe-buying hiatus for six months and plan to make up for lost time. Plus, there's the issue of the clothes ruined by Bruce."

"You drive a hard bargain, Taylor, but I think I can manage that."

I smiled. "I'll have my people call your people."

He crossed his arms over his chest and rocked back on his heels. "Does this mean it's a yes?"

"Under one condition." I held up a finger. "As long as I get to abolish the garlic rule at the company." I smirked.

"That can be negotiated." He swooped me into his arms and pulled me close. His brown eyes melted the rest of my resolve, and when he leaned down to kiss me, I met his lips with hope for the future, hope for us, swelling in my chest.

"I love you, Lainey."

"I love you, too, Brogan."

Epilogue

<u>Lainey Taylor Rule of Life #467</u>
An office with a view trumps a cubicle any day of the week.

Six months later…

"Power looks good on you, Taylor."

I smiled and stared out at the panoramic view of the Seattle skyline. As marketing manager, I had my very own office, and my very own assistant. Sure, the office wasn't a corner one, but my eight by ten window wasn't too shabby. It even came with remote control blinds, which I *may* have been playing with all morning. Mom was coming to visit next week. She'd finished her radiation and was in complete remission.

Brogan walked up to my desk and smiled. "I designed a new employee manual, and I'm going to implement it this week. Would you mind skimming over it and seeing what you think?" He clutched the leather-bound book in his hand.

"Sure. Does this mean I have the power to delete any of the rules I deem arbitrary?"

His lips tipped up in the corner, and he slid the manual across my desk. "Don't let it go to your head. Wouldn't want to have to report you to the CEO."

"What is he going to do about it?" I drummed my fingers along the surface of the table and raised a brow.

"I say let the punishment fit the crime." He pointed down to the book. "Will you just read the last page? That's where I made the most changes." He tugged at the knot of his tie and swallowed hard, uncharacteristically nervous.

I shrugged, not understanding why this last page of rules was so important it couldn't have been emailed to me. "Sure."

He looked at me expectantly.

"Oh. You mean now?"

He nodded. "Yes."

"Okay," I said slowly, still not understanding why this was so important it couldn't wait until after our dinner date tonight.

I flipped open the book to the last page and started to scan down the rules. I could tell a lot had been changed because the book had shrunk by at least an inch.

My breath caught in my throat when I saw the first one was about me. As I read the second one, my pulse beat rapidly against my temples, and I couldn't help the smile that spread across my face.

Rule #762

Lainey Taylor is always right. She's the smartest, kindest person I know, and I don't know what I did to deserve her.

Rule #763

She seems to have horrible taste in movies, but always let her have her pick on Netflix because she ends up

being right.

Rule #764

Don't ever break the four cups of coffee rule. Ever. Under penalty of death.

Rule #765

A woman this amazing shouldn't be walking around unattached.

I looked up from the manual, not understanding what the last one meant.

He took one last tug at his tie and mashed his lips together. In one swift movement, he sank down on one knee in front of me.

His expression changed from playful to serious, and with shaking hands, he reached into his pocket and pulled out a small black box.

My sharp intake of breath was the only sound in the office, and I immediately put my hands to my mouth—something I always laughed about as a cliché, but it really did seem to be an instinct.

"Lainey." His deep voice vibrated against the wall of my chest.

"Brogan." Holy crap, was this really happening?

"You are the smartest woman I know. You drive me insane, make me laugh, and are my complete equal. Will you please marry me and help me continue in my quest to break every single rule in the book?"

"Yes." I pulled him into a kiss and melted as his soft lips swept over mine. I wondered if I'd ever get used to the fact he was mine. Apparently, now, forever.

Acknowledgments

Thank you, to my fabulous agent Courtney Miller-Callihan for always being in my corner. Your continual support has kept me sane through the whole writing process. To my amazing editor, Candace Havens, this all started with a brainstorming session on your hotel room couch at RT. Thank you for letting me run with this fun idea and helping make it shine—I'm so grateful to work with such a talented editor. A big thank you to Rhianna Walker and Linda Russell for being the best PR ladies ever.

Extra smooshy hugs to Lia Riley, AJ Pine, and Brooklyn Skye for reading this book at various stages. Your feedback is always spot on. Love you guys.

Writing friends have gotten me through those hard days stuck in the drafting trenches. Big hugs to Jessica Gunn, Chanel Cleeton, Megan Erickson, Rebecca Yarros, Cindi Madsen, Rachel Harris, and Natalie Blitt. Our chats online have always lifted my mood when I needed it most. Special thank you to Cindi for blurbing my book—you're the best!

Thank you to all the bloggers and readers who picked this

book up! I write for you. Your support means the world to me.

Lastly, to my family. My books would not even be possible without you. Justin, thank you for showing me what true love is. And for pushing me out the door to write.

About the Author

Jennifer Blackwood is an English teacher and contemporary romance author. She lives in Oregon with her husband, son, and poorly behaved black lab puppy. When she isn't writing or teaching, she's binging on Veronica Mars episodes and white cheddar popcorn.

Want to know when Jennifer Blackwood's next book releases? Sign up for her newsletter.

www.jenniferblackwood.com

Also by Jennifer Blackwood...

UNETHICAL

After the medical world was shaken by scandal, with Payton Daniels's family at the center, Payton left everything behind and hid within the anonymity of college. But Payton's ex, Blake Hiller, hasn't forgiven her for leaving, and now he's in her medical ethics class. Forced together again, their passion for each other reignites, but when Payton is asked to testify in her father's high-profile trial, she must choose between risking her acceptance into medical school to help her father, and losing the only guy she's ever loved.

FOOLPROOF

It's been a rough semester and Jules Carmichael needs to get her life together. Pronto. Unfortunately, the only available work is at Office Jax, home of horrid 90s music and the biggest jerk on this side of the galaxy. Then Ryan DeShane discovers the "6 Ultimate Steps to the Perfect Summer Fling"—and Jules is his target. But the "steps" work a little too well, because he and Jules are definitely, uh, flinging. And it's only a matter of time before Ryan's foolproof plan starts to seriously unravel…

Discover more New Adult titles from Entangled Embrace...

BEYOND THE STARS
a novel by Stacy Wise

College-student Jessica Beckett should be spending her junior year in France, eating pastries and sharpening her foreign language skills, but instead she's stuck babysitting Jack McAlister, Hollywood's hottest heartthrob. He's private, prickly, condescending—and makes it very clear he doesn't want a personal assistant. Sparks fly as they push each other's buttons, and soon Jessica is wondering if a sexy, successful guy like Jack could ever find love with a regular girl like her.

ANATOMY OF A PLAYER
a *Taking Shots* novel by Cindi Madsen

Whitney Porter is done with men. She's focusing on her first assignment at the college newspaper: Posing as a sports writer for an exposé on the extra perks jocks receive. But Hudson Decker, the bad boy of the hockey team, is about to test her no-sex rule. With his life spiraling out of control, Hudson is looking for a distraction. When his teammates bet him that he can't land the gorgeous but prickly new reporter, he accepts, boasting he'll have her in bed by the end of the semester. But Whitney is so much more than Hudson expected, and soon enough, he's in too deep.

RUSH
a *Pretty Smart Girls* novel by Shae Ross

Priscilla Winslow has a mouth that spits fiery sarcasm faster than I can throw a touchdown. But I've wanted her ever since I saw her in that Bo Peep outfit on Halloween. Yep, I'm a sheep who will follow that little hottie anywhere. There's one problem...she hates me. Just because we ended up in jail and quite possibly ruined both our futures...

CPSIA information can be obtained
at www.ICGtesting.com
Printed in the USA
LVHW031502181118
597559LV00001B/34/P